Kasey Michaels

Everything's Coming Up Rosie

HQN™

ISBN-13: 978-0-373-77127-1
ISBN-10:   0-373-77127-4

EVERYTHING'S COMING UP ROSIE

To Tammy Seidick, graphic designer extraordinaire,
with love and thanks

Everything's Coming Up Rosie

CHAPTER ONE

THE SEPTEMBER SCENERY in northern New Jersey bordered on magnificent as Douglas Llewellyn navigated his sleek black sedan along the narrow, winding roadways that wended through a civilized forest surrounding the large, manicured grounds of well-hidden mansions.

At any other time Doug would have been slowing the car, peering through the trees, on the lookout for interesting old architecture. Because Douglas Llewellyn was an architect, the senior partner of Philadelphia based Architecture Design, Ltd. (restorations a specialty). His interests were steeped in history, and he'd once lost a hefty commission for refusing to remove a fireplace mantel in a suburban Pennsylvania farmhouse because there were three musket balls in the wood, remnants of an Indian raid in 1763.

Then again, as his friend and partner had pointed out at the time, a man could indulge his love of history to the point of walking away from a mid-five-figure profit, if he'd been born with a silver spoon in his mouth. Hell, Cameron Pierce had said, Doug had been born with a full set of demitasse spoons clamped between his toothless infant gums.

Doug had merely shrugged, then asked Cam to help him unload the massive oak mantel, because he may have turned down the job, but he'd rescued the mantel.

Besides being a highly successful and sought-after architect up and down Philadelphia's Main Line, Doug was handsome, intelligent, urbane, witty—and matrimonially uncatchable.

He prided himself on the fact that he enjoyed all the benefits of female company, while neatly side-stepping the pitfalls—meaning commitment, meaning marriage. He enjoyed life, he enjoyed women. There was, he believed, no harm in that.

Life had been pretty much one big party for Doug, and it was with shock that he woke up one morning with a young blond real-estate agent in his bed and a feeling of utter emptiness in his gut, to realize he'd somehow become forty years old.

How had this happened? Surely it had been only yesterday that he'd been in college, happily working his way through the cheerleading squad.

Where had the succeeding nearly twenty years gone, anyway? He didn't drink more than the occasional beer, so it couldn't be that the years had disappeared in an alcoholic fog. He worked hard, he played hard, and the years had passed in a blur of work and play. Was that a good answer?

Maybe it was learning that his partner, Cam, had at last found his Darcie, and the two were soon to be married—and looking disgustingly happy with each other.

Not that Doug wasn't happy. Hell, he was delirious he was so happy. Wasn't he? A successful business, work that he adored, beautiful women clinging to his elbow, and always with another beautiful woman eager to take her place.

What wasn't to be happy about?

Which didn't explain why he'd become a virtual hermit these past two months, turning down invitations to parties, boating excursions, even a weekend tryst in the Bahamas with one of his semiregulars, the incredibly beautiful Kay Williams, where they'd have the run of her parents' thatched-roof minimansion fifty yards from their private beach. Kay liked to sunbathe topless. And bottomless. And she liked to be oiled, hourly.

And he'd turned her down?

Obviously there was something wrong with him. Not enough iron in his diet, perhaps? Maybe the chase had become too easy, with the result always a foregone conclusion.

Or maybe he was...*old.*

No. No, that couldn't be it. Forty wasn't old.

Then again, forty wasn't thirty-nine, was it?

Cam, standing in the doorway of Doug's office last Tuesday morning—the better to make a quick getaway—had suggested that maybe it all boiled down to the idea that it was time for Peter Pan to grow up.

It was a good thing they were such good friends...and not such a good thing that Cam's words had stuck with Doug ever since.

At first he'd thought, okay, so he was going through a dry spell, a low tide. Something like that. It wasn't the end of life as he knew it, life as he'd always liked it.

He'd just keep his cool, keep his distance from the social scene for a while, until he had his head back on straight, his priorities back where they belonged: work hard, play hard, repeat. He simply needed to be away from women for a few weeks, examine his reasons for—as Cam had also pointed out—dating all the wrong women, and decide what the hell he wanted to *do* with the rest of his life.

Forty was a big year, a milestone, a watershed year. Doug would like to think that forty was just a number, and a number he could ignore, at that. But after two months of kidding himself, he knew that something more permanent had happened to him, some synapse had misfired in his brain, and he was suddenly looking at the soppily happy Cam and his Darcie and listening to their plans to renovate her late uncle's Victorian mansion…and he was jealous.

It was pitiful, that's what it was. And now, with the worst timing possible, he was going to a place where no man of his recently shaken constitution and lifestyle confusions had gone before—a weeklong house party ending in the wedding of his second cousin, Lili-beth.

Worse…yes, things just kept getting worse and worse. Doug had the feeling he would spend that week with a big red-and-white bull's-eye on his back while his cousin Bettie took target practice at him with her matchmaking Cupid's bow.

Talk about being vulnerable. Talk about looking for a way out before he even arrived at the party....

"Come on, Cam, where's your loyalty to your employer? Where's your sympathy for your friend?" he pleaded now into the hands-free cell phone. "There's got to be a disaster brewing somewhere. The Perkins project—he threw a fit over the cost overrun on the tile border and you need me back there to calm him down? Wait—Hildy Forrester. She's always unhappy with something. I'll go check up on the job, smooth her feathers. Hell, Cam, you know she likes me best."

Cameron Pierce's voice came back to Doug through the marvel of the speakerphone. "All married women of a certain age like you best. That's how we get half of our commissions. So, nice try, Doug, but everything's under control here—just the way it was two hours ago. And it's Sunday. We don't even have anyone on the job today. What's the matter? Are you breaking out in hives already? It's only a wedding, and it's not yours, remember? How are you going to be my best man next month if you're allergic to weddings?"

Doug slowed the car as he peered at the archi-tecturally-compatible-to-its-surroundings-but-barely-legible street sign, and then turned right. "I'm not allergic to weddings, Cam, and I've definitely never been allergic to eager bridesmaids. I'm allergic to being set up. Translation, I know my cousin Bettie. She's probably already got someone all picked out for me—one of her tennis partners from the club or whatever."

"And you'd rather chase those bridesmaids."

"You know me so well," Doug said, not yet ready to tell Cam that he'd rather be on a weeklong golf outing at the Greenbriar, thus admitting he was still struggling with this Peter Pan thing and where his usual willing women belonged in the mix. "But not at a wedding like this one, Cam, it would be too dangerous. A week is six days too long to be stuck constantly with the same woman, or get caught switching women in the middle of the stream—party. I don't know where in hell anyone came up with the idea of a weeklong house party before a wedding, but I've got a bad feeling about the entire concept."

"Okay, I get it. A house party is too confining for Casanova."

Doug wished he could smile at the joke. "Exactly. And don't forget Bettie, who I know is setting me up. I'll bet her name is Mitzy, and she's had her silver and china patterns picked since she left finishing school. A week, Cam. A full week of my cousin throwing Mitzy and me together, seating us at the same table, pointing out the woman's stellar qualities. I should have said I couldn't make it until next Sunday, just in time to kiss the bride and take off again for the rest of the month. This is no damn way to start a vacation, Cam. Why did I agree to this?"

"You promised your mother. And, much as I don't like saying this, you're beginning to sound a little unhinged."

Doug sighed. "Right, at least for the first part. Strange how I keep trying to repress that. Representing the Llewellyn name because good old Mom and Dad couldn't change the dates for their cruise. Maybe I should have risked being cut out of their will."

"*Again.* Cut out of their will again. You know, Doug, if I believed you, I'd think your parents were martinets, which I know they aren't, and that you've obeyed them all your life, which I know you haven't. But you're scaring me here, friend—promise me now that you're not going to skip out on being best man at my wedding."

"You're planning a weeklong celebration and mating party before you and Darcie tie the knot?"

"You know we're not."

"Good. Then I'll be there. Damn it, speaking of being there—I'm here."

"How's it look? You told me you haven't visited your cousin since you were a randy college boy. Does it still look like George Washington could have slept there?"

Doug gave the immense structure the once-over with his trained architect's eye. "Standard issue three-story, eighteenth-century colonial reproduction, Cam. Fake history at its priciest."

Cam laughed. "Don't look now, Doug, but that's what *we* do, remember?"

"We restore, augment, enlarge upon. We don't try to build history from scratch. Would you look at this?"

"I'd love to," Cam said, "but I'm not there, remember? Why don't you describe it for me?"

"Gray fieldstone, black shutters, red door. That's not so bad. But, cripes, aluminum shutters and vinyl-clad windows. Oh, yeah, there was a lot of that in colonial America. I'd say at least a dozen bedrooms, by the way, and I remember a tennis court, pool, all the standard equipment of affluent suburbia. So that part's good. It's fine. God, Cam, this pile is my prison for the next week. Why would I care about the damn vinyl windows? If you have any pity in your heart for me at all, you'll call the house by Wednesday—no, Tuesday—and say you need me back in Philly on the double because a roof fell in or something. You have Bettie's phone number?"

"Relax, I have her number, Doug. I had it the first two times you gave it to me. I have to tell you, I still can't believe the tortured wreck I'm talking to is the same man voted Philadelphia's Most Eligible Bachelor and Man About Town, that's all."

"Two years running, Cam, you forgot to mention that," Doug reminded him without enthusiasm because, although he'd once found the awards amusing, they now seemed slightly pathetic. "But that's Philly. I'm stuck here, Cam, seven days of cooing and turtledoves and—okay, I'm over it. I'm a grown man, I can handle a lousy seven days of being the good son, the good cousin.

But I swear to you, Cam, if Bettie throws one too many marriage-hungry debutantes at my head, I won't be responsible for the consequences."

"Right, I remember. The fringe benefits you'll take, but never the consequences. That's our Doug. You know, one day you're going to be old and wrinkled and sorry you never got married."

"Please," Doug said as a teenage boy in a white shirt and red valet jacket opened the car door for him, "let my mother and Bettie give their own sermons, all right? I have to go. Tuesday, remember? And make sure you give the message to Bettie or her husband. What's his name? Oh, right, George. I'm counting on you, Cam."

"You're pathetic, Doug," his friend shot back at him, and Doug smiled as he severed the connection and climbed out of the car.

"Name, please," the valet said, holding a pen poised over several pages stuck to a clipboard.

"Douglas Llewellyn, prisoner 2-4-6-0-1," Doug told him affably as he bent down to hit the trunk release. When he looked at the valet again, he smiled and apologized. "Private joke, and not very funny, huh? You find me on those sheets?"

"Yes, sir, Mr. Llewellyn," the valet said, nod-

ding furiously. "You'll be in the Bachelor Quarter,
sir. That's out back over there, above the garage—
uh, carriage house. See it?" Then he flipped
through the pages a second time. "Hey, you're the
only one who's going to be out there. You the black
sheep or something? Not that they're bad digs. I
was out there earlier, and you've got your own
living room—wide-screen TV, too—even a
kitchen. It's really cool, like your own apartment.
I'll take one of the keys and make sure your bags
get up there, okay?"

Doug took the key the valet handed him, slipped
the kid ten bucks in the hope he wouldn't feel it
necessary to take the car from zero to fifty to get
to the parking lot roped off on the lawn and headed
for the front door before deciding it might be better
to just slip around to the back of the house to re-
connoiter before Bettie saw him.

The Bachelor Quarter? So he hadn't been wrong,
Bettie was definitely up to something. Not that he
hadn't been warned when he'd read the note his
cousin had slipped into his invitation. *I've got such
a lovely woman for you to meet! Bring your best
smile, Douglas, and be on your worst behavior!*

And here he was, an eligible, wealthy, not

hideous forty-year-old male attending a wedding that most romantic of occasions; armed with his own *bachelor* suite out of sight and sound of the other wedding guests, and probably fully stocked with wine, cheese and a few bunches of peeled grapes. What was the feminine of *pimp*, anyway— *pimpess?* Cousin Bettie, the pimpess. If he found a strip of condoms in his bedside drawer he was leaving, and Bettie could find another gazelle to feed to the chosen lioness.

Lost in a daydream in which Bettie was parading him around on a leash while giggling women called out bids, Doug only belatedly realized that he was now at the back of the huge mansion, where it seemed an informal party was in progress. No more than one hundred people, Doug estimated—just a few of Bettie and George's closest friends—and all of them decked out as if it was race day at Churchill Downs.

The grounds of the house stretched out every-where, the trees carefully thinned and incorporated into the landscape that included the tennis court and swimming pool he remembered, plus a brick terrace the size of an NBA basketball court. He couldn't see the stream that he remembered

from his last visit, but knew it was downhill somewhere, through the trees and at least one hundred
yards behind the house. Yes, one hundred yards
long, fifty-five yards wide. Football-field size.

Doug felt the need to think in sports terms,
manly terms, non-wedding terms. He was slightly
ashamed of himself. After all, he'd been slipping
out of matrimonial traps for a long time. He was
good at it, even excellent, a real master of the
game. But, damn, he was a hell of a lot more comfortable on his own turf, and with a quick escape
hatch close by. Bettie had managed to make him
her captive for a week. Worse, he was feeling
strangely vulnerable for some unknown reason.

Had Bettie and his mother put their heads
together and come up with this scheme? No, not
his mother. His mother loved him. Then again,
she'd been on that "when are you going to give me
grandchildren" kick again lately.

Locating the bar and a cold beer was definitely
becoming a priority.

The patio was the center of action at the
moment, dotted with a couple dozen round white
cast-iron tables capped by brightly striped umbrellas, with one side of the patio set up with buffet

tables loaded with chafing dishes and flower arrangements that were all white and coral carnations, or something like that. White and coral colored helium balloons were tied to the back of each chair and just about anywhere else he looked…and he was still looking for the bar.

And then he heard the voice.

"Darling, *there* you are! Why on earth didn't you call? I thought you'd gotten lost!"

She seemed to have come out of nowhere as she launched herself at him, and Doug instinctively held out his arms as they filled with a tall, well-shaped female with a faintly husky voice and a glorious mop of brunette curls that matched the laughing brown eyes of one damn good-looking woman. "Darling?" he asked, folding his arms around her.

"Yes, *darling*. Now don't just stand there—kiss me. And not just a peck on the cheek. *Mean it.*"

Doug Llewellyn had figured out long ago that a smart man doesn't look a gift horse in the mouth. And, speaking of mouths, the red, luscious, smiling lips she was just now reaching up toward him presented an invitation he wasn't about to refuse.

"If you insist," he said, drawing her closer and

covering her mouth with his own. She tasted of zinfandel, smelled like a blend of exotic spices…and felt like heaven. Their tongues tangled as her lips parted in a smile, and Doug kept one hand splayed against her upper back as his other hand ventured lowered, cupped her perfect behind as he eased her against the length of his body.

The pressure of her body reminded his that he'd taken himself off the market for two months, and maybe it was time he got back on the horse—or something like that.

If this was Bettie's idea of a present for her cousin, he was going to have to remember to send her more than a fruit basket this Christmas….

"Okay, that should do it," the woman said, her hands on Doug's shoulders as she pushed herself slightly away from him, apparently unimpressed by his expertise. She wasn't even breathing hard. "And thanks. I think he's got the message now."

"Good for him," Doug said, wildly grabbing at the famous Llewellyn "cool," except that he wasn't getting *his* breathing back under control as quickly as usual. "You want to give me the message now, too?"

Her smile wasn't doing much to help calm

the rest of him, either. She was gorgeous. That shoulder-length tumble of brown curls that glinted almost red in the sunlight. Those huge brown eyes that seemed innocent until he looked more closely and saw the mischief peeking out from beneath her long, thick lashes. That mouth he'd already tasted and wanted to taste again. Skin the color and consistency of cream. Tall, but not too tall, not model skinny, but not overweight, either, as her proportions were perfect. An armful of woman, soft in all the right places.

And she was returning his frank look, measuring him from head to foot and back again. "Boy, I know how to pick 'em," she said, grinning. "I'm Rosie, by the way. Rosie Kilgannon, wedding guest on the blushing bride's side—not related, just a friend. Please tell me the wife and kiddies won't be coming around the corner any minute to spoil our fun."

"Is that what we're doing?" Doug asked, lightly clasping his hands over her wrists as she tried to remove her arms from around his shoulders. "Having fun?"

Rosie bit her bottom lip for a second—nice, straight teeth—and let her body come in contact with his once more. "Weren't you? I know I was. You're a great kisser."

"So I've been told. As have you, I'm sure."

"I'm sure, too. I used to practice on a mirror when I was fifteen, put on a ton of red lipstick and then check the imprint to see if I was doing it right. You know, closed mouth, open mouth, maybe a little tongue—well, never mind, you don't want to hear that."

"I wouldn't have thought so five minutes ago, no, but strangely enough, the idea is growing on me."

"Oh, aren't you the smooth one. Okay, explanation time. I'm here for the wedding, not to be set up with Bettie's idea of my perfect mate. You know Bettie? She's the mother of the bride, and seems to have this fixation about fixing up people she thinks belong together. Anyway, for the last hour I've been stuck with this guy who felt some obviously overwhelming need to tell me how terrific he is and how much money he makes, and then I saw you and—hey, you looked like a good sport. You're also handsome as sin on a stick, and I won't say that didn't weigh in my decision. I mean, I'm not a complete fool. So, handsome, do you have a name?"

Doug was fascinated, absolutely fascinated.

Who told the truth like this? Certainly not any women he knew. "I do. Doug. Doug Llewellyn, cousin of the bride, and probably another one of Bettie's intended victims."

Rosie laughed, her chuckle full-fledged and throaty. "Oh, yeah, you sure are. I love Bettie, but she's the worst matchmaker in the universe. You're the guy I was warned to leave alone because you've already been matched up with Millicent Balfry."

"Not Mitzy, huh? Well, I was close. And what do you mean, matched up? How far has Bettie gone with this? Next question—do I really want to know that?"

"No, you don't want to know, but I'll tell you anyway, because us victims have to stick together," Rosie said, pulling away from him before taking his hand and leading him down three steps and onto the lawn.

Blow in my ear and I'll follow you anywhere. Doug shook his head. What in hell had made him think that? Not that he'd mind if Rosie Kilgannon wanted to blow in his ear. *Man, it has been awhile, hasn't it?*

"Bettie has it all figured out. You should see the lists and charts she's got in her sitting room. Timetables, menus, seating arrangements. You and Millicent Balfry—she's from Long Island, I understand, but I haven't met her yet—are seated side by side at every event. I'm supposed to be stuck with Mr. Big-I-Am, although not for long, because I'll fake an emergency and bail out if I have to."

Doug pulled her to a halt. "Whoa. This Millicent woman—where is she?"

Rosie shrugged her bare, rounded shoulders. She was, he decided, a very physical woman. Always moving, whether it be the near dance of her walk, her mobile facial expressions or the way she seemed incapable of speaking without using her hands. Alive. Bubbly. *Fascinating.* "I haven't met her yet, why? Oh, wait. Don't tell me you're one of *those.*"

"I'm not sure. What those do you mean?"

"You know—the kind who judges books by their covers? Like, if Millicent isn't a real bow-wow, maybe you'll just go with the flow and play escort, maybe have a little fun, break Millicent's little heart and then ride off into the sunset next Sunday night. Shame on you. How could you do that to poor Millicent?"

"Poor Millicent? You already admitted that you

don't even know her," Doug said, beginning to think his earlier idea of locating the bar and getting himself a drink had been a pretty good one. Rosie Kilgannon was a real looker, but she might just be a few shingles shy of a roof. "What do you care about Millicent? And now that I think about it, didn't *you* just dump your table partner?"

Her grin bordered on the wicked. "Oh, but that's entirely different, and eminently defensible. Trust me, that guy has had to have been dumped so many times, he keeps his own brush and dustpan handy to scoop himself back up again. But *I* at least made an informed decision. *You're* planning to cut and run without giving poor little Millicent a chance. Shame, shame on you, Douglas Llewellyn. You cad."

Doug was enjoying himself more and more by the moment. Rosie Kilgannon might be nuts, but she was *fun* nuts. "I'm not a cad. And would you stop with the poor little Millicent routine? I think I'm getting a complex."

She wrinkled her nose. She looked adorable. And sexy. "Sorry. And cad was maybe a little over the top, wasn't it?"

Doug was more than willing to overlook the

wacky parts of the woman in order to concentrate on the adorable and, most definitely, sexy parts. "I don't know you very well, Rosie, but I'd say you don't even know where the top *is*—or care. Do you?"

"No, not really," she answered affably, her smile wide and unaffected. "Now, tell me why, sight unseen, you're going to ditch poor little Millicent."

"First let's go somewhere private, where I can strangle you," Doug said just as affably, taking her hand and heading back up the steps to the patio, and then into the house via the closest set of French doors, preferring to stay out of Bettie's line of sight for a while.

Once inside, he stopped and turned to look at Rosie. "You want to know what I know? I know that my cousin Bettie has sicced five—no, six, I forgot Lillian Armbruster—women on me over the years, sending them to me because they needed a guide to take them around Philadelphia, show them the sights. I've *seen* Bettie's idea of my perfect mate. Believe me, I don't need to see Millicent Belfry."

"Balfry," Rosie corrected. "A belfry is where they keep bells...and bats."

"Exactly, and I rest my case. Damn, I knew I should have found a way out of this."

"Poor Dougie-do-do. Trapped, and with no handy escape hatch," Rosie said, wandering over to a huge square table covered with papers and charts. "And *so* lacking in imagination."

Doug tipped his head to one side for the amount of time it took for the sight of Rosie's incredibly long, straight legs emerging from the hem of the green-and-white polka-dotted flared skirt of her sleeveless dress to jump-start his brain—approximately two seconds—before joining her at the table. "Bettie's war room, right?"

"Uh-huh," Rosie said, pointing to a sixteen-by-sixteen square of paper covered with small yellow Post-it notes. "And here's today's buffet supper planned for the terrace, table by table." She reached out and lifted one small yellow rectangle, waving it back and forth in front of her. "R. Kilgannon. That's me. We understand each other, wouldn't you say? We're here for the wedding—but that's it, we're not here to be pawns in Bettie's romantic schemes. Being of the same mind—not to mention sound minds—it follows that we become allies, correct? So, do we have a deal?"

"Yes, I think we do, although I'm reserving judgment on that of sound mind bit." Doug leaned over and scanned the seating chart. "D. Llewellyn, prisoner 2-4-6-0-1," he said, lifting the Post-it with his name on it.

"Jean Valjean? You know *Les Miserables?* Would you believe my luck—I've found me a man of culture, a real Renaissance man. Tell me, Jean, if we do this, do you think we'll be forced to build barricades around the pool house to keep Javert— I mean, Bettie—from recapturing us and sending us back to our separate matchmaking prisons?"

"I hope not, Rosie. Or have you forgotten how that particular battle ended?"

"True, and with no sewer to escape through, either. So, where would you like to sit? I prefer my back to the wall when Bettie's around."

"The Wild Bill Hickok syndrome. I know it well, and I agree," Doug said, neatly placing M. Balfry where Rosie's Post-it had been. A quick search located two empty seats at another table, and he put his and Rosie's Post-its there. "Not exactly against the wall, but good enough, don't you think? Now, where's Monday?"

They spent the next ten minutes redoing Bettie's seating arrangements for every meal and event, then stood back to admire their work.

"Bettie's going to kill me," Doug said, his lack of concern for that possible fate evident in his voice.

"True, but at least we won't have to spend the week outrunning M. Balfry and Q. Martin."

"Q for Quentin?"

"As if he'd settle for Quentin. *Quint.* He owns an import and export firm in Manhattan, with a satellite store due to open soon in Queens. He calls his business *Quint's Quintessentials.* Isn't that pathetic? His bragging, I mean, although I could probably also be referring to the fact that I've somehow committed the information to memory."

"Close, on both counts. Now, what do you say you and I find the bar and drink a toast to Quint and Millicent—may they be very happy together."

Rosie slipped her arm through his and winked up at him. "Sounds like a plan, Stan."

Well, Doug thought, *at least the week's going to be interesting....*

CHAPTER TWO

ROSIE SAT AT HER NEWLY assigned table on the herringbone brick terrace, her chin in her hand, watching appreciatively as Doug Llewellyn made his way through the crowd to the bar to get them each a cold beer.

He looked as good going as he did coming, a tall, well put-together guy of about forty—a young forty. He probably played golf, maybe even tennis, and worked out three times a week.

Maybe he sailed, or went sculling on the Schuylkill, because she could remember that Bettie had told her that her Philadelphia cousin was to be one of the weeklong guests. He'd gotten that tan somewhere outdoors, and not in a salon. She could tell, because he didn't have that telltale white around his eyes from those funny little plastic eye protectors.

Rosie wasn't a judgmental person by nature,

but there was something about seeing those small oval white patches on a man's face and then imagining him oiling up and lying in one of those coffinlike tanning tubes that…well, that didn't exactly fit her idea of a fail-safe aphrodisiac.

Back to her inventory. She liked his hair, which was thick, nearly pitch-black and just a little too long to be considered Ivy League. But it was his eyes that really got to her. Gray eyes. She was a real sucker for great eyes, and couldn't remember the last time she'd seen true gray eyes. They fascinated her, especially with those small laugh-line crinkles at the outside edges. He dressed like an Armani model, but looked a little bit more like a Ralph Lauren model, now that she thought about it. Smooth, but not too smooth, then again, most definitely never rumpled. Casually, unaffectedly handsome…the sort that didn't have to work at looking great, didn't seem aware of how good he looked. Effortlessly gorgeous.

And he was a good kisser. Possibly even a terrific kisser.

When she considered the thing from every angle, and right now she was considering his profile—that straight nose, the clean cut of his chin—she was pretty proud of her judgment. This could be an interesting week....

"Rosie Kilgannon—*how could you?*"

Rosie reluctantly dragged her eyes away from Doug and turned to smile innocently up at Bettie Rossman. "How could I what, Bettie?"

Bettie sat down with a little too much emphasis, and winced. "Damn that caterer for forgetting the cushions. Who wants to sit directly on cast iron? The chairs in the sun are too hot, the ones in the shade are too cold, and all of them are too hard. Well, he'd better be here first thing tomorrow morning, or he can kiss ten percent of his fee goodbye."

Rosie selected a fat almond from the crystal dish on the table and popped it into her mouth. "No wedding ever goes completely smoothly, Bettie," she told her commiseratingly. "I think everything's beautiful."

"You would. You have no idea of the chaos in the kitchen. Half the quail have burned and all they can find to replace them are chickens. Chickens! They're huge, not at all dainty, like quail," Bettie told her, picking up a pecan and stuffing it in her mouth. "Not that I'm going to eat dinner. I can't afford to put anything past my lips except yogurt and my usual egg-white omelets if I want to have a prayer of getting into my gown next Sunday. As it is, this pecan is probably going to go right to my hips."

Rosie shook her head. Bettie Rossman was nearly as thin as the pole holding up the umbrella over her head. Thin, too tan, a shade too blond, and probably only one or two face-lifts behind Joan Rivers. "I shouldn't remind you, but I think you sat down here to yell at me."

"God, yes, I most certainly did," the older woman said, glaring in Doug's general direction. "Him, I understand. But not you, Rosie. You know who he is, don't you? And I distinctly told you to stay away from him. Stay away from my cousin Doug, that's exactly what I told you. He's a confirmed bachelor, has women hanging on him all the time and breaks hearts at least once a week. I love you, and I don't want you anywhere near him. You do remember me telling you all of that?"

"I do, but I'm confused. You don't want me around him, but you do want him near Millicent Balfry? Don't you love her, too?"

"Of course I love her. I adore her, she's been my friend since forever." Bettie flushed beneath her tan.

"The thing is, Millicent's been divorced for nearly a year. She needs a little personal male...attention."

Rosie cocked her head to one side. "Why, Bettie Rossman, you dirty old woman, you. You're setting your cousin up as her bed partner?"

"As her stud muffin, yes, I won't lie." Bettie leaned closer. "Nearly a *year,* Rosie. They can say what they want about C batteries, I'm here to tell you they're not the same. The woman needs a little fun."

"And your cousin is supposed to provide that fun." Rosie rested her chin in her palm as she leaned her elbow on the tabletop. "That's...well, that's fascinating."

"Yes, damn it, it is. And it isn't as if she wouldn't be grateful. The thing is, Millicent tells me everything, and I've been dying to know what's so special about Doug. You know—does he have special tricks he does, that sort of thing? Maybe he's very good at *certain things?* Maybe, you know, that one very *special* thing? He's certainly never without women chasing him, so there has to be something. I know—money, good looks. But there's something more, I'm sure of it."

Rosie didn't know whether to laugh or be horrified. Or intrigued—she was, after all, human. And

Millicent Balfry wasn't the only one who'd had a slow year. "Oh, okay, I understand now—inquiring minds want to know. Doug takes Millicent into his bed, performs his *tricks,* and you get to find out what they are. Bettie, that's disgusting. He's your *cousin.*"

"Exactly, so I'll never be able to find out anything for myself, will I? I do have my limits. And *you* would never tell me, so I want you to stay away. Oh, shush, here he comes," Bettie said, getting to her feet and smoothing down her coral linen sheath before holding out her arms to Doug. "Darling, darling Douglas—I'd about given you up, you naughty man. Come here and give your cousin a kiss."

Rosie watched as Bettie threw her arms around Doug—a nanosecond after he'd deposited two glasses on the table—and gave him a fairly un-cousinly kiss, then continued to look on with amusement as he untangled himself, taking hold of his cousin's hands, probably in self-protection.

"Don't you look wonderful, Bettie—and much too young to be the mother of the bride. Where's George?"

"George?" Bettie repeated, shrugging. "Know-ing my husband, he and a few of his golf bum friends are holed up in his den, drinking Scotch and watching some tournament on the flat screen. He even played eighteen holes this morning, with everyone arriving today, and expressly against my wishes. I learned long ago that I don't need to know where George is, Doug. I just need to know where he keeps the checkbook."

"There's nothing like honesty. You're such a breath of fresh air, Bettie," Doug said, letting go of her hands. "Once again, I've been instructed to tell you that my parents send their regrets."

"Yes, your mother called the day they left. She's horrified to miss Lili-beth's nuptials—simply beside herself. But they did send the most lovely engraved silver compote for the happy couple. Oh, by the way, Douglas, you seem to be sitting at the wrong table."

Rosie watched, amused, as Doug raised one expressive eyebrow. "You've assigned seats for a picnic? What's next, sweetheart—we all wear those large paper name tags plastered to our chests? Hi, I'm Doug—what's your name?"

Rosie stuffed a knuckle in her mouth to keep from laughing out loud.

Bettie's shadowed eyelids narrowed as she considered the question from the only angle she understood: hers. "Name tags? Don't be ridiculous, Douglas—most of these women are wearing pure, designer silk. Glue would stick to the fabric horribly, and pins would simply ruin good materials, so don't even suggest those. No, that would never work." Then she turned to glare down at Rosie, who had somehow refrained from banging her fists on the table in mirth. "What? What's so funny?"

"Nothing," Rosie promised, quickly reaching for her glass of beer. "You only think I'm laughing."

Bettie, one of those otherwise nice but unfortunate people born without a sense of humor—and definitely no ear for sarcasm—sighed and turned back to her cousin. "And why must you always be so contrary? I've worked hard on this wedding, Doug, harder than you can imagine, and seating charts are a bear—just the very worst. The least you could do is be cooperative."

"Ah, but I know you. You tried to set me up with one of your friends today, Bettie. I'll never be *that* cooperative," he said quietly, "and you should know that by now. But thanks for the bachelor suite. There's a lock on the door, I sincerely hope?"

"Bachelor *Quarter,*" Bettie corrected. "You

know, like the French *Quarter?* And I have no idea what you're implying. You're a guest at my daughter's wedding, and that's all."

Doug bent down to kiss his cousin's cheek. "Now that's what I wanted to hear, Betts."

"Don't call me Betts. I hate Betts. And…and you've ruined everything! What am I going to tell Millicent? I promised her you'd be her escort for the week."

"You shouldn't have done that, Bettie," Doug told her, no longer smiling. "Not for me, and not for Ms. Kilgannon, here, who has just agreed to be my companion for the week. We're considering ourselves rebels with a cause, I suppose you can say, as neither of us is interested in being one of your romantic experiments. Or we could both leave?"

Rosie raised her hand as if she wished to be called on in class. "I think Quint is looking for someone to hang on his arm and look at least half as interested in him as he is—would that make everything all right again?"

Bettie looked at Rosie as if she'd grown another head. "Oh, you don't know, do you? Millicent took back her maiden name—Quint is her *ex.* They *loathe* each other. I couldn't possibly put them together and hope they wouldn't kill each other and ruin Lili-beth's wedding. And you can't leave, neither of you, or you'll upset all the numbers—they're perfect, and they can't be rearranged without unbalancing one of the tables. I planned for all tens and a few eights, but certainly not sixes—the tables aren't the right size for sixes. As it is, I'm going to have to rework all the seating charts. If only priests could marry—but it did work out, pairing him with Aunt Susanna, I suppose. As long as he doesn't mind when she falls asleep over dessert. Father Rourke shouldn't mind that, should he? Don't they take vows of patience or something? Still, I don't have any extra singles, so I'll have to reshuffle the ones I do have, and keep Quint and Millicent at least three tables apart." She threw up her hands. "And I thought the quails were bad? This is a fiasco! Douglas Llewellyn, I will never forgive you for this—never!"

"I'm so sorry, Bettie." Rosie asked, getting to her feet, "If you find out that you can't reshuffle the place cards to work out for you, I'll leave, if that helps?"

"Don't be silly. You can't leave—I told you, *even* numbers. If just you left it would upset things even more. What would I do with a table of seven? I *forbid* you to leave. As a matter of fact," she said, looking from Rosie to Doug and then back again, "this may be just fine. You two deserve each other. Just don't think you can change partners again. You're stuck with each other, both of you, for the entire week."

Doug watched as his cousin flounced off, then sat down and turned to Rosie. "She sure got her shots in, didn't she? Now what do you suppose she meant by that deserve-each-other crack?"

Rosie shrugged. "I'm not sure. She's always after me for dating too many men and not settling down with any of them. You wouldn't happen to be the love 'em and leave 'em type, would you?"

"Some people might think so. I'd much rather consider myself merely as unattached…and very friendly."

"Then that's probably what Bettie was hinting at with her parting shot. Here's to being very friendly," Rosie said, lifting her glass so that they could clink them together. "Why can't people understand that not everyone is in a hurry to get married? Why must they always think they need to set us up with someone? What's so great about marriage, anyway? It doesn't seem to have done much good for Millicent and Quint—and Bettie and George sure don't come off as Romeo and Juliet."

"I hope not—they both died, remember? Tragically."

Rosie took a sip of ice-cold beer, shivering as it hit the back of her throat. "Good point. And I'm not knocking marriage. There's nothing wrong with it. If only I could get my friends to understand that I'm not ready for that sort of commitment, and stop throwing guys at my head. Especially newly divorced guys. Believe me, they're the worst, and who wants to be the rebound woman who gets to hear about the ex-wife every day—how she's bleeding him dry, how she never understood him, how she was so cold in bed, etc., etc.?"

"You don't believe them?"

"Are you kidding? There are two sides to every marriage, and every divorce—and heaven save me from the men who refuse to figure out that they were at least half the problem. What about you? Millicent is divorced. Is that your usual date?"

She watched as Doug seemed to be considering her question. Gosh, he had great eyes.

"How honest are we going to be here?" he asked at last.

"I don't know. We're allies, right, as well as prey? You and me against Bettie's matchmaking schemes? Watching each other's backs until the wedding's over and we can escape? I guess we should be honest with each other, maybe even share trade secrets."

Doug looked at his half-full glass, then drained its contents. "All right. Honesty. I don't have your problems because I'm very…careful about the women I see."

"Do tell," Rosie said, resting her chin in her hand. He looked so serious. "So what you're saying is that I'm not careful enough? How does one go about being careful?"

"For you? I don't know. It's probably different for women."

"Maybe. If a guy has never married he's usually a mama's boy—present company excepted, I most sincerely hope—and I already told you about the divorced ones. As my friends love to remind me— the pickings are pretty slim once you've been out there on your own for more than five or ten years. So come on, give me Doug Llewellyn's patented, surefire way to happy, commitment-free dating."

"I just know what works for me." He shook his head. "And I don't believe I'm talking about this with you."

Rosie deliberately batted her eyelashes at him. "You can't help it. It's this open and trusting face of mine—see? Everyone tells me everything, sooner or later. We just told Bettie we're going to be pals for the week, so you might as well make it sooner."

"Pals? Really? I think I'm looking forward to hearing your definition of *pals*. But all right, here goes. Just remember—you did ask. It comes down to age. I've made it a rule to only date women between the age of consent and twenty-six."

Rosie tried not to laugh because the man did look serious, and because she wanted to hear more. "You're kidding, right?"

"No. Twenty-six. Lately, up to twenty-eight. But that's pretty much the cutoff."

"Okay, twenty-eight. Would you mind telling me why? You have a theory here, right? I'd love to know how you arrived at it before I start robbing the cradle for my own dates. I mean, one of the valets out front is pretty cute, but I'm not sure he needs to shave more than twice a week. So you're going to have to nail this down better for me, Doug, if you don't mind? Do you think age of consent to twenty-eight would work for me, or should I have to operate within more limited parameters?"

Doug used a single finger to root through the nut dish and came up with the last macadamia nut in the assortment. "This is ridiculous. I can't believe we're having this conversation."

"No, no, it's not ridiculous, not if this age thing is a theory you live by, one that's been successful for you. And I'm loving this conversation. I'm considering it an intellectual discussion, even if I am laughing," Rosie pointed out, grinning at him. This was fun, this was a lot of fun—definitely more fun than listening to Quint blow his own horn. "What happens when a woman turns twenty-eight? Does she get too territorial? Oh, and that's the last macadamia, and I want it."

"Well, hell, as long as you're enjoying yourself. And I just turned forty—I might stretch that to twenty-nine now. The ages are just guidelines, but I can be flexible, in the right circumstances." Doug held up the nut as if inspecting it for flaws. "Macadamias are expensive. Do you suppose Bettie had her caterer count them out? You know, three per bowl, and everyone else has to be happy with pecans and peanuts?"

Ah, wasn't that cute—he was trying to change the subject. "I don't know. I don't care. Be a gentleman like your momma taught you and hand over that nut."

"If you insist. Open up."

Rosie rolled her eyes but did as he said, then clamped her teeth lightly around his finger and thumb, ran the edge of her tongue across the tips before letting him go. His reaction was halfway between surprise and pleasure, just what she'd hoped for. "Don't panic. Bettie was looking, and I'm perverted enough to want to tick her off after what she tried to do to me—and to you, of course," she told him. "Now, one more time—why twenty-nine? Do we women turn into hags at thirty? I'm thirty-two, by the way, so you might want to think about that answer before you open your mouth and I have to hurt you."

"Thirty-two? You don't look it."

"Thank you, I guess."

He grinned at her, showing off those sexy crinkles around his eyes. "Making you entirely too old for me."

Rosie sat back against the cast iron that was, as Bettie had said, cold in the shade. Did she just hear what she thought she'd heard? "And you're an old man of forty. Maybe you're too old for me. Have you considered that one?"

"To tell you the truth? No, I never considered that. Women are, as a rule, much more flexible when it comes to age. And it's not really age, Rosie—it's inclination on the woman's part, combined with the need for self-protection on mine. Look—women in their early to midtwenties are just out of the uncertainty of their teenage years, they're on their own, they want to experience life without commitments."

"Girls just want to have fun. I see. Fascinating. And after age twenty-six—or twenty-nine? Don't we want to have fun anymore?"

He refused to look at her, probably because she couldn't stop grinning like a loon. "You still want to have fun, but you also want commitment. You start hearing your biological clocks ticking, and it's not just a good time you're looking for anymore. It's not fair for a man who doesn't plan on ever marrying—that would be me, Rosie—to date a woman who's ready to settle down. So I steer clear."

"Gosh, how generous of you," Rosie said, finally losing her smile. "I'll bet you'll be up for some great humanitarian award anytime now."

He sat back in his chair. "And now you're angry. I knew this honesty business was going to backfire. Laying it all out upfront isn't everything it's cracked up to be, is it?"

"Not on this subject, no, I don't think so," Rosie agreed, holding her beer glass between her palms, watching the foam as it disappeared bubble by bubble. "It's funny. I never thought of myself as being too old for a forty-year-old man. But it's good to know this, it really is. We understand each other now. So what do we do? Switch back the name cards? I mean, I wouldn't want to annoy you with the ticking of my biological clock."

"I thought you said you weren't interested in marriage."

"I'm not. I hate to skew your bell curve or whatever it is, but I'm still having fun. I'm building my business, I like living alone and being responsible only for me. I don't even own a cat. And I really can't dislike you because I'm very much like you—unattached and liking it. We're a good fit for the week, Doug, especially now that we...understand each other. After all, neither of us can say we haven't been warned."

"So we'll watch each other's backs in case Bettie's got some other matrimonial prospects she's thinking of dragging out for us, enjoy each other's company, and when the week is over, go our separate ways? Is that what you're saying? And why am I wondering if I've suddenly lost my capacity for beer and I'm drunk on one small glass?"

Rosie thought this over for a few seconds. The plan seemed sound. And, damn, he was cute. And honest. Honest was something a woman didn't see a lot of out in the dating world. "It will make things easier. Unless you see some twenty-five-year-old bridesmaid or something and beg out of our bargain. Oh, and the same for me, just in case some gorgeous hunk shows up and winks at me. Agreed?"

Doug leaned his elbows on the tabletop. "How...how *together* are you thinking we should be? Sitting beside each other at meals together? Participating in prewedding events together? Spending all our time together? Do we fake a romance to keep Bettie away? Do we do more than fake it if we find ourselves so inclined?"

"I don't know," Rosie answered honestly

because, like Doug, she was nothing if not honest…most of the time. "I'm still not sure I like you. You appeal to me, definitely, I won't lie about that one because you wouldn't believe me, and I'm fairly certain I appeal to you. But maybe you're a little shallow. I know I am, so I recognize the type. So, for now, I don't see any *inclined* stuff going on, sorry."

Doug nodded his head slightly at her words. "So you think I'm shallow? I don't know, Rosie Kilgannon, but that sounded an awful lot like a biological clock I heard ticking just now. I thought you said you were still in the girls just want to have fun category. Shallow should work for you."

Rosie longed to slap his handsome, smiling face. "Don't do that. Don't point it out when I contradict myself. I've…I've just never had a conversation like this before. I doubt anyone has. Face it, how many times does anyone have a warts-and-all discussion like this, reveal this much of themselves to anyone else, let alone someone they just met— unless it's two strangers baring their souls on a plane just before it nosedives into the ocean? I feel…selfish. I think you're selfish, too. Thinking of ourselves first, last and always. It isn't a pleasant realization. I look at you, I listen to you, and I feel like I'm listening to myself as I look in a mirror."

"All right," he answered, draining his beer glass. "You're making sense because I'm feeling pretty much the same way. Some things probably just shouldn't be said out loud—especially to the opposite sex."

"Meaning that business about how you think I'm too old to be happy just dating, having fun? Meaning that any woman over the age of thirty should be thinking wedding gowns and white picket fences? Oh, and two-point-five kiddies?"

"No, I don't mean—well, maybe. What seems perfectly normal and reasonable behavior for me just doesn't seem normal and reasonable for a woman, that's all I'm saying. Does that make me a male chauvinist pig?"

"Very possibly, yes. Or just confused. Let's forget me for a minute, all right, and concentrate on you. You said you just turned forty, right? Doug, do you realize that Lili-beth is twenty-five? You're dating women the same age as your second cousin. It's not unreasonable, but what happens in another ten years, when you've just turned fifty? Then a twenty-five-year-old will be young enough to be your daughter, for crying out loud. Yes, I think you have a problem heading your way down the line, buddy boy. Maybe not yet, but soon. I mean— forty? Don't look now, Don Juan, but you're not thirty-nine anymore. Playtime may soon be over."

Doug looked at her levelly. "You should meet my mother. You two have a lot in common."

"No, thanks. I'm not interested in the meet-my-mother stuff yet, remember? It's like I told you— I'm still building my business and enjoying myself. I don't have any room in my life for anything or anyone else, not on a serious level anyway. But you? I don't know, Doug, but it might soon be time for Peter Pan to grow up. But don't worry, the moment you do, Bettie will be right there with another Millicent for you."

Rosie noticed that somewhere during that last exchange, Doug had winced, actually winced. What had she said that finally penetrated, hit him? Was it when she'd said that thing about Peter Pan? Yeah, that was the moment. Poor guy. Then again, hadn't more than a few female actors played the part of Peter Pan? Was she talking to Doug, but also looking at herself again in that mental mirror?

How had they begun this strange conversation? How could it possibly end?

"Thanks, I'll keep that in mind, but for now, let's change the subject. Tell me about your business."

Ah, he'd been thinking the same thing: change the subject. Good! "Really? So we've still got a deal?"

"We've still got a deal, with a few terms yet to be negotiated. Now tell me the truth—you're a divorce lawyer, right?"

Rosie laughed out loud. "No, far from it. I design Web sites—lately, mostly for romance authors."

He sat back in his chair and fairly goggled at her. "You're kidding, right?"

"No, romance authors. And, wow, you're still not running. Maybe it's that old-age thing creeping up on you. Should I give you a head start? Count to ten, or something?"

"Yeah, it's hard to run these days, dragging this oxygen tank around with me and my walker. Or maybe I'm just too stunned to remember how my legs work. Aren't romance writers the champions of romantic fantasy and happily ever after?"

"Only if you listen to people who don't read romances. The authors write about commitment to one person, about trust, honesty and mutual respect." She grinned. "And sometimes about handsome vampires and sexy werewolves—but we won't go there, right?"

"Vampires? You're right, let's not go there. I think I've had enough information, thank you. But you design Web sites for romance writers while you aren't looking for that commitment, trust, honesty and—what was that last one you said?"

"Mutual respect. And I'm not saying I'm against any of that. It's all good stuff. I'm just not in the market yet, that's all, even at the advanced age of thirty-two. There are exceptions to every rule, Doug, even yours. However, the bridesmaid making her way over here while pretending she isn't probably isn't one of them, as I'm pretty sure she meets your girls who still just want to have fun requirements."

Doug turned in his seat just as a young blonde who must have gotten caps for her birthday and boobs for Christmas rounded the nearest table and headed their way. He looked back at Rosie. "Is she for real?"

"Not all of her, I'm pretty sure," Rosie told him sweetly. "That's Ki-Ki—don't remember if I heard her last name when we were introduced. She's Lilibeth's maid of honor. I love the names some rich people give their kids—probably to punish them for ruining mommy's figure for nine months. Anyway, Ki-Ki's in her midtwenties I'd say, just like Lili-beth, and well within the parameters you've set for your dates. Don't look now, partner, but I'm betting she thinks you're a perfect fit for her, too. Gosh, do you think she has a daddy complex?"

Doug shook his head as he closed his eyes and sighed theatrically. "Please tell me you aren't going to make my dating preferences into a running joke for the rest of the week."

"I can't promise, sorry. Okay, look again, she's expecting you to take a second look. Oh, what am I telling you that for? You know the rules. Heck, you're probably old enough to have written a couple of them."

"See if I ever give you my last macadamia nut again, Ms. Kilgannon," Doug said, grimacing. Then he did as she said and Ki-Ki stopped, posed, smiled and then continued on her way to the table.

Doug turned his back on the smile and the hip wiggle. "Why do I suddenly feel so old? If I get down on my knees, apologizing for every stupid word I've said in the past hour, will you save me?"

"Well, there still are some terms to be negotiated."

"Anything you want. Anything. Lili-beth probably has a dozen more bridesmaids just like her. Thanks to you, I won't be able to look at any of them without thinking about Lili-beth. You found me in a weak moment, Rosie Kilgannon, and you've ruined me—now you have to save me."

"In that case," Rosie said, leaning toward him provocatively, "kiss me, you fool."

Doug grinned in obvious relief, the poor man. "Like I mean it?"

Men were *so* easy. Rosie returned his smile as she breathed, a mere inch from his mouth, "Oh, I'm not worried about that. You will…"

CHAPTER THREE

SHE STILL TASTED GOOD. Different from the first time, now with the sweetness of malt on her breath, but good. Doug wasn't touching her, nor she him, except for where their mouths fused together and their dueling tongues collided, but it had to be one of the most sensual kisses in his memory.

Then he felt her lips twitching into a smile and opened his eyes to see that she was peering over his back instead of keeping her eyes closed as she swooned in passion.

"What?" he asked, pulling away from her, trying to tell himself he wasn't disappointed in her amused reaction to his kiss.

"Nothing. But you're all clear and safe now, Doug. She's gone, headed off at the pass—meaning the pass you just made at me. I told you it would work."

"No, you told me I'd *mean* that kiss," Doug reminded her, adding mentally that, so far in their unique relationship, there had been nothing *safe* about Rosie Kilgannon. "Me, but not you, obviously. How do you women turn it on and off like that?"

Rosie smiled at him. "Centuries of practice, or so I'm told. And who says I'm turned off? For all you know, I could be acting now, and not then. Maybe I'm inwardly a molten mass of lust, just a heartbeat away from throwing myself into your arms and begging you to carry me off to your lair and have your wicked way with me."

"Really?"

"No," she told him, grinning, as she patted his cheek. "But I made you think about it, didn't I?"

"I wish I'd met you years ago, Rosie Kilgannon."

"Oh? Why?"

"Because I would have immediately flown to Tibet and become a monk, instead of deluding myself for the past twenty years that I'm even a little bit attractive to women," he told her as a waiter placed small coral dishes in front of both of them. "You're fairly frightening."

"Oh, I am not, and you are so attractive…in a paternal sort of way." Her grin widened. "Can you tell I've been giving some thought to that idea of dating younger men, the way you do younger women? It just makes good sense for a woman, doesn't it?"

"I don't know, Rosie. How does a woman dating younger men make sense? And why am I asking this question, knowing full well you were going to tell me the answer anyway?"

She shrugged rather eloquently and with all the grace of a Frenchwoman on the flirt. "Well, Doug, if you insist. Think about it. A female in her thirties and forties is just coming into her sexual prime, and there's nobody more *primed* than young males. But you? Ah, after forty there's all those problems that keep cropping up—or not very up, if you know what I mean. At least if we're to believe all those television ads. You guys have it really rough. I mean, you *can't* fake it, can you?"

Doug rubbed at his forehead. If she wasn't so beautiful, and so physically desirable, he'd be gone, outta here. No. No, he wouldn't. He may have somehow taken a left turn this afternoon and landed in la-la land, but he wasn't going to lie to himself. How could he leave now? He'd miss whatever she was going to say next. "I may need therapy after this week is over. Is there anything you *won't* say?"

"Probably not," Rosie told him as she looked down at the contents of her plate. "Isn't this a pretty salad? If only I could stop thinking about how many times someone had to touch each perfect piece to arrange it all this way. Look at yours, it's exactly the same as mine. Little bitty ear of corn just there, cherry tomato five degrees to the left, fancy-cut quarter carrot at nine o'clock, exactly five thin slices of green pepper in the shape of a fan. Touched, touched, touched—and there's probably enough leftover veggies in the trash bins in the kitchen to feed a small town."

Doug relaxed slightly. "Let me take a guess here. We're changing the subject again, right? I know we only met, but I'm fairly certain you want to change the subject."

She picked up her napkin and neatly spread it across her lap. "Oh, no, not at all. I'm merely making an observation, Douglas. A lot of people don't think about this, you know, but I do, because I worked in a high-end restaurant during my summers between college semesters. You only *hope* everyone in the kitchen who had their hands all over your carefully arranged food was wearing gloves. And, of course, that they obeyed that little sign in the restroom—the one that reminds them that all employees must wash their hands before returning to the kitchen."

"Okay, so much for the salad," Doug said, gingerly pushing his plate toward the center of the table. "Shall we go see what's available at the buffet? If, that is, you can refrain from pointing out possible health-code violations with every dish."

"Sure we can. Just as soon as I eat my salad," Rosie said, picking up her fork.

"Whoa. Wait a minute. You're going to *eat* that? After what you told me?"

She spoke around a mouthful of cherry tomato. "I like to live dangerously. Don't you?"

"I'm still sitting here with you, aren't I?" Doug asked, feeling as if he'd gotten in his first real zinger for the afternoon.

Apparently Rosie thought so, too, because she sat back and applauded, then leaned over to kiss his cheek. "You're really adorable. May I have your cherry tomato?"

Doug had an idea. "Is that what this was all about? You gave me that horror story about no gloves and bathroom hygiene—just to get my cherry tomato?"

She popped the tomato into her mouth and let it push out her cheek, and Doug suddenly realized that there was nothing quite as attractive as the sight of a beautiful woman who didn't seem to care that she was beautiful. "Worked, didn't it?"

"You could have simply *asked*."

Rosie rolled her wicked brown eyes. "And what fun would that have been? Come on, let's scope out the buffet before the line forms. I'm starving. Besides, we'd be helping Bettie. Nobody ever wants to be the first in a buffet line, so if we don't start it, all these people will just politely sit on their hands until they faint from hunger. Watch— the minute we're up there grabbing goodies, the rest of the herd will follow."

Doug stood up as Rosie did, then followed after her like a Labrador brought to heel—not that he wanted to dwell very long on that comparison. Sure enough, by the time they'd picked up napkins and cutlery, a line had formed behind them. It was almost spooky the way Rosie Kilgannon seemed to understand human behavior, and he could hardly wait to hear her next observation on the minutia of the world around them—a world he'd obviously not been aware of.

They were only halfway through the line before Doug realized that she hadn't been kidding when she'd said she was starving. She had a method, she'd told him—a How to Navigate a Buffet Method. She'd handed him two large plates, and then directed him to walk behind her as she piled food on those plates.

When she was done ladling and piling—Rosie seemed to believe a person should take a little of absolutely every offered dish—he carried the heavy plates back to their table to see that the other six places were now occupied with an odd assortment of young men in their twenties.

"You know, I wasn't paying attention earlier. Who did we finally end up with, anyway?"

Rosie tilted her head, looked at their tablemates and then grinned. "I don't know. I was just looking for a table near a wall, Wild Bill, as we both seemed to have the same preference. But this is neat. I think we're sitting with the band. Isn't that terrific?"

"Oh yeah, definitely. Yippee," Doug said quietly.

"You're not happy? Come on, Doug, don't be

stuffy. Just think—we could have ended up with Father Rourke and Aunt Susanna."

"True. Aren't we the lucky ones," Doug said, and then realized he was being an idiot. Snobbish, even. "But I'll bet they don't know who Frank Sinatra is."

"*Was,* unfortunately. I cried like a baby when Ole Blue Eyes died. And five bucks says you're wrong."

Doug shot an assessing look at the cadaverously thin, pale young men who seemed to be in the middle of a chicken wing–eating contest, the object of the thing being who could wear the most barbeque sauce. They all had obviously dyed jet-black hair of varying lengths and styles, and they all were dressed in black suits with black shirts and black bow ties. They looked like a not-too-bright gang of penguins after dark.

"I'll take that bet and your money," Doug said as one of the band members employed a denuded chicken bone to scratch an itch behind his ear. "Good afternoon, gentlemen," Doug said brightly as he put down the plates. "Let me guess. You'd be the band? This lovely lady is my companion, Ms. Rosie Kilgannon."

One of the penguins lifted a finger as if to tell

Doug to wait as he finished off one more chicken leg, and then he wiped his hands on the sleeve of the band member next to him before holding his right hand out to Doug. "Anvil. Ear Waxx."

"Doug. Occasional sinus congestion," Doug shot back amiably as he ignored the hand. Instead, he held back the chair for a giggling Rosie—he liked a woman with a sense of humor—and as he slid it forward as she sat down, he whispered close to her hair, "Care to make that ten bucks?"

But she wasn't listening. She was too busy leaning her elbows on the table as she looked from band member to band member. "Ear Waxx? Really? I thought you looked familiar the minute I saw you, but the band I heard was Six Finger Sticky. Or was that Stickies? Sickies! That's it— Six Finger Sickies. And you were all blond. Liked the blond, wasn't so sure about the orange Spandex. Am I right—you're the Sickies?"

Doug squeezed at the bridge of his nose with thumb and forefinger as he mumbled, "Toto, I don't think we're on Earth anymore."

"Shh, Doug," Rosie warned him with a wave of her hand. "Try a chicken wing, they're obviously very good. I gave you two."

He decided to take her advice. What the hell, it wasn't as if he had anything else to do, unless he counted finding the valet, retrieving his keys and pointing his car back toward Philly.

The band member who had held out his hand now grinned at Rosie. He was actually quite a good-looking young man, if one discounted the starving-artist physique, the black eye makeup and the grinning silver skull in his left ear. "You saw us? Where? Oh, wait. We were only Six Finger Sickies for that gig in Wildwood last summer. Right, Floyd?"

The boy to his right nodded furiously as he reached for his glass of beer.

"Yeah, thought so," Anvil said. "So you saw us in Wildwood? Man, the girls were all over us that week. Wow. How'd I miss you? You're bitchin'. Maybe we can meet up later." He winked at her. "Show you why the babes love me."

"Down, boy, I've got this." Rosie's arm shot out to collide with Doug's chest as he actually felt himself beginning to rise from his chair. "Sounds like a lot of fun, Anvil, thanks, but as you can see, I'm sort of taken. He's old, you understand, and I feel sorry for him." She winked at Doug. "Are you guys here just for today, or for the whole week?"

"We're solid for the week. Rooms at the Quality Inn, food and a cool thousand each. Well, a buck and a half for me. I'm the lead, you know. The big draw."

"The bride chose you, right?" Rosie asked, popping a ripe olive into her mouth. "I was with her at that bar in Wildwood. She thought your drummer was pretty hot."

The last penguin on the left, probably a natural redhead if the freckles meant anything, blushed as the guy next to him elbowed him in the ribs. "You hear that, Sticks—chicks dig you." The collective Ear Waxx laughed, and then collectively went back to their food and their beer.

"Guys, I've got a question for you," Rosie said, once again leaning her elbows on the table as if vastly interested in their answer. "Do any of you know who Frank Sinatra was?"

Sticks raised his hand. "I do. He's the guy sang that song with Bono a bunch of years ago, right? Good song, but I never heard of him again after that. U-2 rocks."

"Close," Doug corrected, "but you've got it backward. Bono sang with Sinatra."

"Yeah?" Sticks asked, smirking around a

mouthful of chicken. "Which one's still on the charts, huh?"

Doug leaned in closer to Rosie. "Let me see if I've got this right. Lili-beth chose this band because she thought the drummer was hot? And she's getting *married?*"

Rosie shrugged. "Like mother, like daughter? No, seriously, they're pretty good. I'm not sure about the new name, though. Ear Waxx? It lacks that certain something, don't you think?"

Doug thought about all of this for a few moments. Well, the first part, anyway. He really didn't have an opinion on Ear Waxx, at least not one he could voice in mixed company. "The last time I saw Lili-beth she was maybe sixteen, seventeen? She was a cute kid. Not that I said more than hello to her, but she seemed—" he paused, looked at Anvil again "—normal."

Rosie was efficiently working her way around her plate, taking a bite of minilasagna this time and chewing it before answering him. "Lili-beth *is* normal, which you'll agree is fairly remarkable, all things considered. I lied, by the way. Bettie chose the band. And she wasn't hot for the drummer. She was hot for Anvil. I just didn't want to shock you or them, that's all. Try the Swedish meatballs, they're delicious."

"That 'all things considered' part? That would be Bettie and George?"

Putting down her fork—how had she done it? Her food was completely gone—Rosie looked at him, then sighed. "This is difficult since you're a relative."

"Pretend I'm not. God knows I do whenever I can."

Rosie smiled. "That's what Bettie told me. The amazing, disappearing Douglas Llewellyn. Not that I don't think you have your reasons. I'm Lili-beth's friend, not Bettie's, when you really get down to it. Maybe not her friend, as in her contemporary, her secrets-sharing girlfriend, but Lili-beth is…well, her parents sort of steamroll and… Well, I like Lili-beth, a lot, but I mostly want to shake her for being such a wimp. George figured out how to coexist with Bettie years ago—he ignores her, hides in his golf and his gin rummy—but Lili-beth still folds like a bad poker hand when her mother's around."

"Steamrolls. That's a good description. Bettie talks, the person she's talking to says no, I don't think so…and Bettie keeps right on going. Damn."

He lifted his glass in a mock salute. "Here's to Lili-beth and her soon-to-be husband—may he be transferred to his company's branch office somewhere on the West Coast."

"Oh, I doubt that. George gave Rob a big-title, do-nothing job in his shirt factory—Bettie's orders, naturally—and Bettie told me their surprise wedding present to the lucky young couple is going to be a house they'll build for them here at Happy Acres, or whatever she calls this place. Lili-beth is only going to go as far as her cast-iron umbilical cord will let her, and believe me, Bettie doesn't unreel it too far."

Doug nearly choked on his sip of beer. "You do have a way with words, don't you? I've now got a visual image that may scar me for the rest of my life. Help me try to forget it, and tell me how you met my cousin and Lili-beth in the first place."

"Sure. You don't eat much, do you?" Rosie asked as she speared one of the Swedish meatballs on his plate and popped it into her mouth. She then held up one finger much as Anvil had done until she'd chewed and swallowed. "I told you, I design Web sites. I also teach a class in Web site design at the local community college, and Lili-beth was one of my pupils about eighteen months ago. Not that she wants to design Web sites, but Bettie likes to tell everyone that Lili-beth is still a student. I think Bettie believed that as long as she could say that Lili-beth wasn't getting any older, it meant Bettie also wasn't getting any older. I'm not positive about that, you understand, it's just a theory. But now grandchildren are the next big thing in her country-club circle, so Bettie wants one of those so she can take the kid to Build-A-Bear. I know that sounds cynical, but I have given this some thought. Lili-beth was also signed up for candy making and boating safety. She gave me the cutest little candy-cane anchors for Christmas."

Doug had opened his mouth to say something—he wasn't quite sure what, although the word *help* was forming somewhere in his mind—when they were interrupted by a plump, middle-aged woman carrying a clipboard.

"Excuse me, are you with the band?"

Rosie swiveled around to grin up at the woman wearing the flustered expression. "My friends tell me I do a mean 'Proud Mary,' but no, we're not with the band, Antoinette."

"Oh, my goodness…Rosie, I didn't realize it was—it's just that Bettie has me counting noses and—and aren't you supposed to be with that Quint fellow?" She lifted a pair of reading glasses hanging from a gold chain around her neck and perched them on her childishly upturned nose. "Yes, yes, there you are, right there. R. Kilgannon, table six. I thought I was right. You don't belong here, Rosie."

"Check D. Llewellyn," Doug said getting to his feet. "I'm pretty sure I don't belong here, either. Or anywhere else within a thousand miles." He held out his hand to Rosie. "Coming, *darling?*"

She put her hand in his and gracefully got to her feet. "My master calls. If you'll excuse us, Antoinette?"

"But...but...D. Llewellyn? Oh, my stars, you're table ten." Antoinette began paging through the sheets clipped to the board. "How did this happen? The cushions didn't arrive, the quails got singed, one of the groomsmen threw up in the punch bowl—oh!" She looked at Rosie and Doug in pure panic. "Nobody's supposed to know that. I didn't say that—you didn't hear me. And now people are sitting in the wrong seats and I can't even take an accurate head count to make sure I didn't overorder from the caterer. If this is the way the rest of the week is going to go, I...truly, I don't know what I'm going to do. Have you heard about Eloise?"

Rosie put her hand on Antoinette's arm and gave it a reassuring squeeze. "I checked on the Weather Channel about two hours ago. She's been downgraded to a tropical storm, and she's just paddling around somewhere south and east of Bermuda. Relax, Antoinette, Bettie wouldn't allow a paltry little hurricane to ruin her big show."

"Even if she has to single-handedly blow the storm back out to sea, which she could do," Doug muttered under his breath. He would be so very *gone* from this happy little gathering, if he wasn't already so *into* the intriguing Rosie Kilgannon, who seemed to know everyone, know everything and have an opinion on everything.

Okay, and he wanted to kiss her again, find out exactly what she meant when she said they'd be *together* this week—there was still that.

Rosie turned a delighted laugh into a small cough, then gave Antoinette a quick hug, told her she was the perfect wedding planner, that she was doing a wonderful job, that the food was marvelous, the decorations perfect. *Stroke, stroke.* Except that Rosie sounded like she meant every word.

Which should have been enough to content the woman so that Doug and Rosie could make good their escape. Except that it wasn't.

Antoinette stepped in front of Rosie. "What about that other thing? I can't bear thinking about it. Did you talk to her? Did you convince her? I have to order them by Tuesday afternoon if you didn't convince her, and I don't think I'll last that long without letting something slip."

"I'm halfway there," Rosie assured the wedding planner. "You don't do these things all at once, Antoinette. First you plant the seed, and then you nourish it, watch it grow. I'm planning on a successful harvest by tomorrow night, if not sooner."

"Thank you, Rosie," Antoinette said, hugging her yet again. "I'll try not to worry too much."

"Planting seeds, a successful harvest?" Doug repeated as he took Rosie's hand and led her away from the patio and down the gentle slope to the stream he was sure was still hidden in the trees...unless Bettie had rerouted it for some reason. "Do I want to know about this?"

"Probably not," Rosie said, unearthing a huge pair of black-rimmed sunglasses from her pocket and slipping them on.

"Let me rephrase that. Tell me…just don't ask me to do anything about whatever you tell me."

"I wouldn't think of it, Mr. Llewellyn. I'm perfectly capable of winning my own battles."

"That's *fighting* your own battles," he corrected as they stepped out of the sun and into the thicker vegetation lining a flagstone path beneath the trees.

"No, your way presupposes that I might actually *lose* the occasional battle. I prefer to think more positively," Rosie told him, sliding her arm through his. "Antoinette's the wedding planner."

"I actually figured that one out on my own," Doug said, peering through the trees to see the sun glint on a thin ribbon of slowly meandering water. It was nice to know he could still trust his memory…now that he was forty, and soon to be prey to the frailties of that advanced age.

"Good for you," she said, grinning up at him. "But I'll bet you haven't figured out that Antoinette and I both volunteer at the ASPCA once a month and so I recommended her to Bettie, and that Bettie plans to incorporate fighting fish in the centerpieces the day of the wedding, and that means twenty-four fish on twenty-four tables—plus three more lining the bridal table. Poor, innocent little fish."

They'd reached the banks of the stream that was bubbling rather merrily over rocks that had been placed in the water too carefully to be anything other than planned. Leave it to Bettie to rearrange nature. "Fighting fish? You mean Siamese fighting fish? What's she planning to do with them? They're too small to eat, and stuffing and mounting them is probably out of the question."

"Very funny." Rosie slipped out of her shoes and stepped out onto the first large, flat stone. "Bettie saw a sample centerpiece that incorporates a fighting fish into its design, and now she just has to have it. Gold filigree bowl filled with flowers, then this clear, sealed bag filled with water and the fish—there's a mirror there somewhere, so the fish sees itself and thinks there's an enemy close and puffs out its fins—and then a bunch of helium balloons above that. It's my job to talk her out of the fish part. Personally, I think Bettie's developing a balloon fetish and should lose those altogether, but I'll settle for saving the fish."

"So you planted a seed?" Doug watched as Rosie stepped from stone to stone, clearly working her way to the opposite bank. Leaving him with two options—three, if he considered walking back to the house alone. He could either watch her, or join her. He sat down on a log that had not only been put there by some landscaper, but also scraped free of bark, one side carved into a smooth bench area. Maybe Bettie came here to read the classics, or to write poetry. Then again, probably not.

Neatly stepping onto the facing bank, Rosie disappeared into the trees for a moment, only to return with a blanket she shook out, then spread on the ground before sitting down on it, looking as appealing and inviting as anyone could probably get without holding up an actual welcome sign. Doug was barefoot and heading for the rocks before he realized that blankets don't grow on trees.

"Where'd that come from?"

"Bettie keeps a rather large plastic storage container hidden behind that tree over there. I was sunbathing on the upstairs deck this summer and saw her head down to the stream. She was gone for an hour or more before I realized the pool guy was also gone, although the top was still off the filter he'd been working on. So, later, I came down here to check it out. Bettie's an interesting woman, and with a rather amazing libido. Oh, and I told her they'd clash with the bridesmaids' gowns."

Doug checked back in his mental file and realized he was actually beginning to pick up on Rosie's rather unique conversational rhythms, and even follow along. They had discussed Bettie, who obviously wasn't important to Rosie, and were now back to the fighting fish, which apparently were. Happy to leave his cousin and her amazing libido behind, he joined Rosie on the blanket, sitting with his knees up and his arms wrapped around them. "And that didn't do it?"

"No, but the seed is planted, and it's too late now to change the color of the bridesmaids' gowns and the rest of the decorations, the flowers. It's also too late to change the center-pieces, which is why I changed the order two weeks ago. No fish. I did let her keep the balloons. A person has to choose her battles, you understand."

"And Bettie doesn't know about these changes? How did you manage that?"

Rosie shrugged as if the answer should be obvious. "I called the florist, said I was Antoinette, and I changed the order. Antoinette's a little worried about that, which is why I told her we could still change back, get the fish put back into the centerpiece design—which we can't, obviously. But everything will work out."

"Because of that seed you planted," Doug said, leaning over to nuzzle Rosie's bare neck. If this dizzying, intriguing, fairly off-the-wall beauty was going to drive him insane for the next week, he might as well unbuckle and enjoy the ride. After all, two celibate months of contemplating his navel and reassessing his life should have earned him some fun.

"Do you know that Siamese fighting fish— bettas—excrete ammonia in their waste, and that ammonia is toxic to fish? Twenty-four hours flapping their little gills in the same, unfiltered water, and they're history. By the time the poor things are sealed up in their bags, and worked into the centerpieces, and driven here for the wedding reception, and sit on the tables all day, they'll be a quick emergency change of water away from going belly up while everyone's eating their wedding cake and bar of chocolate, vanilla and strawberry ice cream. Well, not really, Bettie's serving peach sherbet to match the flowers on the icing, but you get the idea. And, hopefully, so will Bettie when I explain everything to her tomorrow. She could care less about those poor fish, but the idea of them floating upside down in the centerpieces for all her guests to see—*and* clashing while they do it—should do the trick. If not, I'll go to plan B."

"What's plan B?"

"I don't know, but something will come to me, it always does. Do that flicking thing with your tongue again, please, it feels good."

God, she was honest. Almost scarily honest. "And you like what feels good?"

She turned her head slightly and they were nose to nose. "And you don't?"

Doug sat back, amazed at himself, but knowing he was doing the right thing. "I don't know. I used to. But maybe we're moving a little too fast here, Rosie. God, did I just say that?"

"You did, and you're right. It's probably those eyes of yours—they really turn me on," she told him, standing up and indicating that he should do likewise. She snatched up the blanket and shook it out, began to fold it. "Anyway, I was trying to be spontaneous."

"Just trying?" he asked, grabbing one end of the blanket, helping her fold it. "I only met you a little over an hour ago, but I think I'm not going out on a limb when I say that you've probably got spontaneous down cold."

She walked her end of the blanket toward him and matched her corners with his before folding it one more time. "You're talking about that kiss I planted on you when you first got here."

"Among other things, yes, I am," Doug told her, aware that the folded blanket might as well be an iron gate that had just dropped out of the heavens to land between them. Had she just told him that his eyes turned her on? What the hell had turned her off? Damn, *he* had, opening his big mouth with that crap about maybe moving too fast. *Nice work, Llewellyn—you jerk.* "I'm also counting the fact that I very much enjoyed that kiss. And the next one. I'd probably enjoy another one."

"In that case, hold that thought," she told him before disappearing into the trees and returning a few moments later, sans blanket. She walked straight up to him and put her hands on his shoulders. "Do you know you have the most fascinating eyes? I meant what I said. Not just sexy, but fascinating. Deep. Are you a deep thinker, Douglas Llewellyn, under all that gorgeous? Anyway, I think that's when I began telling myself that maybe this week wasn't going to be entirely the unmitigated disaster I'd been dreading for months."

Doug began lightly rubbing at her upper arms. "That pretty much says what I've been thinking since I saw you. Disaster averted. After that? I don't know, Rosie, everything after that has been sort of a blur. You're a very unusual woman, you know."

She rolled her eyes. "Oh no, not you, too. *Everybody* says that. Why does everyone say that? I don't do anything anyone else doesn't do. I'm a perfectly ordinary person."

"Really?" Doug said, edging closer, even as he had a flash of memory from some long ago college class, one where the professor explained true eccentrics as people who simply don't realize their behavior was sometimes a couple of ticks off center. The fact that Rosie Kilgannon considered herself to be ordinary, just like everyone else in the world, pretty much proved the professor's definition. "Maybe I'm wrong. Shall we start over?"

Her hands crept up his shoulders and she laced her fingers behind his neck. "We could try, but I doubt it will change anything. Unless you don't think we could have fun together this week?"

"No, I'm pretty sure we could have fun," Doug told her, his eyes concentrated on her wide, full mouth. "As a matter of fact, I think you're just what I need right now. An older woman."

"Oh, a direct hit! You think you're teasing me, but I can understand that. I'd be a change of pace, a sort of peach sherbet palate cleanser before you head back to the kiddy pool. After all, I can name all the Bee Gees—and the fourth brother. I can remember where I was when the Challenger exploded. If you say Festivus for the Rest of Us, I'll know what you mean. I'm a Phillies fan, I hate the Mets, although I tolerate the Yankees. We used to live closer to Philly when I was younger, and I was sitting on the third baseline with my dad when Mitch Williams gave up that World Series ending home run to Joe Carter in 1993, blowing the Phillies' chances for the next—well, we're still a mess, aren't we? I can even—"

"As postforty aphrodisiacs go, I think the Phillies reference just put you over the top," Doug said just before he captured her mouth with his, his arms sliding around her back to pull her close.

She wasn't a wisp of a thing. Her curves were lush and welcoming. Her breasts were full and firm beneath his hands. She knew what it would do to him when she slyly insinuated her thigh between his legs. She wasn't too eager, and she definitely wasn't shy. She was a woman who knew what she wanted and how to take it.

She knew when she was putting out an invitation.

And she knew when to step back, call a halt. Another minute, maybe less, and he would have been cursing the lack of that blanket they'd been sitting on—okay, he was already cursing that—and beyond calling a halt at a few kisses, a few exploratory caresses.

At the same time, Doug was fairly certain Rosie knew where those kisses were leading, and that the road that would take them there was not going to be a long one.

"We'd better get back," she said as Doug ventured a few last light kisses against the curve of her cheek.

"Bettie put me in some small apartment over the garages," he told her as he held her hand, guiding her back across the stones to the other side of the stream. "Are you staying at the house?"

"Yes. I only live about twenty minutes from here, but Lili-beth asked me to stay in the bedroom next to hers for the week. I told her I'm past the bridesmaid stage, so when she asked me to be involved with the wedding I couldn't turn her down a second time. I think she sees me as a buffer between herself and her mother. Will you do me a favor?"

There it was again, that sudden whiplash change of subject. He had to be careful or he'd find himself agreeing to kidnap a bunch of fighting fish from the reception while he and Rosie sang the chorus of *Born Free.* "I don't know. Will there be a reward?"

"I think that can be arranged," she said, brushing up against him as she stepped ahead of him on the narrow path. "In fact, I'm sure of it. What I want you to do is to talk to Rob—the groom. Sort of vet him, give me your opinion of him."

"Isn't it a little late for that? The wedding's in six days."

"I know, but Lili-beth has been acting strangely for over a month now. Sad. It could be prewedding nerves, but I want to be sure. Bettie's been pushing this wedding hard, you know, and Lili-beth isn't the sort who knows how to push back, even if she's unhappy."

Doug stepped in front of her on the path, blocking her way. "Rosie Kilgannon, tell me you aren't planning to throw some kind of monkey wrench into this wedding."

Rosie's eyes were so wide, so innocent, so amazingly golden brown. "Stop the wedding? As if I'd do anything like that." Then she smiled. "Unless, of course, you and I find a good reason for us to do it."

He watched her as she walked away, not letting her get far before he caught up with her—after all, she already seemed to be three steps ahead of him.

CHAPTER FOUR

ROSIE WANDERED THE GROUNDS after excusing herself when George Rossman spied Doug and invited the two of them into his den for a few hands of gin rummy.

Not that George really wanted Rosie to play—he still owed her twenty bucks and a full minute of standing on one leg, flapping his arms and clucking like a chicken, from their last game. No, he wasn't going to do that again. He wanted her to sit beside Doug and distract him from the game, and he'd said so. George Rossman wasn't a rocket scientist in anything but French cuffs and innovative collar design, but he was honest.

She'd made her way through the tables still littered with plates and glasses and the twenty select guests who had been invited to stay at the house for the duration, and had actually put one foot on the grass when Bettie Rossman spied her, grabbed her and unceremoniously pulled her back across the patio and into her sunroom.

"So? I saw the two of you go down to the stream. So what happened? Did he make a move on you? Of course he did. How does he do it? I've got him pegged as a smoothie, but you never know. He might use the caveman approach. A lot of women like that."

"I don't. But you already knew I wouldn't tell you anything, so stop drooling," Rosie said with a smile that almost hurt, skirting the large table and wondering, just for a moment, what Bettie would do if she tipped it over and all the woman's carefully laid-out plans skidded to the floor. Except, if she did that, she wouldn't put it past Bettie to pull out an Ouzi and blow her away. This was, after all, the war room, and if she'd ever met anyone with a General George Patton complex, it was Bettie Rossman. She probably had a pair of ivory-handled pistols stashed somewhere in here.

So Rosie contented herself with slipping the woman's all-important electronic organizer beneath a pile of material swatches while Bettie poured herself a drink at the bamboo bar in the corner. It was a petty move, but sometimes you just had to go with whatever you could get.

"Don't be touchy, Rosie-Posie. And that's not really why I dragged you in here, so we'll talk more about Doug later, if he hasn't already dumped you for Ki-Ki. Have you seen her wiggling around here? I think the girl's in heat. I keep expecting her to get down on the ground on her belly, yowling, with her tail stuck in the air. You want anything?" Bettie asked as she held up a bottle of vintage Scotch. "No? Only an idiot or a very brave woman would dare go through this week sober. You sure you don't want a belt?"

"Positive, thanks. Is this still about the cushions? Or the quails? Is quails the plural of quail? Or is it another of those deer-deer things?"

"Who cares? And those dumb birds are old news. That twit Antoinette overdid it on the champagne cocktails, and I had to have two of the waiters pour her into bed about an hour ago." She shook her head. "I don't know what her problem is…she was muttering something entirely inappropriate about poor Rob, as if he'd just ruined her life, which is ridiculous. He's only the groom, he has no say in anything, now does he? So how could he possibly ruin anything, unless he backed out of the wedding, and he certainly isn't about to do that, not with what we're paying him to—never mind. Antoinette likes you. You'll see what that's all about, won't you? There's a dear."

"Sure, I'll check with her first thing tomorrow." Rosie slipped behind Bettie and reached into the small stainless refrigerator under the bar to pull out a cold soda, then popped the top and took a long drink. "Ah, that's better," she said, motioning for Bettie to lead the way to the overstuffed floral seating arrangement on the other side of the room. "No, sorry, never mind. It didn't work. I can't swallow my question, Bettie. What you let slip? You're *paying* Rob to marry Lili-beth?"

"No, don't be ridiculous," Bettie said, downing half her Scotch. "What we're paying for is this *wedding,* Rosie. That's all I was going to say. Pay Rob to marry my baby? You make Lili-beth sound like some unattractive *loser,* or something. She can't be a loser, she's *my* daughter. I wouldn't allow it. Honestly, Rosie, you have the strangest ideas."

Rosie looked at her levelly. "Right. So, I'm right, you *are* paying him. The job I understand, in a way. You and George want the business to go on once you're gone. That makes sense. I even understand the house, although it ought to come with a free five-year, unlimited visits contract with a shrink for both of them. But that's not all, is it? My God, Bettie, you *bought* Rob for Lili-beth. Didn't you?"

"Oh, don't be so dramatic. We *encouraged* him, that's all. He was already interested. It's just that he'd been downsized just before he relocated here and he and Lili-beth met, and felt he wasn't economically sound enough to ask for Lili-beth's hand, and so George took him on at the company and…well, and he settled a few debts for the boy, that's all."

"And when was this? That you paid off Rob's debts, I mean."

"I don't know. Let me think." Bettie finished her scotch and got up to pour another one, weaving her way across the room in her stiletto heels. "You mean the first time?"

Rosie rubbed at her temples, a sinking feeling invading her stomach. "Meaning there's been a second time? Maybe a third? Bettie, that's not helping the kid—that's bordering on blackmail. Both ways. How could you do this to your own daughter?"

Bettie wheeled about on her thin heels, pointing a shaking finger in Rosie's direction. "Don't do that. Don't sound like that. Don't sound like George. Rob will work his way out of this—he made some bad business investments, that's all. I've been planning this wedding for twenty-five years, since the day Lili-beth was born, and nobody and nothing is going to rain on my parade. When I go down that aisle next Sunday, Rosie Kilgannon, I'm going to look like the *sister* of the bride—not the freaking *grandmother.* And if that costs George some of his stupid shirt money, so what?"

"*Your* parade? When *you* go down the aisle, Bettie? Are you listening to yourself here? I don't want to knock you out of your happy, delusional world, but you are not the bride, Bettie, and *you* are not the center of attention. It's Lili-beth's day."

"Which would never come, if I waited for her to show some spine, some backbone. She saw Rob, she wanted him, but she didn't have the faintest idea as to how to get him. Oh, let's not argue, Rosie. We both love Lili-beth. I just happen to know what she needs, that's all. You'll see, it will all work out. Look at George and me, for pity's sake. Do you really think I married him because I couldn't live without his clumsy love-making? People in our social strata marry for practical reasons. Love on one side is one more side than usual."

Rosie got to her feet. "And it's practical for Lili-beth to be married to a loser who'd take money from his in-laws—over and over again?"

"I told you, he won't do that again. George put his foot down a month ago, when he gave him that last check. And I'll admit it, I do have a few qualms, as George certainly pays Rob a generous salary, yet he still seems to need more from us. I'm sure everything will change once they're married, and Lili-beth is going to have the wedding of the year. People will *talk* about it for years." Bettie shrugged. "Besides, there's always divorce."

"Oh, really. Why do I get the feeling there's a prenup agreement already signed?"

"Because you're bright? George and I are not entirely stupid, you know," Bettie answered as she kicked off her heels and propped her feet on the glass-topped coffee table. "Believe me, Rob knows what's good for him. He'll fall into line."

Rosie felt herself seething, her anger building. How she longed to back Bettie against the nearest wall and tell the idiot woman just what she thought of her arrogance and insensitivity. But all that would do would be to get her tossed out on her ear, and that wouldn't help Lili-beth.

Besides, Lili-beth loved Rob. Rosie knew she couldn't lose sight of that one important fact. She could still remember how happy and glowing Lili-beth had been the day she'd shown her the three-carat marquise diamond Rob had given her. Hmm...who had paid for that? Was this entire wedding all for Bettie, with Lili-beth simply there for window dressing?

It was time to change the subject. Being Rosie Sullivan Kilgannon, only child of the wealthy, powerful and socially prominent fifth generation private banking Kilgannons, could only take her so far with Bettie, who seemed to see nothing wrong with buying a groom. But she really was feeling mean at the moment, so why not get in a few licks on that other subject—the centerpieces for the big day?

"Bettie, did you get a chance to talk to Antoinette before she was carted away?"

"No, why?" Bettie sat up **straight**. "Don't tell me something else is wrong. **I don't** want to hear that anything's wrong, Rosie. The quail were quite enough, believe me."

Okay, so she couldn't resist a parting shot at the groom. "And whatever Rob did that had Antoinette diving into the champagne cocktails."

Bettie gave a dismissive wave of her hand. "Antoinette was sloshed when she said that. I put no credence in people who can't hold their liquor. Rob's fine, I'm sure of it—although I am holding you to talking to the woman once she's sobered up, finding out what's bothering her. I just don't want any more problems."

"Then I won't tell you that Siamese fighting fish wilt in the heat. Poor little things—their pretty fins go all green and droopy. And then there's the smell, but you don't have to worry about that. I understand that only a few people think the smell reminds them of skunks."

Bettie sniffed. "That's nonsense. They're all locked up in those containers. They can't smell."

Okay, fish led to water, now to watch her swim. Rosie didn't know why she hadn't thought of this before—but this one small fib was going to work wonders, she was sure of it. "That's what I thought. But that's what Sharon Westcote told me when she gave me the deets on the Bridgerman wedding last week."

"The Bridgermans? The *Bridgermans* had fish centerpieces? And you waited until now to tell me? Rosie, how could you! Half the people I've invited were also invited to the Bridgerman wedding, although I was out of town last week, for that quick chin lipo. I can't have those stupid fish now! Everyone will think I copied the Bridgerman wedding. And they clash with the bridesmaids' gowns, too—that's been on my mind ever since you mentioned it the other day. Rosie, what am I going to do? I can't possibly do something that's already been *done*."

Sometimes Rosie felt a twinge of conscience as she maneuvered selfish, self-absorbed people like Bettie Rossman—but not today. Cruelty to fish? Bettie could care less. You had to hit the woman where she lived, and Bettie lived in very shallow water. "Gosh, I don't know. Unless…"

"Yes, yes, unless what?"

It was time for the coup de grâce. "I created the Web site for a novelties company last year. Very new, very innovative company. They do the most amazing designs with a sort of light stick shaped like candles, things like that. I'll bet we could just substitute something like that for the fish—as you said, fish are so being *done,* so last week. I mean, the Bridgermans? God, Bettie, Gussie Bridgerman's still driving last year's Mercedes. You're right. You can't do anything she did. Shall I handle everything for you, with you being so busy with everything else? I'm sure I could get them to ship something to your florist, and in plenty of time."

Considering the fact that she'd ordered the things the same day she'd cancelled the fish, and the florist already had them...

But Rosie couldn't be happy about her victory as she headed out across the grounds once more, leaving Bettie behind with a glass in one hand, the bottle of Scotch in the other. The fighting fish had been a small victory when compared to what she'd learned about Lili-beth's groom. She really couldn't even feel very happy about the electronic organizer she'd slipped out from beneath the fabric samples and dropped into her pocket.

All she could think about was Lili-beth. What was the matter with the girl? Had she been blinded by love? And wasn't it up to her parents to at least *try* to open her eyes?

"There you go—thinking like a Pollyanna again," she muttered as she made a U-turn and headed for the buffet table in the hope that the waiters hadn't already taken away the Swedish meatballs, only to be waylaid by Anvil and his high opinion of himself.

"You looking for me, babe?" he asked, taking another step forward after Rosie had stopped, thus invading her personal space—something wise people never did. "I saw you looking at me earlier. We could, uh, you know, go somewhere? Have some fun? You know—get it on? You older ones, you like that, right? Really *grateful* and all?"

Oh, yeah, she was going to try dating younger men. Not for the sex, but for the scintillating conversation and the flattery. "Ah, gee, Anvil, that sounds totally wild, you know, but I've seen you move onstage. You're just too much man for me. I'll just stick with the old guy I've already got. Old guys are grateful, too."

"That guy you were with before?" Anvil tipped his head to one side, as if considering her words. "He's not too bad. I mean, I'm no *Brokeback Mountain,* you know, but he's not bad. So you like the way I move?"

"You'd ruin me for all other men," Rosie said, straight-faced.

Anvil shrugged. "Yeah, okay. You seen the blonde?"

The blonde? "Ki-Ki?"

"Nah, had her. You know—the blonde. The skinny one. I saw her with you awhile ago." He grinned. "She says she can break me. That's a challenge, right? Like I'm some wild horse she's going to—"

"Okay, I got it," Rosie interrupted. "And she's back there, through the last set of French doors."

"Total," Anvil said, adjusting his black bow tie. "We all square here? I mean, no harm, no foul, you know?"

Rosie held up her hands as if to indicate that she was fine. Devastated, never to be the same again—but fine. "We're solid, Anvil. Oh, and her name's Bettie."

"Bettie? Hey, thanks. I should probably know that, huh?"

"Not necessary, believe me," Rosie muttered under her breath as Anvil went loping off toward the sunroom. "It's not like she's going to remember yours."

And she had expected maternal common sense

from Bettie? Hamsters had more of a maternal instinct…and definitely better morals, higher standards. Wasn't that why Rosie had gotten so involved with Lili-beth in the first place? Because nobody else *was?* Because nobody else seemed to *care?*

Rosie forgot about the meatballs, her appetite gone—and it took a lot to kill her appetite—and redirected her steps to the French doors at the far end of the house, the doors that led to George's inner sanctum.

She knocked twice on one of the panes and stepped inside, to be immediately assaulted by the aroma of fine cigars. She liked the smell, although when she'd tried smoking a classy-looking Panatella herself about five years ago, the experiment had ended in a mad dash to the bathroom, where she had proceeded to lose her lunch.

Now she knew not to inhale.

There were five men in the room, seated around a green felt–covered game table, cards in their hands, glasses at their elbows. None of them had heard her knock, or they'd chosen to ignore it.

George Rossman sat facing her, a small stack of red and white chips in front of him, and a thoughtful frown on his florid face. To his right were the cardiologist, Fred Baines, and the stockbroker, Thaddeus T. Thompson, III (affectionately known as T-Three). To his left were Rob Hemmings, free-loading groom, and, with his back to her, Doug Llewellyn, hunk.

As yet another hand ended, Rosie slipped into the last empty seat, directly beside Doug—after watching Rob play for a full five minutes. She already knew all she needed to know about George, Fred and Thad…and she'd concentrate on Doug's play as the game went on. "How much to buy in?"

Doug smiled at her, and she liked the way her stomach did that funny little flip thing. "One hundred to start. Do you need me to spot you?"

"No, thanks, that won't be necessary. George, my love? *Cluck-cluck-cluck?*"

George Rossman's eyebrows shot up on his forehead. "You think that's worth a hundred?"

Rosie rested her chin in her palm as she propped an elbow on the table. "Don't you?"

"Hell, yes!" he said, counting out chips and shooting them across the table. "Gentlemen, a small announcement, as us men have to stick together. We now have a ringer sitting at the table with us. She looks like she's selling Girl Scout cookies, but she'll beat your balls off before you know what hit you. You've been warned."

"Nice, George. Very nice," Rosie said, rolling her eyes. "Now shut up and deal the cards."

Doug leaned over to whisper next to her ear, "I'd be worried, except that I've been playing with George for over an hour now. A six-year-old could fleece him. And the rest of them."

"I know," Rosie whispered back at him. "Thad saves sixes—I don't know why, but he always does—and Fred starts blinking like mad when he's one card from gin."

Doug grinned at her. "Marry me," he said with mock passion. "Together we could rule the world."

"Sorry," Rosie told him, picking up her cards, shielding them from his slyly meandering gaze. Yes, she really liked this man. "I already rule the world. At least the parts that interest me. But you could be my slave."

"Isn't everybody?" Doug asked, and then turned his attention to his own cards. And, to his credit, he didn't even blink when she leaned back in her chair to grab a cigar from George's nifty humidor and then asked him to light it for her—after she'd bitten off the end, of course, and *p-tuii-ed* it unerringly into the fireplace.

Doug held a lighter to the end of the cigar as she clamped it between her teeth. "All you need now are black silk garters on your sleeves and a leather visor."

Rosie closed her lips around the cigar and drew on it several times—which seemed to please Doug Llewellyn, a lot. Not that she had supposed otherwise, or she wouldn't have done it. "Make jokes all you want, Llewellyn. I'm going to fleece you."

"That almost sounds like fun," he shot back at her, his voice low, intimate.

"Could be, could be." She took the cigar from her mouth, checked the rosy tip and then clamped it between her teeth once more. "I wanted to make sure it stayed hot."

"You don't have anything to worry about, Rosie. I imagine most everyone around you stays pretty hot," Doug whispered. "And that's enough of that. We're playing cards here, remember?"

"Ah, and just when we were beginning to have fun," she said, winking at him. Flirting was such a kick. It ought to be illegal.

Because she was in a man's world now, and men seemed to take their gin rummy rather seriously, Rosie played the next few hands quietly, winning one, losing one to Doug, another to George. Fred Baines excused himself before the next deal, when his pager went off, calling him back to the hospital, and the game went on.

Next to go was T-Three, an hour later, when his wife battled her way through the cigar smoke—it had to have been a battle, for she advanced only as she waved her hands in front of her and made annoying little puckery expressions that almost moved her surgically tightened features—to tell him that he'd had enough for one day, whatever that meant.

T-Three seemed to know, because he got to his feet, called to heel and cashed out his small stack of chips.

"You beat him again, didn't you, Rosie?" Gina Thompson asked as she waited for her husband to slip back into his sports jacket.

Rosie grinned up at the woman, who was a large, jolly, likable grandmother in her early sixties. Shame about the face-lift, actually—in Rosie's opinion it hadn't been at all necessary. "You know me, Gina. No mercy, no quarter."

"Good. I'll expect a check in the mail by the

middle of the week, then," Gina said before giving her slightly lit husband a gentle shove toward the French doors.

"And that means...?" Doug asked as he gathered up the cards, because it was his deal.

"Nothing," Rosie told him, carefully flicking more ash from the cigar into the crystal dish they were sharing. "Gina volunteers at a shelter for abused women. I sometimes donate my winnings, that's all. The wives don't mind if I play with their husbands, as long as it's for a good cause."

"Playing with their husbands," Doug repeated, and Rosie detected what might have been a teeny-tiny note of sarcasm in his voice. "And gin rummy is *all* you play with their husbands?"

All right, two could play this game. Rosie drew some smoke into her mouth, then leaned her head back, arranged her lips in a slightly openmouthed O, and then very deliberately huffed three perfect smoke rings before lowering her head again to look at him. "No, that's not all I play with their husbands. I'm *very* talented."

"Don't tease the boy, Rosie," George said, tossing his ante chip into the pot. "She plays, all right. Golf. Tennis. Horseshoes. Badminton. Volleyball. Hell, she's even beat me at croquet. She's never beaten me at volleyball, but that's because I don't play volleyball. I'd have a coronary."

"I'm really not that good, you know," Rosie told Doug. "It's just that George is *so bad*. Right, George?"

Doug grinned. "Then I suppose we're just going to have to get you a more worthy opponent."

"You're challenging me?" she asked him, feeling her blood warm in anticipation. Look at those eyes! She could swear they were actually smiling. Lordie, she had good taste!

"You like challenges, Rosie?"

"I *live* for challenges," Rosie told him, resting her chin in her hand as she blinked outrageously. "Are you throwing down a gauntlet?"

"I am. Let's say golf, tomorrow. I'm a five handicap."

"Not scratch? I would have thought scratch. Maybe when you were younger?"

"Ha-ha. Are we playing or not?"

"Very well. I'm an eight. Give the poor defenseless lady three strokes, and we're on. My club, ten o'clock. The course is closed to the membership on Mondays, but I often go out with the caddies, as long as I put my share in the pot and play from the blues. Maybe you'd better give me five strokes. That seems fair."

"Wait a sec. You can't do that, Rosie," George told her, pulling a folded sheet of paper from the inside pocket of his sports coat and unfolding it. "Yes, here it is, right here. Monday. Breakfast served on the terrace from eight until eleven, luncheon from noon until two. Excursion bus leaving at one o'clock for some upscale shopping, for those willing to make a dent in their credit cards. Croquet on the south lawn from ten until three for all who are interested. No golf until— here it is—Tuesday. You can wait until Tuesday, right? Just so Bettie doesn't blow her cork?"

"I'm good. Doug?" Rosie asked.

He nodded his agreement. "Wait a minute. What's your handicap at croquet?"

"Oh, that's easy. An uncontrollable urge to go after other players and whack their balls off the course instead of going for the win," she said, because she liked to be honest.

Doug spread his hands in mock defeat. "Oh, no. I'm not touching that line."

Rosie grinned at him, and he grinned back. He

was still gorgeous, and getting more gorgeous by the moment. Not only that, but he was still here, still appeared interested—which was a good thing, because she was definitely interested. Rosie was an expert at weeding the wheat from the chaff as it were, and Doug Llewellyn was passing all of her tests with flying colors. "All right, but you've been warned."

His smile slowly faded, his gray eyes intense with hidden meanings. "No. Challenged. There's a difference. I don't care for warnings, but, like you, I'm always up for a challenge."

"Cripes, you two, get a room why don't you? Are we going to play here, or what? I need a chance to get even."

Rosie glanced across the table to Rob Hemmings, the complaining groom-to-be. He was a good enough looking kid—he was twenty-six, and that made him a kid as far as Rosie was concerned. Not all that tall—but then neither was Lilibeth—with thick, sandy-colored hair, and the sort of complexion that tends to go red cheeked in moments of exertion or emotional stress. Right now, his cheeks were blazing.

The pile of chips in front of him had dropped steadily lower as Doug's had grown higher, and the stress was beginning to fray the kid's nerves around the edges. Rosie had been content to win when the cards were good, not bothering to bluff when they weren't, but Doug had gone after Rob like a barracuda goes after—well, after whatever turned barracudas on. He'd been quiet about it, not obvious, but he'd been picking the kid apart for the last hour, either instinctively or by cleverly holding on to the one card the kid needed until he made it his final discard.

Which made Rosie pretty sure that Doug Llewellyn didn't much like Rob Hemmings. Now she had to find out *why*.

CHAPTER FIVE

DOUG TOOK ROSIE'S HAND as they made their way through the maze of outdoor tables now being set up for a casual supper for the house guests. She didn't resist as he led her onto the lawn, and he hadn't expected her to. She'd just seemed to assume that they were buddies for the week, and since he had no complaints, why the hell not?

"Interesting couple of hours," he said, bending over to pick up a well-chewed rubber ball and toss it in the general direction of the tennis court. A nanosecond later, a large golden Lab with a tongue long enough to be considered a birth defect appeared out of nowhere to go in hot pursuit.

"Oh, now you've done it," Rosie told him, shaking her head. "Congratulations, you have a new friend for life."

Sure enough, the Lab had grabbed the ball in its

jaws and was already on its way toward them, his body wriggling as he ran, his tail doing a fairly impressive pinwheel imitation. "What's his name?"

"Marmaduke Wisdom Longstreet, poor thing. But Lili-beth calls him Marmie. Marmie—down!"

"Yeah, Marmie, down," Doug repeated, stepping back so that the dog wasn't standing on his toes. "Cute."

"Adorable," Rosie agreed. "And nearly indefatigable when it comes to retrieving. And how can you deny those trusting, eager eyes? Throw the ball anywhere near Marmie, and resign yourself to throwing it again, and again, and again. Do you have a handkerchief with you? The ball gets pretty soggy after about the fourth retrieval."

"You don't like dogs?" Doug asked as Marmie went loping off after the ball once more. "I would have taken you for a dog person. And you volunteer at the ASPCA, if I remember correctly."

"Oh, I love dogs. Dogs, cats, bunnies, you name it. Well, not all animals. I've never been able to work up a real affection for creepy-crawly things. And speaking of creepy-crawly things…?"

"Well, that was indirectly direct, wasn't it? You

want to know about our eager groom? That was my assignment, correct?"

"Actually, I've already learned a lot on my own, but I would like your opinion. You really sliced and diced him back there, didn't you? How much did he lose?"

Doug picked up the ball Marmie deposited in front of him. Rosie was wrong. It only took two retrievals before the ball got soggy. "A little over two hundred, I think. George spotted him the second hundred. I felt bad about that, but the kid was so damn eager to lose his money."

"Very good. And, of course, you'll want to donate all your winnings to Gina's charity." She held out her hand, palm up. "Give. Trust me, you'll feel better. Besides, except for Atlantic City and all those state lotteries, gambling is illegal in New Jersey. Really, you'll sleep much easier knowing your ill-gotten gains have gone to a good cause."

"I'm always interested in feeling better." Doug reached into his pocket and pulled out the bills he'd put there when the game had broken up for the evening. "Rob told me he drives down to AC twice a month, by the way. I'll bet they roll out the red carpet for him."

"You think he loses a lot of money at the tables?"

Marmie was back for yet another encore. This time, Doug put his entire right side into his throw, sending the ball bouncing into the trees. "Damn, I didn't mean to throw it that far. And let's just say I don't think Hemmings is the sort who knows when to walk away. You can see it, if you know what to look for—that certain desperate gleam in the eye, that hopeful moment of hesitation as he reaches for the last card in the deal, the one that will break his losing streak, make his world all right again. The big score, the big chance. I just can't believe George doesn't see it."

"So you don't like Rob?"

"Who said I didn't like the kid?"

"I did, just now," Rosie said, walking toward the woods. "And you don't, do you? I know what to look for, too, you know—like that certain hard set to your jaw, the excessive energy you put into throwing that ball. I don't think all that energy was directed at Marmie."

"You're something else, do you know that, too?"

"Of course. Come on, before Marmie gets lost. He's cute, but he's just another dumb blonde."

Doug followed, as she knew he would—he'd

think about that one later. "You're right, I don't like him, but it has nothing to do with what I'd consider to be his gambling problem. That's no skin off my nose. I don't like the way he talked to Lili-beth when she came into the room earlier, before you showed up. And, speaking of showing up—your turn."

Rosie picked up the soggy ball Marmie had brought back to them and wound up, throwing it in a girl's version of a wicked sidearm, in the general direction of the buffet table. "There. Now, pray somebody decides to feed him. Table scraps trump rubber ball for Marmie any day. And what did he say to Lili-beth?"

Doug thought about this for a moment, reliving the short scene in his mind. "It wasn't what he said, it was the way he said it. The way he looked at her when she asked him to take a walk with her. As if she was no more than an annoyance he didn't have time for at the moment. Lili-beth pretended not to be hurt, but I saw her eyes. She looked…she looked a little like Marmie, I suppose. Begging for attention. Needy." He shook his head. "I don't think George noticed that, either."

"George doesn't notice much. I think it's his self-defense mechanism. But you did notice. That's nice."

"Yeah, I'm a real prince. Now tell me what you know."

Rosie lowered her chin for a moment, then looked up at him. "I don't know if I should. You're family."

"Really? A couple of hours ago I thought I was a potential coconspirator."

"True," she said, nodding her head. "So you're in? You'll help me get rid of him if we're right?"

"I already know our friend Hemmings is a main-chance kind of guy. I've met that animal before. I already know I don't like the way he did everything but flip off Lili-beth, or the way she just seemed to accept it, as if she's used to that sort of treatment from him."

"That's the one that really bothers you, isn't it? That you agree with me that Lili-beth isn't exactly the bubbly, giddy bride-to-be, and you didn't like to see her being treated like yesterday's newspaper?" Rosie asked him. She leaned her head against his shoulder and smiled up at him. "That's so knight in shining armor of you."

"Is that better than a prince? Never mind. Before I'm in, and knowing up-front that Bettie will probably sic a hit man on me if I screw up her big party—and my own mother will pay for him—

I think I need to know what you know. So convince me. Lay out your evidence."

"My evidence?" Rosie grinned up at him. "I never asked—are *you* a lawyer?"

"Now I'm insulted. Do I look like a lawyer?"

Rosie stepped back a few paces, looked him up and down and up again, then smiled. Well, leered, but on her it looked good. "You'd win a lot of cases if you were smart enough to stuff the jury box with females between the age of puberty and three-days dead. No, you don't look like a lawyer. You look like a comfortably wealthy man who's never had to worry about what other people think of him because he's happy in his own skin."

"Really. All right. And you look like a fabulously beautiful woman who definitely looks great in her skin."

"Oh, and smooth, too. You forgot wealthy."

"You already told me you're a working woman, remember?"

"And you don't work? I don't believe that. I know a sloth when I see one, and you do a lot more than work to maintain your five handicap. Don't tell me, though. I want to guess. Gynecologist? Please say no."

"No," Doug said, trying hard not to smile. "And you're avoiding the original question. What have you learned about our obnoxious—what the hell is that?"

He and Rosie both watched as somebody wearing a pith helmet and swimmers' goggles stumbled out of the trees, clomping heavily in rubber fisherman waders held up by red suspenders. It was a guy, Doug was fairly certain of that much, but that's all he could figure out as Rosie grabbed onto his arm and buried her head against his chest, giggling.

"It's…it's, oh God, it's Delwood. I know she asked him—but I didn't think he'd actually *do* it!"

"Who's Delwood?" Doug asked as he did a quick inventory on the rest of the fellow's outfit. He wore a heavy, long-sleeved camouflage shirt, and a pair of yellow rubber gloves secured to his forearms with rubber bands. He carried a large wooden box with a mesh front in one hand and a clear plastic bag filled with crackers, a butter knife and a large jar of peanut butter in the other.

Delwood put down the box and bag and removed his pith helmet and goggles, revealing a long, thin, youthful face. "Hi, Rosie."

Her back still to the young man, Rosie passed her hand in front of her face, doing one of those forehead-to-chin "erase the smile and try to look serious" gestures.

She turned to Delwood, in much better control of her amusement than Doug knew himself to be—and he wasn't even in on the joke.

"Delwood, sweetie," she told him as seriously as possible, "always listen to Bettie. That's a given, because she won't shut up until you do. But that's it—listen. Agree. But never actually *do* what she says. Didn't I tell you that when she asked you?"

Delwood began attempting to remove the rubber band from his left arm, the fat rubber fingers of his gloves not helping him with his dexterity quotient. "I know, Rosie, but if I didn't do it Mrs. Rossman would have hired one of those companies, and they would have put out poison or inhumane traps. Besides," he added, flushing beneath his wild shock of blond hair, "Lili-beth made me promise I'd do it."

"Give me a clue here," Doug whispered from behind Rosie, who was now helping Delwood with the rubber bands. "What did Bettie ask this poor kid to do?"

"Lili-beth," Rosie corrected, successfully removing the rubber bands so that Delwood could strip off his gloves. "Delwood would do anything for Lili-beth. Wouldn't you, Del?"

"It's not like that, Rosie," he protested—another guy who should never try to bluff at cards. "I'm just helping out, that's all."

"I know that, Del, and I'm sorry. So, you're using peanut butter and crackers for bait?"

Bait? Doug thought about this for a moment, another part of the puzzle that was Delwood and his outfit, and came up with an answer. "You're trapping something?"

"Squirrels," Rosie told him, nodding. "There's a million of them scampering around here. Bettie's worried about them running wild during the wedding ceremony. She was nagging George to get out his BB gun and take target practice, so I offered an alternative. I suggested the peanut butter pate to lure the little buggers into traps she could borrow from the animal shelter. But I didn't think anything would come of it. Bettie picks up and drops so many projects. I'm really sorry, Del."

Doug gestured toward the pith helmet and goggles. "Okay, I'm getting this so far. But why the outfit? They're only squirrels. Oh, by the way, Del, I'm Doug Llewellyn, Lili-beth's second cousin."

"Pleased to—" Delwood wiped his palms on the front of his shirt. "Sorry. Baby powder. So the gloves slipped on easier." He held out his right hand. "Pleased to meet you, sir. Mrs. Rossman told me all about you. You're her favorite cousin."

Doug shook the young man's hand, and then manfully resisted the urge to wipe his hand on his slacks. "Also her only cousin, in case she didn't mention that. And you're Lili-beth's friend?"

"Since grade school," Delwood said rather wistfully, blinking his huge brown puppy-dog eyes. The kid had to be about Lili-beth's age, and he and Lili-beth had obviously taken their self-confidence lessons from the same flawed correspondence course. "I'm best man."

"So far," Doug whispered to Rosie, "although I'm not sure if that's saying much." Then, to Del, he said, "So you're Rob's friend, too?"

"Not really, Mr. Llewellyn. Rob only moved here from Wisconsin about a year or so ago, and doesn't know too many people. Lili-beth asked me to step in."

Rosie stood up on tiptoe to kiss Delwood's

cheek. "You're too good, Del. And I mean that. Seriously."

Doug waited for the kid to scuff his booted toe in the dirt, but he didn't. He did, however, do just about everything else that helped peg him as a good kid who needed a large double shot of self-confidence. Blushed, lowered his chin, swung his hands back and forth as if trying to grab an answer to Rosie's praise out of the air.

What he finally came up with was an answer to Doug's earlier question. "Squirrels can be very aggressive, you know. And they get pretty angry when they're locked up, at least once the crackers and peanut butter are gone. The one I caught yesterday tried to run up my pants leg when I let him out of the cage. So Lili-beth and I figured out this protection. You never know when one of them could show up with rabies. I've managed to trap seven of them so far, and now I'm moving this trap over closer to the tennis court because I saw one run that way earlier."

"Go get 'em, tiger. You're driving them over to the park to release them?" Rosie asked him.

"Yeah. That's a good five miles from here. Do you think that's far enough?"

"Not for Lassie," Rosie said seriously. "But for squirrels? I think so, Delwood."

"Yes, well, fascinating as all this is," Doug said as Delwood began to suit up once more, obviously about to fling himself back into his role as Squirrelmaster. "Rosie? I've been told there's a stocked refrigerator in my apartment over the garages. Would you care for a soda? Del—great work. A pleasure to have met you."

"Uh, yes, certainly. Back…back at you, Mr. Llewellyn," Delwood said as he pulled the swim goggles over his head.

"Isn't he sweet?" Rosie asked as they headed for the garages. "And desperately in love with Lili-beth, obviously. Not that he'd ever *do* anything about it. And Lili-beth considers him the brother she never had."

"I don't know, Rosie," Doug said as they rounded the corner of the garages and headed for a flight of wooden stairs. "She might see him in a whole new light, now that he's Delwood the Squirrel Slayer. Maybe we should help the kid out—get him a cape to go with that outfit."

"You just couldn't wait to say something like that, could you?" she asked him, pausing on the landing. "But thank you for holding on until Del was out of earshot."

"You're welcome, but it wasn't easy. Hey, where are you going?" he asked as Rosie skipped past him, heading back down the steps once more. And he'd almost had her where he wanted her...

She stopped halfway down, pointed up at the door behind him. "I still don't know what you do for a living—but you did strike me as a college man. You have to know what that means."

Doug turned around to see the coral silk scarf tied to the doorknob. It took only a second to remember that Bettie's coral dress had been tied at the waist with a matching silk scarf. The age-old warning that the apartment—and the bed in particular—were *occupado.*

He followed Rosie back to the grass. "I don't believe this. Bettie gave me this apartment so that she could use it? Bring her lover up here?"

Rosie nodded. "Sounds like Bettie. Oh, and it's worse than that. *I* know who her lover is."

"And you're going to tell me?"

"No, I don't want to shock your sensibilities. She is your cousin, after all. She's got the morals of a cat, but she is your cousin."

Doug took one last look up at the apartment. "Please let there be a stocked linen closet up there, or I'm sleeping on the couch."

Rosie laughed. "I wasn't sure what you'd say—there was a lot to choose from—but that's about the last thing I expected. Don't worry, there are two bedrooms to the suite. Weren't you in the least suspicious when Bettie put you out here all by your lonesome? Everybody else is staying at the house. You're her alibi, her diversion, I guess. Her reason to be out here, if anyone should see her either coming or going. I'm *so* glad I took her organizer."

Doug whipped his head around to goggle at her. "You took her what? Why?"

"Her electronic organizer—she can't function without it. And I did it because of what she's doing to Lili-beth, of course. She made me so *mad*. I don't like getting mad. I like getting even. Oh, wait, I didn't tell you yet, did I? Bettie and George have *bought* Rob for Lili-beth. More than once."

Doug didn't know what he'd expected to hear, but he was pretty sure this wasn't it. "You're kidding."

"I wish," Rosie said, shaking her head. "I don't know who's worse, Bettie for selling, or Rob for buying. And Lili-beth is so in love. Or at least I used to think she was. Should we kidnap her?"

"Kidnap Lili-beth? That's your solution? I'm glad I haven't signed on to the Stop Lili-beth's Wedding caper yet, if that's all you can come up with, Machiavelli."

"Hey, relax, that was only my first idea. Admittedly, not a great idea. But we do have to do something, don't we?"

"We. Again with the *we*. You know, if I had half a brain, I'd go find Quint's ex and introduce myself."

"Except that we've already agreed we're going to stick together this week," Rosie said, stepping closer, reaching up to fiddle with his open collar. "Besides, I've ruined you for all other women. Haven't I?"

"You did that when you pointed out that most of my dates are Lili-beth's age. I don't think I'm over that one yet. Now tell me more about this buying a groom thing."

"Why? It's happening. Isn't that enough?"

Doug considered her question for a moment, and then shook his head. "No, actually it isn't. I'm not sure I trust you, Rosie. You want Rob gone, and I have a feeling that when you want something you find a way to get him…it. I meant *it*."

"No, you didn't," she said, moving closer to him. "You think I want you, Douglas, don't you? You think I saw you come around the corner and up onto the terrace, and decided to make you my private property for the week. Go on, admit it."

He brushed the back of his fingers down her sun-warmed cheek. "I'd be wrong?"

"No," she said, dancing away from him. "You looked like fun. Of course, as you pointed out, you're too old for me, and I'm too old for you. But it's only for a week in any case, right? Now you're frowning. What's wrong?"

"I'm not sure," Doug said honestly. "Part of me is wondering if Bettie should rename this place Sodom and Gomorrah, and the other part of me is pointing out to me that it's a little late in my career to start being squeamish about a lifestyle I've pretty much embraced for the past—well, for a lot of years. Maybe it's looking at you, and seeing myself. I'm probably damning myself in admitting this, but I've never looked at my life and considered that there could be a woman out there anywhere who looked at life the same way. It's…uh…it's eye-opening."

"Yes, I know. That's because we have wombs,

and you men don't," Rosie told him, nodding her agreement.

There she went again, saying something totally unexpected, totally outrageous and off-the-wall. "What did you just say? No, never mind. Just don't repeat it."

"No, really, it bears repeating," she told him, sitting down on the bottom step of the stairs leading up to his Bachelor Quarter, also known as Bettie's Boff spot. "Sit down, I'll explain."

Doug looked out over the grounds, to see Delwood holding a large cage above his pith-helmeted head as Marmie danced around him, barking wildly. "I think Delwood caught another squirrel."

"Good for him, but you're not getting out of this quite so easily. Sit down."

He joined her on the step. "Last chance to change the subject," he pointed out, not with much hope of success.

"Nope. I've put a lot of thought into this, so just listen. Women have *wombs*," Rosie told him, her expression serious. "Women bear children. And, according to this male-dominated society, while it's perfectly all right for the one who makes the deposits to make them anywhere he wants, it's somehow not all right for the recipient."

"Because women have wombs and bear children. I remember. Are we done now? Please?"

"Not quite yet. There's more. According to the way you men think, we women are not supposed to actually *enjoy* sex. We're supposed to wait on our pedestals for Mr. Right to come along—after making his deposits willy-nilly for years without a thought to the recipient. You're all alike. You all want a virgin…after doing your best to make sure there aren't any virgins left within a thousand miles, that is."

Doug rubbed at his forehead, avoiding Rosie's gaze. "Why is this making sense?"

"Because *I'm* making sense, that's why. It's a double standard. Oh, you all talk a good game— equality of the sexes, encouraging a woman to explore her sexuality. Let's all hear it for adult, probably transitory, mutually consensual relationships based on little more than physical attraction, dinner and a chick-flick. But scratch deep enough, and you all want the woman you eventually choose to honor with marriage and your progeny-producing deposits to never have wanted anyone but you, have never *really* enjoyed her sexuality until you came along and turned on all her switches, or whatever. And you men have the audacity to call *women* hopeless romantics?"

Doug couldn't think of a quick rebuttal, and was pretty sure he wouldn't find one if he had a week to think of it, either. "I apologize. For every man in the world. Truly."

Rosie grinned at him. "Ah, that's sweet. For all the women of the world, I accept. Which is not to say that you and I are going to do anything more than watch each other's backs until the wedding is over—one way or the other—and we go our separate ways. I want to be clear on that."

Doug got to his feet, holding out his hand to her. "And you have been—when you're not rubbing up against me, of course."

"You mean like this?" she asked him, rising to her feet and easing her body against his, all in one fluid movement.

He slipped his arms around her waist and pulled her even closer, looking down into her beautiful, laughing face. "Yes, exactly like this. Except for the part where you should be kissing me like you mean it."

"You mean like this?" she breathed against his lips just before he lifted a hand to the back of her head and all but mashed their open mouths together.

She was a flirt. She was a tease. She was maddening, as bad as he was, and he'd never been so turned-on in his life.

"Oh, for God's sake, you couldn't wait another ten minutes? I know you have quite a reputation, Douglas, but nobody's *that* good."

Bettie.

Doug broke the kiss—not the easiest thing he'd ever done—but didn't let Rosie go because Bettie was bound to say something vulgar as she leered at the front of his slacks. Thankfully, Rosie seemed to understand this, and merely looped her arms loosely around his shoulders as she looked up the stairs toward Bettie.

"Hi, Bettie. Where's Anvil? You didn't kill him, did you?" Rosie asked, and then leaned forward to whisper in Doug's ear. "Black widows do that after they mate, you know. And maybe scorpions? The only reason George is still alive is because she lost interest in him years ago."

Anvil? Bettie and *Anvil?* Well, *that* took care of Doug's raging libido. Hell, it might take care of it for a couple of months. "It's safe to let go now. Thanks."

"Anvil?" Bettie said as she tripped down the stairs in her Ferragamos, her heels clicking on the wood. "How did you—no, don't answer that. I don't want to know. What a disappointment— rockets take off slower. Just go away for a while, the two of you, so he can leave without you seeing him, and then it's all yours."

"I'm going to go get a hotel room," Doug said as he watched his cousin walk away, the coral scarf now tied around her throat and trailing behind her in the light evening breeze. "Preferably in another state."

"And Lili-beth?" Rosie asked him, heading up the steps.

He followed her, but not because of Lili-beth.

"How long has Bettie been—no, never mind, I don't want to know. I like my life the way it is. I send her Christmas and birthday presents, she sends me a box of Omaha steaks once a year and one of her single girlfriends in even numbered years. I can live with that. Lack of information has gotten me this far and I don't want to jinx that."

"Hi, Anvil," Rosie said, standing back as the

lead singer of Ear Waxx slipped past her in the doorway, still buttoning his shirt. "Shame on you. What would your mother say?"

Doug watched, finally finding some humor in the situation as Anvil raced down the stairs and took off at a run for the front of the house. "Ten bucks he doesn't stop until he's locked in his room at the Quality Inn."

"Where he will proceed to brag about his sexual prowess to his bandmates, no doubt," Rosie said, shaking her head. "Still, I imagine Bettie can be pretty scary. You want a soda? Ice?"

Doug nodded his head in agreement to both offers, and then went off to inspect the apartment while Rosie pulled two cans of soda from a small, under-the-counter refrigerator in the kitchenette that was part of the large, well-furnished living room.

Rosie had been right, there were two bedrooms. He closed the door on the one with the rumpled sheets, happy to see that his two pieces of luggage had been deposited on the mattress in the other bedroom. He went into the adjoining bathroom and washed his hands, splashed some cold water on his face and then rejoined Rosie in the living room.

"There is a dead bolt," she told him commiseratingly as she handed him a glass filled with ice and soda. She had taken off her shoes, obviously having no problem making herself at home. "Once you're in here, she can't get in. Or you could just loop your tie over the doorknob."

"Don't sound so happy at my misery," he told her, collapsing onto the soft flowered couch, lifting his feet onto the coffee table before saying what was on his mind, what was bothering him. Really, really bothering him. "Bettie's forty-eight, forty-nine, tops. She married young, had Lili-beth young, but she's still pushing fifty hard, I'm sure of it."

"Agreed. And she's fifty-one, as a matter of fact. How old do you think that kid is?"

Rosie sat down beside him, propped her feet up beside his on the coffee table. Her toenails were painted a deep red, and she wore a thin gold chain around her right ankle, a small tattoo of a butterfly on her left. She had terrific ankles. Narrow feet. There was definition in her calves, indicating that her legs were strong as well as wonderfully long and straight. It wasn't much of a mental stretch to imagine them clamped tightly around his—what was her question?

Oh, right. How old was Anvil. "I couldn't be sure. Twenty-six? Twenty-eight? Too young for Bettie."

"But if Anvil was fifty-one and Bettie was twenty-six? How shocked and outraged would you be then?"

Doug took a long drink from his glass, vaguely wishing he'd opted for something alcoholic. "Do me a favor, Rosie, and don't hammer on that nail anymore. It's in. Believe me, it's in."

"I do believe you. After all, I saw the look on your face when you realized what was going on up here. Although I doubt Bettie cares whether or not Anvil knows any songs by Frank Sinatra."

Doug laid his head back against the pillows of the couch. "And I'm not being sexist. I'm not saying that society has a double standard on older women with younger men and older men with younger woman—although I guess it does."

She leaned back, too. "So what *are* you saying?"

Doug blew out a frustrated breath. "I don't know. Maybe I'm just saying that you—and Bettie, unfortunately—have made me take a look at myself today, and I'm not exactly thrilled at what I'm seeing." He turned to look at her, her face mere inches from his. "I'd say you started this, but

I've been…thinking about this for a while now. Do you suppose I'm having a midlife crisis?"

She wrinkled her nose, then grinned. "With a male life expectancy of around eighty, forty would be midlife, wouldn't it? Poor baby. Maybe it's time you took stock of your life, looked at where you've been, where you're heading. I'll help you. There must be pen and paper around here somewhere."

She was off the couch before he could grab her, tell her no, thank you, he'd rather not take stock of his life right now…that he was much more interested in taking stock of her, inch by inch.

"Rosie, I don't think—"

"Got some!" she said, closing one of the kitchen drawers. Then she sat down at the small glass-topped table halfway across the room, one leg tucked up beneath her, her smile telling him that she was feeling delighted with herself. "Well? Aren't you coming?"

"Apparently not," Doug muttered under his breath as he pushed himself up and out of the couch and joined her at the table. "Okay, Doctor Phil, where do we start? And if you say the first thing I have to do is to *own* my feelings, you can leave now, okay?"

"You watch Doctor Phil? My, you are a man of many surprises, aren't you?"

Doug rubbed at his forehead, not because he had a headache, but because he wanted to make sure he hadn't opened a hole in his head and his brain was leaking out. "Only a few times, last winter, when I had the flu. Okay, where do we start?"

"I have no idea," Rosie told him, the pen poised over the paper. "Where you've been? That sounds familiar. So, Douglas, where have you been?"

He didn't want to do this. It was perilously close to contemplating his own navel, or the time his mother had thrown one of those *Cosmopolitan* magazine self-tests at him, having generously filled it out for him, and telling him that he had scored in the high nineties. He'd asked her if that was a good grade, and she'd told him it was, if he liked majoring in Fear of Commitment, with double minors in Selfish and Exists To Frustrate His Mother. His mother had missed a great career in stand-up comedy.

"Doug? Come on—where have you been?"

"Okay, okay. Where have I been in my first forty years. I've been building my career, my business."

"No, no, don't go there yet. I still want to guess what you do. Not a lawyer, not a doctor. Stockbroker? No, that can't be it—you have a sense of humor. Well, I'll guess some more again later. What we're doing here now, Doug, is finding out where you've been, emotionally—not what you've accomplished in your career."

"No, sorry, I still don't get it. That's a woman question. Men don't ask questions like that. We're more prone to slap each other on the back and then go get drunk."

Rosie put down the pen. "You're right. And maybe where you've been isn't all that important." She folded her hands together on top of the paper and peered at him curiously. All that was missing was a pair of tortoiseshell half-glasses perched on her nose. That adorable nose. "So, Douglas, where do you want to go?"

"Dinner," he said, getting up so that he could stand behind her chair and pull it, and her, out from under the table. "Dinner, some time playing the good guests, then some kissing, possibly some heavy petting…after which I'm going to come back up here—*alone*—and try to figure out just what the hell is happening to me."

She patted his cheek as she walked ahead of him to the door. "I do love a man with a plan. I hope they still have more of those Swedish meatballs…."

CHAPTER SIX

ROSIE WOKE ALL AT ONCE, as she always did. Asleep and happily dreaming one moment, and then wide-awake and happy with the memory of that dream the next.

She never had nightmares. She never dreamt she was standing in front of her eleventh grade English class naked on oral report day, or that her teeth were falling out. Monsters never chased her while she felt as if she was running in quicksand. Deceased relatives never spoke to her, and if any dream did dare to even hint that it might turn sad or frightening, some internal editor simply changed the script.

Instead, Rosie's dreams were full of silly things, mostly comic turns on the events of the previous day. These were all jumbled together and flipped on their heads—rather like a sitcom made up of

mixed-up bits and pieces from *I Love Lucy,*
Friends, Sex and the City and maybe a few one-
liners from *The Simpsons,* and most definitely
Seinfeld, a show both she and her father watched
faithfully in reruns, often phoning alerts to each
other when a favorite episode was to be aired.

Last night's dream, at least the part she remembered as she lay in the four-poster bed in the room
next to Lili-beth's, had featured a kick line of high-
stepping squirrels in pith helmets accidentally
knocking over a pyramid arrangement of Swedish
meatballs. Anvil, dressed in a blue baby bonnet, had
clapped his hands in glee at the sight, while Sinatra
sang *My Way* and a huffing, puffing Bettie danced
around him the best she could, using her walker.

Rosie had watched it all while Doug Llewellyn
pushed her in a giant swing that hung from a dis-
embodied tree branch, the seat of the swing
actually a larger version of an electronic organizer,
the ropes adorned with coral silk streamers. Each
time the swing came back toward him, Doug had
kissed her, his hands gliding cunningly over her
breasts before sliding around to her back as he
pushed her high into the air once more. Let her go,
bring her back, let her go, bring her back…

"I'm driving the poor guy insane, and I'm pretty sure the feeling is mutual," Rosie happily told the Tudor roses woven into the canopy above her bed as she kicked off the covers and began her morning routine. First she raised her hands over her head and stretched as hard as she could, arching her back before slowly sliding her arms out to her sides as if reaching for the edges of the mattress even as she lifted her legs one at a time from the hip, knees locked, her toes pointed toward the canopy.

She'd been on the diving team in college, and she'd always practiced her dives in bed. This particular dive called for her to now neatly tuck her knees to her chest, her feet pushed tight against her buttocks as she held on to her calves and flipped backward, somersaulting three times, and then stretching out her body again so that she was now an arrow, breaking the water hands first, barely making a ripple.

The somersaults themselves were, of course, out of the question, but the extension, contracting, stretching of her muscles as she visualized her form as she left the platform and neatly sliced through the air always served to get her heart pumping.

She pantomimed two more dives of varying difficulty quotients as she thought about her late-night stroll with Douglas Llewellyn.

He was so sweet. He'd spent two entire hours being polite to the other wedding guests and pretending not to notice when she crossed, then recrossed her legs, or when, complaining of the heat and humidity that had hung on even after the sun went down, she had pulled the neckline of her dress slightly away from her body and then blew on the skin of her breasts.

He'd shot her a dirty look, one that had all but screamed, "Just you wait until I get you alone, woman!" but he hadn't cut short Aunt Susanna's colorful description of her gallbladder operation or George Rossman's hole-by-hole recitation of the eighteen holes he'd been lucky enough to play at Pebble Beach a year earlier.

No, he'd been good. Then, at last, they'd gone off on their own, to the tennis court, and he'd been bad.

Wonderfully bad. Deliciously bad.

She could only hope he would be even *worse* when they were alone again tonight, once he'd been able to clear his mind of what had to be libido-crushing thoughts of Bettie and Anvil.

"I'm a terrible person," Rosie told herself as

she rolled out of bed and headed for the en suite bathroom, not having to bother with discarding her nightclothes because she didn't wear night-clothes. "But somebody has to help the poor guy fight through his midlife crisis, and it might as well be me. Twenty-five-year-olds? No wonder the man is floundering. What he needs right now is a *real* woman."

She was soaping her body as she stood back from the spray of the shower when she felt cool air enter the room and grabbed the shower curtain, peeking out to see who had entered the bathroom. Blinking at the rivulets of shampoo that ran down into her eyes, she asked, "Doug?"

"*Doug?* You mean my cousin Doug? Oh, Rosie, that's gross, that's just gross."

"Lili-beth? Hold that thought," Rosie said, letting go of the shower curtain and stepping under the spray to rinse off, then extending her hand beyond the curtain. "Towel? Two of them, okay?"

She wrapped one long fluffy white towel around her body, tucking an end in above her breasts, and then wrapped her hair in the other, smaller towel before stepping out of the tub to confront the younger woman. Nobody would believe it, she always thought, but, basically, she was a very modest woman. Enjoying her sexuality was one thing—parading around in the altogether, however, didn't do a thing for her. "I can assume the house is on fire?"

"Oh. No, I'm sorry," Lili-beth said as she sat on the toilet lid, doing a really good impersonation of a Victorian maiden wringing her hands in some sort of mental agony. Lili-beth was a lovely girl, petite and blond like her mother (minus the artificial tan and hair dye), with the sort of profile that belonged on a cameo. That she'd spent her entire life under the thumb of Bettie Rossman was just a crying shame.

"You're sorry the house isn't on fire?" Rosie asked as she rubbed the smaller towel on her head.

Lili-beth smiled, as Rosie had hoped she would, then allowed her shoulders to slump. "No, of course not. I'm sorry I interrupted you. I…I'm hiding."

"Really," Rosie said, tossing the towel in the general direction of the tub even as she reached for her comb amid the jumble of toiletries on the counter. "What did your mother do now?"

"Oh, no," Lili-beth said, raising her head as she looked up at Rosie. "Bettie didn't do anything wrong."

"Bettie?" Well now, that was a new one. "And what happened to *Mama?*"

"Mama—*Bettie* says that was all right when I was younger, but now I'm grown up, going to be married, and she and I should be friends. More like sisters. I'm, uh, I'm getting used to it."

"Uh-huh. Sisters. What does George say?"

"Daddy?" Lili-beth shrugged her slim shoulders. "You know Daddy. He doesn't say much. And don't think I don't know what M—Bettie is doing, Rosie, because I do. She's trying to stay young, feel young. I don't suppose I can really blame her."

"No, of course not, sweetie. Let me do that for you," Rosie told her, her mouth now full of toothpaste. "So, if it's not Bettie—precisely whom are you hiding from? Ki-Ki? Antoinette?" She spit into the sink. "Rob, your wonderful bridegroom?"

Lili-beth nodded, her normally peaches-and-cream complexion going pale. "He...he's being unreasonable. He wants us to elope. Now, this morning. To Las Vegas. He even showed me the airline tickets. I can't do that, Rosie. The wedding is this Sunday. Mama would have a cow."

Rosie rinsed and spit once more, then rubbed at

her right cheek because, when Lili-beth had said *Las Vegas,* she'd momentarily lost control of her toothbrush and jammed it hard against her gums. "Did he say why he wants to elope?"

"He says he can't wait another day to make me his wife," Lili-beth said, blushing now. "We…we haven't…*done it,* you know. I…I wanted to, but Rob says that true love shouldn't be…well, that it shouldn't be sullied by premarital sex." She blinked up at Rosie. "Isn't that romantic?"

"Oh yeah, sure, it's something all right. Your Rob should write verse for greeting cards. Tell you what, you hang out in here for a few minutes while I get dressed, and then we'll talk about this some more. Because I take it you aren't flying off to Vegas?"

"Mama—Bettie—would have a cow," Lili-beth repeated, obviously believing this was true, as did Rosie, at least a little bit. Not that it wouldn't be fun to watch…

In five minutes she was dressed in a simple rose linen sheath that only looked simple because the fabric had been cut by a master. She returned to the large, old-fashioned bathroom to grab her brush and hair dryer, to see Lili-beth dabbing at her eyes with a length of toilet paper. Really, this kid just broke her heart.

"Ah, sweetheart, is it that bad?"

"No-o-o-o," Lili-beth wailed piteously, and then buried her head in her hands.

Rosie looked at her reflection in the mirror above the sink, pushed at her damp hair a few times with her fingers and put down the hair dryer. She'd go for the loose curls, windblown look today…and only hoped the early September day could muster up a few breezes to cover for her.

She knelt down on the plush rose-colored rug—right on a damp spot where's she'd stepped on it getting out of the tub—and took hold of Lili-beth's slim arms, her plan being to urge the young woman to her feet, only to have Lili-beth grab onto her with a strength surprisingly like that of a barnacle clamping onto a hull.

Linen wrinkled when you looked at it crooked; now she'd be windblown, wrinkled and even a little damp…and her day had just started.

"What am I going to do, Rosie? Rob's going to be devastated when I say no. He loves me *so much!*"

"He does? Uh—of course he does," Rosie corrected quickly, awkwardly patting Lili-beth's back.

She'd never been really good at this female-bonding thing. "There…um…there, there. We'll fix this. I promise. We will. We'll fix this."

Lili-beth finally released her, to reach over and pull on the end of the toilet paper, unrolling a good two feet of double ply she then bunched up and pressed to her mouth and nose. "W-w-w-we?"

"Right," Rosie said bracingly, getting to her feet before Lili-beth could grab her again, and before she could change her mind. "Doug and me. We. Us two. We'll fix it."

"H-h-h-how?"

Great. Now the girl wanted details. She held out her hand and this time Rosie managed to boost Lili-beth from the bathroom to the bedroom. "It may be better if you just left the how of it up to Doug and me. What you have to remember is that you can't say a word to your mother about any of this. Not a single word."

"Oh, God, no," Lili-beth agreed, wide-eyed. "She'd have a—"

"A cow. Right, I've got that," Rosie cut in, still moving Lili-beth toward the door to the hallway. "So mum's the word, okay? You just go back to your room and take a bubble bath and I'll have someone bring up some fresh cucumber slices you can put on your eyes while you follow your bath with a nice long nap. Have you had breakfast?"

Lili-beth shook her head. "I couldn't even *think* about eating anything, Rosie. And I haven't slept all night."

"See? All the more reason for that nap. We can't have the bride looking tired, now can we? I'll have some light breakfast sent up along with the cucumber slices, and tell everyone you had a small touch of food poisoning or something last night and need to be left alone today. You do want to be left alone today, don't you?"

"God, yes. I can't see Rob yet, not until after that plane takes off at least. We'd have to leave for the Philadelphia airport by three this afternoon. And Ma—Bettie wants me to be in charge of Aunt Susanna at Lord and Taylor and I'd rather throw up for real than do that."

Lili-beth motioned for Rosie to lean closer. "I'm never supposed to say anything, but she *takes* things," she whispered. "My great-uncle left her half of Fort Knox, but she shoves cheap jewelry into her underwear. And *I'm* supposed to take her into the ladies' room and go fishing for them to give them back? I don't think so. Oh, I'm sorry. I shouldn't give away family secrets. What must you think of us? It's so embarrassing."

"Then we'll just have to trade secrets, so that we're even. My maternal grandfather used to take out his dentures and use them to pretend he was a ventriloquist," Rosie told her. "Sometimes it was funny, but then he put on his act at a fancy White House dinner during the Carter administration. There were those who thought he was poking fun at Jimmy Carter's mouthful of very white teeth, but he was just being Grandpa Sullivan. The rich *are* different, Lili-beth. Ah, that's what I wanted to see—you're smiling. Now go on, I'll report back when Doug and I have completed our mission."

Lili-beth bit her bottom lip between her teeth for a moment, and then asked: "About what you said…?"

Rosie opened the door and stepped into the hallway to make sure the coast was clear. "About what I said when?"

"You know. When I first walked into the bathroom? You thought I was my cousin Doug, didn't you? Did you really expect me to be him?"

"No, of course not. I was actually hoping on

Matthew McConaughey. Admit it, Lili-beth, that man is *hot*. And that Southern accent?"

"But you said—"

"Antoinette!" Rosie exclaimed, delighted to see the wedding planner bustling down the hallway toward them. She took hold of Lili-beth by the shoulders and rather roughly turned her in the direction of her bedroom. "Scoot. You don't want her to see you looking so healthy, do you? It'll blow our whole story."

"Rosie, I'm so glad I caught you," Antoinette said as Rosie stood in the hallway, putting herself between the woman and the retreating Lili-beth. "Did Lili-beth tell you what Rob did? He ruined the entire seating plan, that's what he did. You have to help me—Mrs. Rossman's incensed over today's flower arrangements, and I'm just not brave enough to tell her something else has gone wrong."

Rosie was beginning to think she should have been put on the payroll for the week. Not only that, but she really needed a cup of coffee, fast. "Wow, that's too bad. Let me just slap on some lipstick and mascara, Antoinette, and I'll be right with you," she said, leaving the wedding planner in the hallway to work on her harassed expression.

"Okay, lead me to the closest coffeepot," Rosie said a minute later, still fluffing her loose natural curls with one hand as she closed the door to her bedroom and locked it with the large metal key she then slipped into her pocket, because Bettie had a habit of borrowing anything that took her fancy— possibly some of Aunt Susanna's influence handed down through the genes? "Now tell me, what's the catastrophe du jour?"

"It's actually yesterday's catastrophe, but I…I wasn't able to cope with it yesterday."

"Okay, I remember now. Because you dove into the champagne cocktails?" Rosie suggested, grinning back at the woman as she headed down the curved staircase to the foyer.

"She told you that, didn't she? I didn't mean to. They just sort of snuck up on me, that's all. I had one when the cushions didn't arrive, and possibly two more when the quail burned. But when Rob insisted I find places for his two last-minute friends? Well, I may have gulped the fourth or fifth one a bit too fast. What am I going to do, Rosie? There's nowhere to put two single males, not at this late date. Everyone fit so well—boy-girl-boy-girl-boy-girl, you know—

and they simply throw everything off. And they're...*strange*."

Rosie paused in the foyer and looked back up the staircase to where Antoinette had paused, holding on to the banister with one hand, the ever-present clipboard with the other. She was dressed in one of her usual cotton shirtwaists, but she'd misbuttoned the top two buttons, and her reading glasses were hanging crookedly on their golden chain. Clearly the woman was still coping with a champagne hangover. "Are you all right, Antoinette?"

"No, I'm not. I've been planning weddings for fourteen years, Rosie, and my share of bar-mitzvahs and retirement parties, but I have *never* encountered anyone like Bettie Rossman." Antoinette carefully made her way to the bottom of the staircase and looked left and right before whispering, "I think the woman's insane. And *evil*."

Rosie laughed. "Intense, Antoinette. The woman's intense. Oh, and you can scratch one problem off your list. Bettie has abandoned the fighting fish idea, and I've already spoken with the florist, arranged a replacement for the centerpieces. There, does that help?"

"Oh, yes, it does, it does! Rosie, can you do calligraphy? My usual calligrapher refuses to come back here after Bettie told her she was too damn slow and she'd be damned if she'd pay her by the hour. Which is what we'd agreed to, you understand. Frances was in charge of name cards for each function, as well as those little cards we set up in front of the wedding gifts displayed in the library. Now the name cards are only half done, and there are more gifts arriving every minute. I don't know how I'm going to find another calligrapher at such short notice, so do you—?"

"Gosh, sorry, Antoinette, but no, I don't. Not freehand anyway. But I could probably whip out something nearly as good on my computer, if that's okay. I've got my laptop with me, and I know George has a printer in his study. Just find me some good stock paper and we're golden."

"*Would* you? Oh, Rosie, that would save my life. Now if only you could tell me what to do with those two men. I've already moved them into the second bedroom in the Bachelor Quarter, but—"

Rosie made a counterclockwise motion with her right hand. "Could you sort of back up there a minute, Antoinette? You put Rob's unexpected guests in with Mr. Llewellyn?"

"Why, yes, of course. They'll have to share one bed, but it is king-size, and nobody spends that much time in their rooms anyway. Oh dear. Do you think Mr. Llewellyn will mind?"

"Mind? I can think of at least three people who might not be too choked about the arrangements," Rosie told her as they made their way out onto the terrace, and to the large metal coffee urn at one end of the semipermanent buffet. It was sort of like camping out—but with real silver and crystal. She took her coffee strong and black, and had a feeling she was going to need more than a single cup. "So these two guests—you put them there last night? In with Mr. Llewellyn?"

Antoinette shook her head, then winced, as if that hadn't been a very good idea. "No, I really wasn't up to much last night. I don't know where they stayed last night, but this morning Mr. Hemmings made it very clear that accommodations must be made—at least for tonight."

"What about the rest of the week?" Rosie waved her hands in front of her as the words *Las Vegas* slammed back into her brain. Was Rob Hemmings running off to Vegas with his blushing bride—or running away from his two unexpected guests?

"Never mind, Antoinette. I think I already know the answer to that one. And here comes Mr. Llewellyn now, so I can ask him how he feels about sharing the Bachelor Quarter. Oh, wait, George just cornered him. Is there anything else I can do for you?"

"You can pray that Eloise continues to wander around near Bermuda until she falls apart," the wedding planner said. "The tents aren't scheduled to go up until Wednesday morning—all the good ones are booked through tomorrow for that antique show at the country club—and Bettie insisted on scheduling nearly every event out here on the terrace. I think the woman believes she can control the weather, and nobody can do that. Although I must admit, when I checked the extended forecast this morning, they're calling for sunny skies through the weekend. It's just that Sunday seems so far away. Especially when I hear Bettie calling my name."

As if on cue, Bettie Rossman tottered toward them, dressed in a white silk pantsuit with coral accents—clearly her color theme for the week. "Antoinette? *Disaster* has struck! *Please* tell me you have my organizer!"

"Why, no, Mrs. Rossman. I haven't seen it. But I've got everything on my clipboard."

Bettie looked at Rosie, her expression clearly saying *did you ever hear anything so stupid?* "And what am I supposed to do with your stupid clipboard? My *life* is on that organizer."

"Good God, Bettie," Rosie asked, aware of the weight of the organizer in the pocket of her dress. "Surely that's an exaggeration?"

Bettie rolled her eyes. "No, Rosie, it's not. My private e-mails, my telephone book, my entire social calendar, all my hair and tanning appointments. I know I have a Botox on Wednesday, but I can't remember the time, and the office never does those day-ahead reminder calls, and the office number is on my organizer, and I can't remember the name of the group. Basking Ridge something-or-other, but *everything* is the Basking Ridge something-or-other, and I just changed cosmetic surgeons and I'm not even sure of the address, except that it's on my organizer. See? I can't *function* without that organizer."

"Gee, that's too bad," Rosie said, feeling guilty. Sort of—but she'd get over it. "I'll be sure to keep my eye out for the thing. Oh, and I should tell you that Lili-beth isn't feeling too well this morning.

I told her to take a nap, just stay in her room and take it easy for the day."

"Well, she can't," Bettie said with some force. "She's the bride. She has obligations."

The organizer would stay where it was for a while, Rosie decided. "But, Bettie. She's really sick."

"Oh, she is not. It's just nerves. She gets those from her father. She'll get over it by the time we all leave for the mall. She knows she's in charge of Aunt Susanna. Now, anything else?"

If Rosie couldn't get a rise out of Bettie about her ailing daughter, she was pretty sure she would get a reaction with her next news: "Antoinette moved Rob's unexpected guests into the second bedroom in the Bachelor Quarter," she told her brightly. "That works, doesn't it?"

"She *what?*" Bettie rounded on Antoinette, who cringed behind her clipboard. "You *what?* Well, you're just going to have to move them the hell back *out* again. For pity's sake, they're only Rob's friends. Find them rooms at the Quality Inn. I cannot…that is, my cousin insists upon his privacy. Damn, there's Millicent. She was at me all of last night to move her to another table, away from Quint. I have to disappear before she sees me.

Antoinette—do something about that. Put one of Rob's friends next to her, why don't you? Now, I've got a hairdresser appointment at nine, and it's already past eight-thirty. Oh, and go tell Lili-beth that she'd better be waiting on the driveway in front of the house at precisely—whenever I said— to be Aunt Susanna's mall partner. And find my organizer! You have that? Write it all down on your clipboard or something, and *don't forget!*"

"I really don't like her," Antoinette said quietly as Bettie turned on her heels and headed back into the house. "I mean, I really, *really* don't like her. I don't know how Lili-beth stands any of this. If I were her, I'd have eloped by now."

"Uh...right," Rosie said, waving to Doug, who had just extricated himself from George, who was now swinging an imaginary golf club as he spoke with another male guest. "Could you see that some buttered toast and tea and a couple of slices of cucumber are sent up to Lili-beth's bedroom, Antoinette? Thanks. Oh, and if you could point out Rob's guests? They're the only two from his side, right?"

"An orphan," Antoinette said, nodding her head. "We're going to have to ask guests to fill in on his side of the aisle for the wedding ceremony." She stood up on tiptoe and looked across the expanse of the large terrace. "Ah, there they are," she said, pointing with her clipboard. "See? Over there, with Mr. Hemmings. The dark-haired one is Rizzo, and the big blonde is Leslie. Mr. Hemmings didn't give me more than that. I don't even know if it's Mr. Rizzo and Mr. Leslie, or if those are their first names. These things are important. Which reminds me. The calligraphy? Can I count on you? I promise to get their full names for you, once I decide which table to put them at, of course."

"Put them with us, Antoinette," Rosie said, noticing the way Rob Hemmings was gesturing almost pleadingly with the smaller man, his cheeks blotchy red. And the cords of his neck were standing out, as if he was yelling at the man, but in a whisper. "We're already sitting with Ear Waxx, remember? That'll make an even ten."

"Of course! That would be perfect! You're not family, although Mr. Llewellyn is, although for some reason I've been getting the feeling that Mrs. Rossman is rather angry with him at the moment. And you'd be the only woman at the table, Rosie. You wouldn't mind?"

"I think we'd actually prefer it, Antoinette. Oh,

and don't waste any of your valuable time looking too hard for that organizer. I have a feeling I know where it is. Now, if you'll excuse me?"

Before Antoinette could come up with another problem, or another plea for assistance, Rosie filled a second coffee cup and met Doug halfway across the terrace.

"Hi, sailor, you just drop anchor?" She held out one of the cups. "I've decided you take your coffee black."

"And I know better than to contradict you, don't I?" he said, taking a quick sip, then wincing. He was dressed casually, in a black golf shirt and tan slacks, and he looked scrumptious. "That's hot. I put an ice cube in mine. Try to remember that for the next time, okay?"

"I'll make a note of it on Bettie's organizer," Rosie told him as they turned and headed for their assigned table. "I guess the collective Ear Waxx is sleeping in this morning," she said as Doug held out a chair for her. "How about you? Did you sleep well?"

"After I finally gave up hoping you'd change your mind and sneak over in your pajamas after bed check, yes."

"That could have proved difficult. I sleep

naked," she told him, then grinned as he did a little choking thing on his latest sip of coffee.

He wiped at his mouth with the back of his hand, and then said, "Ask me how well I'm going to sleep tonight."

"Hey, at least you're going to sleep alone. Antoinette tried to stick Rob's two wedding guests into the extra bedroom, but Bettie ix-nayed that. Which is another way of saying I think she still has plans for that room. Six members of Ear Waxx. One down, five to go. You should be free by Saturday night. Shall I consider that a date?"

"Saturday night? No, you shouldn't. You should consider tonight a date. I'll talk to Bettie. She reacts fairly well to threats."

"Tonight?" Rosie looked at him overtop her coffee cup. "You're a confident son of a bitch, aren't you?"

"I'd prefer to say I'm optimistic. Am I overly optimistic?"

Rosie grinned. "No, I don't think so, Mr. Llewellyn. And aren't you glad I'm not coy?"

"You'll never know how much," he told her, his expression serious. "I've been thinking about what we discussed yesterday."

"Really?" She moved slightly closer to him. "And

here I was thinking about our time down at the tennis courts. And that little thing you did behind my ear with your tongue. That was very nice."

"Yeah, well, that, too," he told her, his hand having found its way to her left thigh. "Between our conversation and the tennis court, I spent most of last night thinking about you. I don't remember the last time that happened, if it ever has, at least not since high school. You do have a way of getting under a man's skin, don't you?"

She laughed softly as she covered his hand with her own. "Am I really supposed to answer that?"

"I suppose not. If you tell me yes, then I'll wonder how many men you've knocked sideways the way you know damn well you're doing with me, and if you pretend not to understand what I'm saying, I won't believe you. Let's just live in the now, Miss Kilgannon, if that's all right with you. Enjoy the *now*. All of it."

Rosie was having a slight problem controlling her breathing, but she didn't mind, because the rest of her was beginning to feel so *good*. Douglas Llewellyn was the most naughty, honest, *fascinating* man. "No more thinking of where you've been, or where you're going?"

He shook his head before moving in for a kiss, stopping only a whisper away from her mouth. "If that's all right with you, Rosie. Do you really sleep in the nude, or were you just pulling my chain?"

She looked deeply into his incredible gray eyes. "You'll just have to wait and see, won't you?"

She felt his hand move up along her thigh, edging closer to dangerous territory, before he moved both it and himself away from her.

"Is something wrong?" she asked him, feeling cheated out of a kiss, at the very least.

"Not a thing. It's just that frustration isn't my favorite game. Last night was the last time I intend to start anything I know we aren't going to finish. The next time I kiss you, Rosie, we're going to finish what we start."

"So if I'm going to back out I should do it now, because I've been warned? Is that it?"

He smiled at her, obviously very much in control of himself, which was really rotten, because she wasn't all that in control of her own self. "Let's just say I think you talk a good game, Rosie, and that maybe I goaded you into pretending something that isn't really true. You're no Bettie."

"All right, you've got me there. But I'm no Lilibeth, either," Rosie told him honestly.

"No, I suppose not. You're just Rosie," Doug said, lightly running the back of his hand down her cheek and throat, as he'd done before; a soft, intimate gesture she quite enjoyed. "And I think I like that. Not too fast, not too slow, but just right."

"Is that so? If I remember my 'Goldilocks' correctly, I think that would make me Baby Bear."

"Really? Okay, I'll work on it, find a better comparison."

She grinned at him. "Comparison shopping?"

He was suddenly serious. "Not this week."

Rosie got to her feet, probably too quickly. "I think I'll go grab goodies for us from the buffet. You stay here, take a few deep breaths or something. You're dangerous this morning. Not that I'm complaining…."

CHAPTER SEVEN

"YOUR HAIR'S DIFFERENT this morning," Doug said as Rosie took a bite of the strawberry mini-Danish she was using to wash down the chocolate mini-croissant she'd just polished off a moment earlier. He'd never realized how incredibly sexy it was to watch a woman who truly enjoyed her food. "I like the curls. They're, um…touchable. And still a little damp, in case you hadn't noticed."

"Actually, I was hoping for more of a breeze, but if you like the curls, then we're good." She licked out the center of the Danish, all but rolling her tongue around the strawberry filling. "Rob is pushing Lili-beth to elope with him today to Las Vegas. What do you think of that?"

Doug mentally sorted through yet another of Rosie's verbal puzzles and decided to ignore the breeze comment and center on the proposed elopement. "Not a whole hell of a lot. How do you know this?"

"Lili-beth told me," Rosie said, licking sugar from her fingertips…a job he would have volunteered for, except that he was aware he was probably already in too deep, if this was supposed to be a fun, but casual weeklong fling. "I sent her to bed."

"Alone, I hope," Doug said, dipping his linen napkin into the glass of water a waiter had placed on the table earlier, along with the pastries, and then taking Rosie's hand in his and wiping at her fingers. "Did you have to lock her in, then go find Delwood in his pith helmet and tell him to go to the garage and lock up all the ladders?"

Rosie shook her head. "She doesn't want to elope. Bettie would have a cow—Lili-beth's words—for one thing. And, for another, although she didn't come out and actually say the words, I think Lili-beth is having second thoughts about her groom. In which case," she said, curling up her nose, "Bettie would have a litter."

"Calves don't come in litters," Doug told her, dabbing the damp napkin at the corners of Rosie's mouth, not because she had crumbs on her lips, but because he just wanted an excuse to hold her chin in his hand and look into her eyes. "The most she could have would be two, I think, unless she's trying for the *Guinness Book of World Records*. Come to think of it, she'd make the list if she just had one cow—calf. What do you say we walk down to the stream to talk about this? There are too many people around here, and Anvil could show up at any minute. Call me a coward, but I really don't want to see him this morning—my memories of yesterday are too fresh."

"I wonder if he feels the same way? If so, I doubt we'll see him again unless he's performing."

"As long as he isn't *performing* in my apartment."

"Poor baby. All your innocence shattered. Do you think you might need therapy?"

"Oh, I signed up for that the minute I met you. Anvil would only be an afterthought."

"I'll take that as a compliment." She slipped her hand into his, reminding him how tactile she was, how she seemed to enjoy touching, being touched. Then again, what had he just been doing?

"Eyes left—nine o'clock," she said as they strolled through the still-dew-wet grass. "Two men, standing with Rob Hemmings. One blond, one dark. Give me your first impressions, just

KASEY MICHAELS 171

straight off the top of your head. And be discreet, okay? Don't gawk."

"Bite your tongue, woman. I never gawk." Doug did as he was instructed, slicing a quick look to his left, taking in as much as he could in a few seconds and then pretending to point to a bird high in the limbs of a tall oak tree. "Look, Rosie, I do believe that's a black-on-brown wing-tipped Florsheim. They're very rare."

"Considering Florsheim's are *shoes,* yes, I agree. You don't see many of them in trees. Unless they're shoe trees," Rosie said, laughing. "And I suppose you think you're being subtle? And you couldn't have seen anything worth seeing that first time. Take another peek, they're not looking this way."

Once again, Doug slid his gaze to the left. This time, because Rosie was correct and nobody was looking their way, he stopped where he was, put his hands on her shoulders as he turned her so that her back was to the men and gave her his impressions as they hit him.

"Hemmings. Looking harassed. Nervous. Ah…now angry. But not as angry as the short dark-haired guy. Excuse me—vertically challenged guy. But he seems to make up for it with that menacing way he stands, legs apart, chin jutting forward. Bantamweight and fast on his feet."

"Very good, although I would have said junior welterweight. That's Rizzo," Rosie said, taking a quick peek at the trio of men. "And he's not angry—he's smiling."

"You're half-right. He's smiling with his mouth. But not with his eyes." Doug decided to have a little fun. "Is it just me, or does he look a little like a knockoff version of the guy who plays Tony's nephew on *The Sopranos?* I mean, we are in Jersey."

"Oooh, I'm scared," Rosie said, rolling her eyes at him. "Keep pretending you're talking to me. Now, moving right along…what about the other guy? Leslie."

Leslie was about six-eight and weighed roughly five pounds less than a pickup truck. "This is just a shot in the dark, but if we're going to play Name That Thug, I'd say he's the enforcer of the pair, the knee breaker. Oh, wow, he's cracking his knuckles. Such an endearing trait, don't you think? Leslie, you said? He must have had to beat up a lot of kids on the playground before he grew into that name."

"And he's blond. He doesn't look at all… Soprano-like. Not that I'm buying anything you're selling, buster. Although," she said, pulling him toward the tree line, "they both do sort of stand out in this crowd, don't they? Do you think that's Rob's problem? He's embarrassed by his own friends? That's so incredibly tacky. At least they aren't going to be your roommates. What do you think they have on him?"

Doug shook his head in amused disbelief. "Now who's coming up with gangster scenarios? Why can't they be his friends from Harvard, or wherever Hemmings went to school? No, scratch that. Harvard grads don't wear triple-pleated sharkskin slacks, do they?"

"Leslie isn't wearing sharkskin slacks. He actually looks fairly natty, in an I-saw-it-put-together-this-way-in-a-magazine sort of way. Shame his jacket is two sizes too small. So they're bookies, right? I mean, I could be wrong, but I think they're bookies. Not that I've ever seen a bookie before, but they do have that central casting bookie look to them, don't you think? Oh, wait, maybe they're loan sharks?"

Doug grinned. "Well, there are the sharkskin slacks. But that still might be a stretch."

"In any case, they're here for their money,

money Rob doesn't have until he and Lili-beth are married, so they're sticking around for the ceremony—and the payoff. Which Rob doesn't want to give them, so he wants Lili-beth to run off to Vegas with him before anything can happen and wake up George to what's going on and he stops the wedding and—well, I think that's enough for now. What do you think?"

They'd reached the carved-seat log and Doug sat down, pulling Rosie onto his lap. "I think...I think...give me a minute. I don't know what I think. No, wait, yes I do. I think you're beautiful. And nuts, although I'm willing to overlook that in favor of my libido if you promise never to mention any of what you've just said again. Is it a deal?"

"No, I don't think so. It *fits*, Douglas. It all *fits*. You don't like Rob. I don't like Rob. Rob doesn't love Lili-beth."

"I never said that. He was rude to her. Once, while he was losing at gin rummy. That doesn't warrant a leap of logic that has him not loving her, just marrying her for George's money."

"All right. Here's something that should hit home with you. They haven't had sex," Rosie said smugly as she slipped her arms around his shoulders. "Not once, even though Lili-beth told him she'd be agreeable. A year, Doug. People in love can't keep their hands off each other for five minutes, let alone a year. There, chew on that one for a minute while I gnaw on your earlobe. You have the cutest earlobes."

Doug sat very still while Rosie did just as she'd said she would, mixing a little tongue in with her nibbling bites, a little warm breath blowing that sent an immediate Stand By for Action message south of his personal border. He closed his eyes, called himself seven kinds of fool, a slave to his aforementioned libido and the armful of lush, willing woman. "No sex. For a full year, no sex. Not even once?"

"Nope. And they've been engaged since Easter, which came early this year, and the wedding's the first week of September. Because Rob says love shouldn't be sullied by premarital sex." She did something truly remarkable with her tongue behind his ear. "That's a direct quote from the groom-to-be. Hmm, you taste good. So, do you have anything to say now?"

"Not a lot, no," he said, turning his head in order to look into her soft brown eyes. "How about this? I want you."

Rosie smiled, and Doug was instantly reminded of the Cheshire cat from *Alice in Wonderland.* "Back at you. At least we agree on something. We are the quintessential consenting adults. But I think we need to investigate Rizzo and Leslie more first, don't you?"

"No," Doug said honestly. "I think we need to pack our bags and get the hell out of here, go somewhere with twenty-four-hour room service, and do whatever comes naturally. Several times."

"Well, that was blunt."

Doug pressed his forehead against hers. "You should know. And I'm an idiot. What in hell are you doing to me?"

"Being a woman," Rosie breathed quietly. "Not a girl, Doug—a woman. A real woman. Over thirty, reasonably intelligent, knowing what she wants and not afraid to go after it. And, at least for the moment, I want you. I *am* you—just the female version. Scary, huh?"

Doug felt a self-depreciating chuckle gathering in his chest and stood up, Rosie still hanging on to him as she slid her feet to the ground. "You don't mean a word of that, do you?"

"I'll never tell," Rosie said, moving away from

him. "Do you think Rizzo and Leslie play croquet? I remember Antoinette said she was going to post a sign-up sheet down at the tennis court. Let's go see."

He followed after her as she started off along the path back to the house. "You're not going to give up on this one, are you?"

She turned to him, suddenly serious. "Lilibeth's unhappy. Your cousin is unhappy. You saw her. She's never been a real outgoing type, but right now she looks like Bambi in headlights, for crying out loud. She cried on my toilet this morning, Doug. *Sobbed.* How can I turn my back on that?"

"You can't," Doug said quietly, letting the toilet reference just sort of slide over his head, because he was pretty sure it wasn't important—at least he hoped it wasn't important.

He didn't know this woman. He probably never would. There were too many sides to her; she was like quicksilver, running through his fingers. She had him off balance, wondering, questioning. But he had learned one thing, at least he hoped so: she was sincere. Sincerely sensual. Sincerely herself. What you saw was what you got, even when you didn't have a clue what that *what* was. And sincerely caring. Rosie Kilgannon *cared.*

Did *he* care? Maybe. Possibly. When the mood suited him. When the moment suited him, served him. He was Douglas Llewellyn, and he cared about Douglas Llewellyn, about his work and about his pursuit of pleasure. For all his hard work, for all that he'd built an impressive business, he was, at forty, very much alone—just the way he thought he liked it.

He dated silly young women because there was no future in it—only an enjoyable present. He skimmed along the surface of life.

So did Rosie—skim, that is—at least to hear her tell it. But that wasn't all of Rosie Kilgannon. The "free spirit" thing just didn't ring true, not when he saw how involved she was…with charities, with her friends' lives. With Lili-beth, who had basically been little more than her student. She wasn't nosey, or pushy (well, maybe a little bit pushy). She was frank about wanting to enjoy life, but she also *cared*.

What did he do?

Laugh at Cam when he'd gotten himself turned all inside out over his Darcie, and then tell himself he never wanted to be where Cam was then or now, as Cam planned his wedding.

Be named Philly's Most Eligible Bachelor—

twice. At thirty, that could be considered an honor, or at least a good joke. Maybe. But at forty? Wasn't that beginning to border on the pathetic?

"Doug? You look a million miles away."

He smiled, shook his head. Okay, he was in— where Rosie led, he'd follow, and if he was lucky he wouldn't have to think this deeply about his miserable life again for at least a week. "Sorry, Rosie. I was just wondering—do you think Bettie owns a gun?"

"Because she's going to kill Rob if we're right?"

"No…because she's going to kill *us* if we screw up her big day."

"Then it's settled? No more discussion? We're doing this? We're breaking up this wedding? Oh, Doug, that's terrific, really terrific. I knew you'd see reason."

"Not so fast, Kilgannon," he told her as they walked out into the sunshine and headed for the tennis court. "First we have to make sure we're right. One hundred and ten percent sure, Rosie."

"All right. That's only sensible." Her frown bordered on the adorable. "How do we do that?"

"I have no idea," Doug said, shaking his head. "What have we got so far?"

She immediately began ticking off a mix of fact and supposition on her fingers.

"One, Bettie and George bought Rob for Lilibeth. They paid off his debts, gave him a cushy job, and he's come back needing more money at least twice. George cut him off last month—but not before he gave him even more money. Although I'm betting—get that? Betting?—he's broke again."

"Two," Doug said, "Hemmings likes to gamble. He goes to Atlantic City all the time. And, if the reckless way he played yesterday means anything, the casinos comp him free rooms and meals, give him a fat line of credit and then take him for every last penny."

"Logical conclusion—he's not only broke, he's in debt again after George's last handout. He's in over his head, and Rizzo and Leslie aren't his old college buddies from home, but his Mutt and Jeff friendly neighborhood loan sharks, and they've come looking for their money and won't leave until they've got it. Or maybe his bookies. He also bets on the horses, or baseball, or something. I mean, we've decided at least this much—those guys are not insurance salesmen."

"We can't prove any of that, Rosie," Doug

pointed out as they reached the chain-link fence around the tennis court and she picked up the pencil tied to the fence and wrote in their names for the first croquet match, then scribbled *Rizo* and *Leslie* on the next two lines. "We need to stick with facts, not suppositions. And I'm pretty sure Rizzo has two Z's."

"Oops—he'd know that, right?" she said, grinning as she picked up the pencil again, added a Z. "All right, back to facts. Fact three: he's not acting like a groom. Fact four: Lili-beth isn't acting like the blushing bride. Fact five: Rob feels a crushing need to get the hell out of town, even while he feels a crushing need to marry George's money."

"I don't know why I ever thought you might be a lawyer," Doug said, shaking his head. "You keep blending facts and suppositions."

Rosie pulled a face…a comically beautiful face he really, really longed to kiss. "Picky, picky. Now come on, let's go locate our victims and get this show on the road."

The woman was like a force of nature as she stormed the terrace, grabbing George and Rob, then Leslie and Rizzo, and then ordering them all onto the south lawn.

George went willingly enough, but it was only when Rosie suggested they play teams—for money—that Rob agreed to the plan, quickly downing the remainder of his Bloody Mary before sticking the stalk of celery into the corner of his mouth like a cigar. And, Doug noticed, as Rizzo and Leslie seemed to think their mission in life was to go where Rob went, all six of them were soon at the designated croquet field, choosing mallets and balls.

"Oh, wonderful, Rosie," Antoinette trilled, coming at them with her clipboard clutched to her breasts. "I was so worried no one would sign up. Delwood's almost finished—aren't you, Delwood?"

"Two more wickets and one post and we're ready," Delwood said, hefting a rubber mallet.

Doug was still trying to figure out Delwood's place in this strange menagerie. Was he a guest of the wedding, or an employee? Whichever, he sure was a helpful sonofagun, wasn't he?

As if she could read his mind, Rosie leaned close to him and said, "His full name is Delwood Armbruster. Armbruster Electronics? I think I remember you saying that you've already met his sister, Lillian, when Bettie sicced her on you. Relax, she's married now, with a baby on the way, and living in Phoenix. Delwood just likes to be helpful. Of course, he's also madly in love with Lili-beth. But you already guessed that."

"Would it be a stretch for me if I thought Delwood is part B of your planned coup? Delete Rob—insert Del?"

Rosie looked at him with a comically shocked expression. "Me? Don't be ridiculous. I'd never even think of such a thing." She stood on tiptoe and kissed him on the mouth. "That's *your* job."

"My—" Doug backed up a step. "What am I supposed to do? Lock them together in a closet?"

"No, that wouldn't work," Rosie told him. "Delwood needs self-confidence. He needs a few pointers. Okay, a lot of pointers. He needs to be tutored by an expert. You know, by the two-time Most Eligible Bachelor and Man About Town in the City of Brotherly Love?"

"Who told you that?"

"I looked you up online. What do they give you for that? Free cheesesteaks for a year?"

Doug dropped his ball and used the mallet to lightly tap it toward the first wooden stake. "Cute. But here's a lesson for you, Kilgannon. Never piss off an ally."

"Am I doing that? I'm sorry. And I know I shouldn't have done it—cheated, that is, but I wanted to sound brilliant when I guessed that you're an architect. So all I've really done is admit I don't always play fair, and you already knew that."

"Don't always play fair? You mean there're times you do play fair? Gee, now I'm shocked."

She smiled brilliantly. "I know, I know. I'm so ashamed. Oh, and it's too bad you missed the trifecta. I saw this year's winner. Not bad, but definitely no Douglas Llewellyn."

"Are you done now?" Doug asked, his small spurt of anger dissipating as he finally saw the humor in the thing. "And you'll never mention my infamous past again?"

"Or your sad fall from fame? Do you think that next year the magazine that chooses these guys will run a sidebar on 'Whatever Happened To Doug Llewellyn'?"

He growled at her.

"Okay, okay, I'm done now. Well, I have one more—a real zinger—but I'll be kind. *If* you promise to tutor Delwood."

"Oh, sure. I'll just run right over there and give him pointers on how to seduce my second cousin.

How many centures in purgatory do you think that would get me?"

Rosie rolled her eyes. "No, not Lili-beth. *Ki-Ki*. Goodness, Doug, don't you know *anything* about women? You must have just been really, really lucky all these years. Delwood's been following Lili-beth like a lovesick puppy since they were kids, and she only sees him as a friend. But that all changes when it looks like he's about to become Ki-Ki's love monkey. Lili-beth will start looking at him with new eyes…and just as Rob is getting his walking papers. It's simple physics, or something."

"Or something. Love monkey, huh? And thank you for these almost frightening insights into a woman's mind."

"You're welcome. Oh, look, isn't that cute? Leslie picked the green ball—to coordinate with his tie, which is really ugly, by the way. The man may have a softer, more feminine side."

"Let's take that a step further, all right? Rizzo chose the black ball, and I don't think it's because it goes with his slacks."

Rosie wriggled her eyebrows as she whispered portentously, "No. It goes with his *soul*. Be afraid…be very afraid."

"I'm really glad to know you're taking this seriously," he told her. "Play your games, Rosie, but not with Rizzo. The more I look at him—and I'm trying not to—the more I think you may be onto something. Our boy Robbie could be in some serious trouble."

"Ah, I'm getting through to you. Not that I ever doubted it for a moment."

Antoinette came up to them, handing Rosie a printed scorecard. "Here you go, my dear. We've made up our own rules. Five points for each wicket successfully navigated. Minus five points if you go through backward. Ten points for sending an opponent's ball off the course, minus ten if yours is sent off the course. Double wickets count for fifteen, and hitting the stakes after successfully completing each length of the course is a fifty point bonus. Any other arrangements are left up to the players and I don't want to hear about them. Next game is at eleven, so please try not to dawdle."

"I didn't take her for a drill sergeant," Doug said as Antoinette and her nervous efficiency headed back toward the house and George walked up to them wearing, dear God, a golf glove.

"We've got it all figured out. Dollar a point.

Front nine for a hundred, back nine for two hundred, sweep both and it's five C-notes. That boy Rizzo calls them that. Rob's trying to go double or nothing, but I don't think that's going to happen. You two still game? It's going to be cutthroat."

"Cutthroat croquet," Doug said, shaking his head. "Do you think Rizzo takes Mastercard?"

"Oh, don't worry," Rosie assured him as George walked over to place his ball two mallet lengths in front of the stake. "I'm the Tiger Woods of croquet. Here's the plan. You take Rizzo, and I'll take Leslie. Just follow where they lead, and keep hitting their balls off the course. Piece of cake. Oh, and don't forget to milk him for information while I do the same with Leslie. Just be subtle, we don't want them to know what we're doing."

"That will be easy—since *I* don't know what we're doing. You're so lucky I want your body," Doug told her as George tapped his ball through the first pair of wickets, then gleefully announced that he now had two shots still coming to him, one for each wicket.

"Liar. You'd help me in any case. And you know why? Because you're a great big softie at heart, and you're worried about Lili-beth. That makes you *very* sexy, did you know that?"

"Don't believe it for a minute, Kilgannon. I'm only doing this so I can get into your—"

George cut Doug's words off with a bellow. "Rosie, pay attention, please. You're up!"

She stood on tiptoe and kissed Doug on the mouth. "Liar. But feel free to hold that thought."

He watched, fascinated, as Rosie, her red-striped mallet on her shoulder, strolled over to the starting point and introduced herself to Rizzo and Leslie, shaking their hands, saying something that made Rizzo laugh and Leslie dip his head and look embarrassed. When it came to easy self-confidence, Rosie was the undisputed champ.

And it was time he joined the party.

Rosie placed her ball two mallet-head lengths in front of the stake, hiked up her skirt so that she could straddle the stake and shot the ball through the first two wickets and far enough into the field to have a great chance to use her two shots to make it through the second wicket.

Which she did, playing the croquet field like a pool table, each completed shot setting her up perfectly for the next one. With her bonus shot for making it through the wicket, and her great set-up—not to mention her great legs—she was now through the middle wicket and heading for the next one…and would have made it, too, if she hadn't dubbed the shot.

Doug was pretty sure she'd done that on purpose, but he was also pretty sure he was the only one who thought that.

"Dames," Rizzo told him as Leslie put down his ball. "They can get lucky, but they can't get good. For cripes' sakes, Leslie, take off your jacket. You look like a moron."

"Can't," Leslie said quietly, which was when Doug realized that only most of the man's bulges were courtesy of his girth. One of them, under his left arm, Doug suddenly felt certain had been man-made.

While Leslie lined up his shot, Doug walked down the side of the chalk-outlined field to talk to Rosie. "Don't look now, partner, but I think the Jolly Green Giant is packing heat."

"Pardon me? Oh." Her eyes went wide. "*Oh.*"

"Yeah. *Oh.* Change of plans. You get Rizzo, I get Leslie. And, once this is over, *darling,* we both get serious psychiatric help."

CHAPTER EIGHT

ROSIE SAT AT THEIR ASSIGNED table on the terrace, her elbows on the table top as she gleefully counted out their winnings. "Five hundred and ten, five hundred and twenty—hey, what are you doing? Now I'll have to start over again."

Doug had pulled the bills out of Rosie's hands and scooped the pile from the table and onto her lap. "Fine, you do that. But later, okay? Never count your winnings where your marks can see you."

He looked serious. Wasn't that cute? "Is that like knowing when to hold your cards and when to fold them, or something like that? From that old Kenny Rogers's song?"

"Same song, different verse," Doug told her. "Now put the money away. I don't think our new pals Rizzo and Leslie react well to shameless gloating. And where in hell did you learn to play croquet like that? That last hit, Rob's ball didn't stop going until it caught the downhill slope of the driveway—a good thirty feet away. It's probably still rolling."

"He should have gone chasing after it instead of Delwood. I don't know who I'm more upset with—Rob for being such a poor loser, or Delwood for being such a nice guy. As for your question, it's all in the wrists. And the follow-through, of course. Oh, and I've found that hiking my skirt halfway up my thighs works very well when I'm playing against men. But okay, I'll count the money later. Half for the ASPCA, half for Gina's abused women. I think this is going to prove to be a profitable week for everyone's favorite charities. Thanks for handing over your share of the winnings."

"Did I have a choice?"

"Not really," she said, leaning in to give him a quick kiss, except that Doug didn't seem to believe in quick kisses. "Wow," she said when she finally sat back blinking, and definitely a little shaken by her instant, almost visceral reaction to this man. "You really are extraordinarily good at that, you know. Kissing, I mean."

His grin was positively evil, and a real turn-on.

"Practice makes perfect, they always say. And I do have an ulterior motive. You can't help yourself—you're putty in my hands."

"Oh, really. Now who's gloating—and just because you're right?" She was about to suggest they grab some sandwiches and go up to his rooms above the carriage house to partake of a picnic…and anything else that might occur to them, when she looked past Doug's shoulder to see that Rob was standing behind him. "We've got company, Mr. Hickok," she said quietly.

"I want to go again," Rob said, tapping Doug's shoulder, none too lightly, either. His expression didn't actually mar his college-boy good looks, but that was only if Rosie didn't look too hard at his eyes, which were all but shooting sparks at both of them. "Double or nothing."

Doug looked at Rosie, who could only shrug, and then slowly turned around. "No, thanks. We'd like to, you understand, but I'm afraid we've got other plans."

"They can wait, whatever they are. You have to give me a chance to get even. It's only fair. George can't play worth crap. This time I'll take Rizzo as my partner."

Doug stood, giving him about a four-inch advantage over the younger man, and when he spoke Rosie lost her smile. Who would have thought Doug could be so good at *stern?* "I said, no, thank you. Why don't you go find your bride, hmm? You know—at least make it look good?" Oh, not just stern. His sarcasm was pretty impressive, too.

Rob immediately had a hard set to his jaw, and his hands had bundled into fists. Belligerence personified. "What do you mean by that? You mean something by that?"

Rosie coughed into her fist, pretty sure that it would take more than the butter knife beside her plate to cut the sudden tension in the air. It might take a referee. "Hey, guys…?"

Rob leaned around Doug to glare at her. She knew a glare when she saw one, and the jackass was actually *glaring* at her. "This time, I'm really going to watch you. I think you cheat."

Rosie was on her feet before she even thought about it, and back in her chair a millisecond later, courtesy of a semigentle shove from Doug, who was now standing toe-to-toe with Rob Hemmings.

"That was in very poor taste, Hemmings,"

Doug said, nearly purring the words. "Apologize to the lady."

"The hell I will. She's too damn good. I demand a chance to get my money back," Rob said, his voice rising, so that Rosie took a quick look around to see who might be within earshot.

There was only one other person within thirty feet. Unfortunately, that person was Father Rourke. "Umm…Doug?"

"Wrong answer, Hemmings. There's not going to be a rematch. I said, apologize. Now."

"Yeah? And who are you to tell me what to do? Just because you're banging her doesn't mean—"

Rosie's eyes went wide as Rob slowly crumpled to the brick terrace. She hadn't seen Doug move, hadn't seen the punch, but Rob was most definitely down, his arms wrapped tight around his gut, his face turning red, all his breath knocked out of him.

"Rosie to Doug. Come in, please. Hard-of-hearing priest at six o'clock," she said quietly.

"Well, hell…"

Obviously he didn't need to be told twice. She liked that; the man was definitely quick on the uptake. He was also chivalrous, and packed a pretty mean punch, which were both pretty nifty, too.

"Hey, that was some trip you took, Hemmings, old pal," Doug said in an almost booming voice, grabbing Rob's left arm and hauling him to his feet in one powerful motion. "You really have to watch where you're going. Are you going to be all right?"

Rob was still sucking wind, and didn't respond.

"Oh, would you look at that?" Rosie said, her voice also loud enough to carry a good third of the way across the terrace. "There it is, a loose brick. Gosh, Rob, it's a good thing you're going to be a part of the family soon, or you could sue George for pain and suffering, huh? I mean, nothing's broken, right? Doug? Maybe you want to help poor Rob up his room?"

"Don't…you…*touch* me," Rob managed, still fairly well bent in half. "Rizzo isn't…isn't going to like this."

"True. Because if we kill you, there goes a hefty chunk of the guy's accounts receivable, right?"

"Rosie, if you don't mind," Doug told her, "I'll handle this."

She made a face. "But you heard him. He said Rizzo. That just about proves that we're—oh, all right, all right. But why do you men always get to have all the fun?"

"Rosie…"

She held up her hands in mock surrender. "Okay, okay, I was merely saying…"

"You're crazy. You stay away from me," Rob said even as he was backing up, which was pretty funny, actually. "I mean it. You both stay away from me." Then, keeping his eyes on Doug, he turned and made for the French doors leading to Bettie's command center.

"Oh, pooh. He's going to go tattle, you know, try to get us in trouble with his future mama-in-law," Rosie said when Doug sat down once more, surreptitiously rubbing at the knuckles on his right hand. "I wanted to hang on to the organizer a while longer, but now I'm going to have to give it back, just to divert her. Darn."

"You're welcome," Doug said, definitely with another endearing touch of sarcasm. "I think I caught a knuckle on one of his ribs."

"Oh, I'm sorry. Does it hurt, is it swollen? Shall I kiss it, make it all better?"

"I'll take a rain check if you don't mind. You're dangerous to be around, do you know that?"

Rosie couldn't help herself; she felt positively

delicious. "Me? I was just sitting here, minding my own business—"

"You'd come across as more sincere if you weren't grinning like the village idiot, you know?" Doug warned her, shaking his head. "I don't get this. I'm the champion of minding my own business, of never getting involved. When in hell did I turn into a knight in shining armor?"

"I don't know. But you're very good at it. I missed the punch. What did you use? Was it a right cross?"

"An uppercut to the solar plexus. I would rather have hit him with a right cross, but Bettie would kill me if she thought the groom was going to show up for the ceremony with a shiner. So I settled for the uppercut. Pretty much a cheap shot, frankly, because he wasn't expecting it, but that's just too damn bad. And that boy's going down."

"Don't look now, champ, but I think he already did."

Doug helped her to her feet. "You know what I mean. Whether you're right or wrong on the money angle, he's got to go. Lili-beth can't marry that jerk. What the hell is the matter with George?"

"I think George gave up believing he was the head of his own household about twenty years ago," Rosie told him in all seriousness as they walked across the lawn toward the carriage house. They hadn't said a word about their destination, but both of them seemed to know just where they were going, which was nice. Really, really nice.

Doug mumbled something nice girls probably should pretend they hadn't heard.

"He's sort of like those three monkeys now, Doug. You know—sees nothing, hears nothing, says nothing. We all know who's in charge around here, and it isn't him."

Doug stepped back and indicated that Rosie should precede him up the staircase. "That's no excuse. Lili-beth's his daughter, for crying out loud." He stepped past her to unlock the door. "You have children, you damn well pay attention."

Rosie turned and slipped her hands around his shoulders as they entered the living room, barely waiting for him to kick the door closed behind them. "I really do like you, Douglas Llewellyn. Really and truly. It's not just those gorgeous eyes of yours, although they don't hurt, believe me. Or this great body. I'm not lodging a complaint about either. Do you need some ice for those knuckles?"

He put his hands on her forearms. "I seem to remember an offer to kiss it, make it better."

"You know, Mr. Llewellyn, I think I do remember that," Rosie told him, slipping her arms free to take hold of his right hand, lift it to her mouth. "Is it this one?" she asked, pressing her lips against his skin as she focused her attention on his eyes. They seemed to darken a shade even as she watched. Fascinating. "Or maybe this one…?" She flicked at his knuckles with the tip of her tongue. Once. Twice.

"Okay, lady, that just tipped the scales on my frustration level," Doug said, and somehow his hands were locked around her waist as he began backing her toward the hallway leading to the bedrooms.

Always wanting to be helpful, Rosie clapped her hands on his shoulders, using his strength for balance as she executed a small jump, lifting her legs up and round his back.

Doug may have staggered a little, but recovered nicely—and didn't even go *oomph* at her added weight, bless him. She knew she was more a lush Kathleen Turner than she had ever been a reed-thin Kate Moss type, but she wasn't all that big. What was five foot seven and a mere one hundred and forty-three well-toned pounds between friends, anyway? And, hubba-hubba, they were soon to be *very* good friends.

Their mouths were pretty well mashed together as Rosie pushed her fingers into Doug's hair, her whimpered moans partly theatrical, partly deadly serious as he still half walked, half staggered backward toward the hallway. She only laughed a little when he banged into the doorjamb and swore under his breath.

"Just…just a passing bit of information—I'm getting too damn old for this," he told her as he turned around, attempting to look past her as he aimed them toward the bed.

Rosie was nibbling on his right ear now. "It's a little late to tell me that, you know, Casanova," she said, then stuck her tongue in his ear as they tumbled together onto the quilt-topped bed.

He lay half on top of her, his elbows braced on either side of her head. "I was referring to the carrying part. I think I can manage the rest," he said, his mock leer *so* cute, such a turn-on. Not that she wasn't already turned-on. She'd been pretty much on *simmer* since that first impetuous kiss.

"So I didn't throw your back out or anything?" Rosie asked, realizing that she still had her legs wrapped around him. So that's what she'd heard earlier—not her breaking his bones, but her skirt seam ripping. That was going to be fun to explain if anyone saw her on her way back to her room at the main house. *Oh well...*

"Not yet," he murmured against her throat, "but we can always live in hope."

It was a game. They were both playing a game. The same game of mutual seduction.

And how great was this—they both seemed to be winning!

Doug caught her mouth once more, their tongues dueling as their hands were busy with buttons and zippers, snaps and clasps. Clothing was an impediment, and it was all quickly gone, as was the genuine, manufactured to look like a family heirloom quilt.

He was as gorgeous naked as he was in designer clothes. Hard muscled. His tan darker on his arms; a golfer's tan on top of already sun-lit skin. The sun-bleached hair on his chest arrowing down, down...down. A thin white scar. An appendectomy scar? Did it matter? She'd ask later. Right now, she was busy.

Delightfully, wonderfully, hungrily busy.

As was he.

He had slight calluses on the fingertips of his talented fingertips. A man who worked with his brain, but also with his hands.

A man who enjoyed his work…

Firm, sure caresses.

Mouth, teeth and tongue, all employed with expertise, and to their best advantage.

She adored a man who enjoyed his work…

And he tasted good. All over.

Making love was fun. Making love with Doug Llewellyn had begun as fun, the two of them nipping and touching, laughing and joking, learning each other. Likes, dislikes. Turn-ons.

There seemed to be a lot of turn-ons, turn-highers.

He raised her hands above her head and began nibbling at the side of her rib cage, treading dangerously near her underarm. She'd never had anyone lick her *there*. Until this moment, had there ever even been a *there* there? If so, it had been sleeping for thirty-two years.

Her turn now, and she rolled him onto his back, began an exploration of his chest and belly.

And lower.

She'd never dared touch any man *here*. Had never wanted to, either. Not with her mouth.

His low moan sent a fire racing through her blood, and then they were rolling together, coming together, pausing only a moment as Doug reached into the bedside drawer even as she lay beneath him, nibbling at his rib cage, his *there.*

"Cut that out."

"You're talking. Don't waste time talking." She slid her tongue over his nipple.

"Then for cripes' sake, hold still. God, I want you."

"I know. I know…"

And then he was on top of her again.

Deep. Full. Hard. As their hands moved. As their mouths devoured. Deeper. Fuller. Harder…

Exploring. Learning. Experiencing.

This was fun, more than fun. This was glorious. Maybe even beyond glorious.

This was…this was…

Rosie lay on her back, her eyes closed, her breasts still rising and falling rapidly as she tried to come back down from a most splendid exertion and even more magnificent release.

Doug kissed her one last time and then slowly rolled off her, to collapse onto his back beside her on the bed.

She could feel his arm beside hers, and tucked her hand into his while they both lay there. Breathing.

At last she summoned the strength to open her eyes, looking up at the ceiling, at the twin skylights that had poured early-afternoon sunshine on them as they'd…as they'd…

"Wow," Rosie said quietly, blinking. "Just… *wow*."

Doug squeezed her hand. "I don't think I could have said it better. What the hell just happened here?"

Rosie closed her eyes against the sunlight as well as a dawning suspicion that she may have just gotten in a little over her head. "I don't know. But you, too?"

"Yeah…you could say that."

"Do we want to dissect it?"

"A postmortem, you mean?"

She tried to smile. "A post-something. Do you?"

"No. I don't think so. Do you?"

Rosie shook her head. "I…I think I'll just, um, I'll just go take a shower, if that's all right?"

"Join you?"

They were speaking in half-sentences. Why were they doing that? Why weren't they looking at each other? As Doug had said: *What the hell just happened here?*

"No, that's okay."

"There's another bathroom. I'll use that one."

"That's…good. Good. I'll…I'll be back."

"I'll be here. Rosie?"

"Hmm?"

"Thank you."

Rosie frowned up at the skylights. Gosh, it was bright in here. Maybe he'd keep his eyes closed while she located the quilt and pulled it around her. "For what?"

"I haven't the faintest idea," he said, and his bewilderment was clear in his voice. "But… thank you."

Suddenly Rosie saw the humor in their strange dialogue, and her laugh rose soft and throaty—damn, she sounded like a contented cat. "You're extremely welcome, sir. Now turn your head or close your eyes, or something. I'm getting up."

"Been there," Doug said, and she actually believed she could feel his wince. "Sorry. Bad attempt at humor, huh?"

"It wasn't great, no," Rosie said, grateful to see

that the quilt had somehow landed on the floor on her side of the bed. "Doug? Are you nervous, too?"

"Nervous? No, Rosie, I'm not nervous."

She was on her feet now, the quilt wrapped around her. He looked so adorable, lying there with his forearm over his eyes. As for the rest of him, naked on the bed, sunlight playing over his muscles, merely *adorable* didn't quite cover it. "Oh."

"I'm terrified."

Rosie relaxed. "Oh, good. I know we agreed there'd be no postmortem, but it's still nice to know I'm not the only one who— Doug, did you lock the door?"

Doug's arm dropped to his side as he levered himself up on both elbows. "I was a little distracted. Why? Did you hear something?"

"I'm not exactly sure," Rosie said, looking toward the hallway as if there might be a neon sign out there with some sort of answer written on it, like, *For God's sake, Rosie, it's only your imagination.* "I thought I may have heard something—"

Wait! There it was again. Voices. Definitely voices. Two of them, and she recognized one of them. She wheeled around and snatched up her scattered clothing even as she ran for the bathroom, nearly tripping over the quilt as she whispered fiercely, "It's Bettie, and she's not alone. Duck and cover—especially *cover!*"

Rosie managed to close the bathroom door without slamming it, and then subsided with her back against the wood, realizing she'd just ruthlessly abandoned Doug to his semirapacious cousin. *Yeah, well, at times it just came down to every man for himself in this cold, cruel world. At least until she had clothes on anyway...*

Clapping a hand over her mouth to hold back a near hysterical giggle, she pressed an ear to the six-panel door, praying it was one of those hollow ones, hoping to hear Doug say something brilliant.

"Hi, Bettie. Come here often?"

She should have realized this man would never be at a loss for words. Rosie shoved a corner of the quilt into her mouth as she slid down the door until she was sitting on the tile floor, almost convulsed in silent laughter at the double entendre. *Oh, that naughty, naughty man!*

"Doug! What are you doing here?"

"Taking a nap in my assigned room, obviously," Doug answered. "But I can leave if you're here to change the sheets, empty the waste cans. I'd think you were here to bring me some clean towels, but I don't see any towels. Hello—Sticks, isn't it?"

Rosie's eyes went wide as she mouthed, *Sticks? The Ear Waxx drummer?* She closed her eyes again, shook her head. *What was he? Twenty, twenty-one? And, with Bettie in her fifties, that made her—hell, that made her borderline depraved!* "And a lot more confident about her body than I am about mine," she told herself quietly. "How much work has the woman had done, anyway?"

Then, realizing that she was talking to herself and could be overheard, Rosie quickly slapped both hands over her mouth and put her ear to the door once more.

"…put a towel or a tie or something over the doorknob when you're in here, and then I—"

"I'm not going to play that game. I'm not living in a frat house anymore, Bettie. And you're married."

"Oh, right. I'm *marr-ied*. And you're my judge and jury? I don't think so, Douglas. Not a man with your reputation. Oh, come on, Doug, we're having a *party* here. Relax. Loosen up."

"I don't know, Betts. I think you're probably loose enough for the both of us."

"I told you—don't you judge me, Douglas. You have no right to do that. Do you know what it's like having to shepherd a dozen boring-as-warm-spit women around a mall? Aunt Susanna? God, I lost her twice in the food court, and only found her after she'd downed most of a huge bean burrito. She belched all the way home, not to mention the farts. Saying *excuse me* does *not* make up for that. I'm under a lot of stress this week, so what's a little stress relief, hmm? You used to be a good sport. You had to know why I stuck you out here by yourself. Don't be so greedy. *Share*."

Rosie had both hands over her mouth now, her eyes tearing with suppressed laughter as she listened for Doug's next words.

"Sorry about the bean burrito, Bettie. I'm sorry for you, and even more sorry I had to hear that story. Oh, and don't look now, but I think your stress relief du jour just bailed."

"What? Oh! Now look what you've done! Thanks a lot, Doug. You big party pooper!"

Rosie waited for Doug to say something else, but the only thing she heard was the stamp of Bettie's high heels against the hardwood floors, followed by the slam of the outside door.

"Olley-olley-umpstead-free. Or whatever that saying is," Doug said, knocking on the door to the bathroom. "Ms. Hot-to-trot just trotted out of here, so it's safe to show yourself."

Rosie opened the door a crack and grinned out at him. "Olley-olley-umpstead-free? That isn't frat house. It's barely even grade school. But cute, definitely cute. Thanks for not giving me away. Bettie would have driven me nuts, asking for details."

"She'd do that? *She'd* get the postmortem? Never mind, of course she would. But you're welcome. How about sharing your shower? Just to show your gratitude?"

"I don't think so," Rosie told him, feeling hot color running into her cheeks. "I know you may not believe this—and why should you—but I'm sort of a…sort of a prude about some things."

His grin was plain-out devilish. "Now *that's* a turn-on. Take your shower, Rosie, and let's get out of here. Otherwise, fair warning, I might lock us in for the rest of the week."

"Lock Bettie out, you mean," Rosie said, grinning. "And we can't. I checked the schedule earlier. There's going to be a wine-tasting party on the terrace in about an hour or so and we both have to change—the affair is black tie, as per your cousin's delusions of grandeur. We'll leave here separately and meet up there, all right? You know, like nothing's happened?"

He reached his hand past the door to stroke his fingers down her cheek. "So, Miss Kilgannon, grabbing you in front of everybody and putting my tongue halfway down your throat is out, hmm? Too bad."

"Yes, isn't it, Mr. Llewellyn?" Rosie said as she closed the door, thinking it really, *really* was too bad. But, hey, they were back to two consenting adults—flirting, teasing, poking fun at themselves and their wedding-week, mutually indulgent fling. This was a good thing.

Wasn't it?

Of course it was!

Wasn't it…?

CHAPTER NINE

DOUG WASN'T A wine-tasting-party kind of guy. Too many people standing around, posing and talking about woody aftertastes, fresh bouquets, fruity flavors—all as if they knew what in hell they were talking about, which none of them ever did.

Because Rosie was still nowhere in sight, and because Aunt Susanna had cornered him and kept jabbing at him with her gnarled, be-ringed finger, scolding him for missing her eighty-fifth birthday party—no amount of explanation could prove to her that he wasn't his father, who'd had the good sense to flee to the Greek Isles—he was quick to excuse himself at the first opportunity and attach to George Rossman, who was at least sane.

"Was this your idea, George?" he asked. "Swishing different wines like expensive mouthwash, spitting into cups? Not to mention the paper bibs with Lili-beth's and Hemming's names stamped on them, to catch any drool. They're a nice touch."

George grinned at him. "This bunch of drunks? No spitting here, Doug. Bettie calls it a wine-tasting party. Everyone else sees it as a good excuse to get sloshed before dinner." Then his smile faded. "Tell me something, Doug, what do you think of Rob? You played cards with him for a couple of hours yesterday, and then that jack-assed croquet match today. What's your take on the boy? You should have an opinion by now."

Doug neatly lifted a glass of red wine from a passing waiter's tray, idly wondering how much it cost George to let Bettie convince the waitstaff that they'd all look great in Italian peasant garb. "I don't know, George. It really doesn't matter what I think. He's not going to be my son-in-law. What do you think of him?"

George took a sip from his wineglass and made a face as if he'd just sucked a lemon. "I don't get it, Doug. They've been stomping grapes to make this crap since man walked upright, and they still can't come up with one that tastes as good as an ice-cold beer before starting out on the back nine. What did you ask me? Oh, right, what do I think of my only child's fiancé? I used to think he was a whiny, annoying little prick with a pretty face that loved my daughter. But lately? Lately I'm not so sure."

Ah, now this was interesting. Rosie should be here to hear this. Yeah, well, maybe he could take notes. Because he was pretty sure Rosie was the sort who would demand all the gory details, line by line. "That he's a whiny, annoying little prick, you mean?"

"No, Doug, that he loves Lili-beth. Try to follow along here, okay? I'm not sure he loves her. Bettie sent me to bring Lili-beth down to the party, but she wouldn't come out of her bedroom, just poked her head out the door to tell me she's still sick. She looks like hell, I'll give her that. But she also looked all red-eyed and splotchy, like maybe she's been crying. Lili-beth was never a pretty crier. I know I don't pay attention if I don't have to, but something's going on here."

"The proverbial cold feet, maybe? She'll get over it—if you're even right."

"That's the damnable part of this, Doug—I'd better not be right! Let me tell you something— that little prick tries to back out of this wedding, I'll break both his legs. Well, not me, but I'm damn near thirty-five years in the garment business, you take my drift? I *know* people."

Doug found himself now doubly wishing Rosie was here. She'd have loved this conversation. "You *know* people? Is that right? Playing up there with the big boys, are you, George? Or maybe just watching too many episodes of *The Sopranos?*"

George shot him a dirty look. "You laugh, Doug, but it's not so damn funny. You have to go along to get along in the garment business. It's always been that way. Not that I'm paying outright protection money to some thug in a cheap suit or anything like that, but a man could, for instance, decide to change shipping companies or garbage haulers, and all of sudden two hundred dozen tapered-fits bound for Michigan accidentally get dumped in the river. That's just a for instance. That's the real world, Doug, a world far away from Bettie's society world here. But that's all right. You draw pretty little houses, what can you know?"

"Not a lot, obviously," Doug said, wondering when George was going to either wipe at his nose with the back of his hairy hand or hike up his tuxedo pants and belch. *For instance.* "I'm impressed, George, I really am. You've actually met some of these dangerous guys? I mean, like, if you saw one, you'd recognize the type, at least?"

Damn. George did it—he actually wiped the back of his hand under his nose, and then sniffed. There were a lot of flowers around, so it could be an allergy attack. But Doug was pretty sure it wasn't, that good old pudgy George Rossman, who'd probably had to duck playground bullies all through grade school, was trying to look *tough*. Rosie was going to be mad as hell to have missed this. "I suppose so. They're hard to miss."

"Interesting," Doug told him, depositing his empty wineglass on the same tray that had passed by earlier. "Educate me, George. If one of these guys doesn't look like any of the cast of *Goodfellas*, what does he look like?" He made a big deal out of looking across the terrace, and then pointed at a man who was in the act of tying a bib around his neck. "Like that guy over there in the double-breasted? How about him?"

George sniffed again, but this was the offended sniff of a clothing connoisseur confronted with inferior tailoring. "Teddy Bishop? Are you kidding me? And here I thought you came from the bright side of the family. Come on, Doug, would you look at that tux? More money than Trump and he's been stuffing himself inside that same tux for ten years now. That's a decade, Doug. I've seen better-looking sausage casings."

"Clothes do make the man, I suppose," Doug said, trying hard not to laugh.

George dramatically lifted his hand, rubbed his thumb and forefingers together. "If you ever get close, check out the collar. It's pilling. You know, from rubbing against his neck stubble? Not one of mine, let me tell you, but that doesn't matter. Who the hell wears the same shirt for ten years? Oh, and no, not a wiseguy, trust me. The closest Teddy's ever gotten to seeing any kind of violence was the day I caught him using his size elevens to grind my ball into the rough on eighteen when he thought I wasn't watching. Damn near saw violence up close and personal that day, let me tell you. But I took him for five big ones so I'm not complaining. Teddy won't ever shoot his age until he turns the century mark, and we all know that's not happening."

It was all coming back to Doug now. Golf, or the shirt business. George's conversation had never seemed to go much beyond either for more than five minutes. This recent verbal side trip into

Sopranos land had been fun, but it was obviously over now, and George was heading back to Conversation As Usual. He was a nice guy, he really was, but Doug could also feel at least a little sympathy for Bettie who'd started hunting, if not conversation, at least her diversions, elsewhere.

He'd just have to reel him back in because he wanted George's opinion of Hemmings's pals.

"Okay, so not Bishop. What about—" Doug searched the terrace for the tallest, broadest body "—those two over there. Hemmings's old college buddies or whoever they are. Do they look the part? Just out of curiosity, you understand, as long as we're on the subject."

"Really? Ah, hell, it beats talking about Teddy Bishop. Where are—never mind I see them. Not the big one, no. I tried to have a small, friendly talk with him, earlier. Slip him a few tips on jacket size, you know? And those high-water slacks he had on? Every time he bent over on the croquet court you could see his ankles. White socks, if you can believe that, and you could because you were there. I tried to get him to take off his jacket later just so I could measure him—even offered him a few shirts—but the other one pulled him away.

Now, the other one? The little guy? Him, I'd believe. But he's Rob's friend from back home, and whoever heard of those guys living in flyover country? They're pasta guys, not macaroni and cheese. But, yeah, him. Russo."

"Rizzo," Doug corrected quietly, hiding a smile as it occurred to him that, for Rosie's sake, he probably should have stuck one of those miniature tape recorders in his pocket. With George, in his own way, of course, every word was a pearl. Who would have thought a weeklong society-wedding party could be so entertaining?

George finished off his wine. "Rizzo, huh? Okay, if you say so. And at least the name fits, doesn't it? And why the hell are we talking about this anyway?"

"I have no idea, George. You brought it up," Doug said, figuring that George was at least four glasses of wine ahead of him and wouldn't bother to count back, figure out who had begun this conversation. "So you're thinking Hemmings might back out at the last minute? Really?"

"Yeah, that was it—that's how we got started. I don't know, Doug. I love Lili-beth with my life, but she's no movie star stunner, you understand—

four years of teeth braces and they still couldn't really fix all of that overbite. To tell you the truth, Rob's the first guy she ever really wanted who seemed to want her back. So who am I to say yes or no? It's her life, right? Got to give the little princess what she wants, right?"

"I'm not sure, George. Maybe *not right*. Certainly not right if he makes your daughter unhappy," Doug said, sticking his foot in a situation he would have avoided like the plague a few days ago—and all thanks to Rosie. "And you called him a little prick. You really want Lili-beth marrying a whiny little prick? Whiny little prick grandchildren with overbites running in and out of your study while you're playing gin rummy, driving you crazy? The overbites could be cute— Lili-beth's is cute—but the whiny part? You really want that? I don't get it, George."

"Cripes, no. But it's what Lili-beth wants, what Bettie wants. And look around you, Doug. You have any idea what all this is costing me? I gave Bettie a budget of one hundred thousand dollars. She doubled that without breaking a sweat. It's too late to call it off. This show is damn well going on, or that boy's balls are in a wringer."

Doug was learning so much about his cousin's husband, some of which he wished he hadn't learned. Sure, the guy cared—but not enough to actually *do* anything, and that was unsettling. "And if it's Lili-beth who wants out? I'm not saying she is, but what if she is, George? What then? You'd force her to go through with it?"

"Lili-beth? I was thinking it was Rob." George looked at Doug intently. "You know something? Does Rosie? Wait a minute. Rosie, of course. Lili-beth talks to her, and you two have been joined at the hip since you got here, to hear Bettie tell it—she's mad at you for that by the way. Something about screwing up her seating charts. But Lili-beth? Is that what's going on? Is it my daughter who's getting cold feet, and I'm barking up the wrong tree?"

Doug had no idea. How had a nice guy like him gotten into such a mess in the first place? Him, Douglas Llewellyn, the man who'd prided himself on being uninvolved at all times. Again, the answer was Rosie. The woman was like some larger than life, unstoppable force of nature. She led, you followed, and it wasn't until you were in it up to your knees that you even realized you were too far gone to get out again.

At any rate, both he and George had come to somewhat the same conclusion: look deep enough, and there stood Rosie. "Rosie hasn't told me that Lili-beth doesn't want to go through with the wedding, no," he said, finding it easiest to stick with the truth as far as he knew it.

"But you said—"

"Right, I was just *saying,* making conversation. I don't want to go poking my nose in here, George. But now that you brought it up, asked my opinion, I'd feel guilty if I didn't tell you I'm not all that impressed with Hemmings. After all, you did ask. But that's only me, George. You and Bettie both know him better than I do."

George nodded, his expression a mix of anger and confusion. "I know. I do. He's a bit of a problem, I admit it, but I hold the purse strings. I can keep him in line just by giving those strings a good, healthy tug when I feel like it. But if Lili-beth is having second thoughts, if she really doesn't—damn it, where's Rosie?"

"Rosie?" Bettie said, slipping her arm around her husband's elbow even as she avoided Doug's eyes. "Honestly, George, I'd be jealous if I didn't know you'd never stray. Would you, Snookie-oogams?"

Some things just shouldn't be heard on an empty stomach, not if you had hopes of eating dinner that same evening. Doug looked at Bettie as she continued to ignore him, flirting with her husband, who seemed to know what was expected of him in this public venue, because he flirted right back at her.

If Doug's mother hadn't told him that Bettie and George had actually separated for three years when Lili-beth was in junior high, and only gotten back together because divorce was too expensive in George's income bracket, or seen Bettie in action this week, he'd be inclined to think something along the lines of *Ah, isn't that sweet—still sappy after all these years.*

But unfortunately for Doug, he knew better. He also knew about Anvil. And Sticks. And the pool boy. And Lord only knew who else. Bettie had so many notches on her bedpost it had to look as if a giant woodpecker had gone postal on it.

Still, she looked good, he'd give her that, in the usual borderline emaciated way of women of a certain age in her income and social circles. She was wearing peach or coral or some color close to it again, probably because someone had told her it was her best color, and not because that was, as

Rosie had informed him, the main color in the wedding theme—or whatever colors in a wedding were called.

Hell, that's probably why the wedding colors had been chosen in the first place: to flatter Bettie. Hadn't Lili-beth had any voice in decisions concerning her own wedding? He shook his head slightly at his mental rhetorical question. Lili-beth could consider herself lucky if she liked the food they'd be serving at the reception.

But he still had to hand it to his cousin, the woman did look pretty damn good.

So he said so. What the hell, she couldn't ignore him for the next six days. "You look beautiful this evening, Betts," he said sincerely, tacking the *Betts* on because, well, because he felt like it, and she had tried to turn the Bachelor Quarter into her personal love nest.

"Why, thank you, Doug," Bettie said, her mouth smiling even as she spoke through clenched teeth. "And please tell me you're enjoying yourself at our humble little house party. Everything seems to be going fairly well so far, don't you think?"

"A well-oiled machine, Bettie. I know you have a professional event planner on board, but I'll bet you're behind each decision, down to the smallest detail. The business world lost a fine manager when you decided to dedicate yourself to your family as a devoted wife and mother, but I'm sure they're grateful."

"Oh, George, did you hear that?" Bettie trilled, her eyes cold as she stared at Doug. "Now you know why Douglas is my very favorite cousin. Um, George? Darling? I'm really parched, and I haven't seen anyone passing by with a tray, have you? Be a sweetheart and go find me a glass. Something white and dry?"

"Now? A couple of us were going to try to fit in a few hands of—oh, all right. *Sweetheart.* I'll be right back."

"I'll be counting the moments," Bettie called after him.

Doug, too, was counting. Counting silently as George headed for the large white linen–covered table strewn with wine bottles and a towering arrangement of champagne glasses that had been turned into a fountain. He got to four before Bettie, who had been turned around, smiling at her husband's departing back, turned back to him, fangs bared.

"What did you do to Rob? You *hit* him? That's what he said—he said you *hit* him. He said he was just standing there, talking to you, and the next thing he knew you were sucking a punch at him."

"Sucker punch, not sucking punch. Granted, he might have made a few sucking *sounds* as he tried to get his breath—but the correct term is *sucker punch.* And your boy Hemmings is right about part of his story. I did sort of take advantage of him. But don't ask me if I'm going to apologize to him, because that's not happening. Besides, think back to our childhoods, Bettie—nobody likes a tattletale."

Her voice remained low, her tone intense. "Tattletale? Don't be stupid. Of course he told me. He had to tell me. You *hit* him. The *groom,* Douglas, Lilibeth's betrothed. You just admitted as much. How could you do something like that? Is that the way you welcome a new member into our family?" She closed her eyes, shook her head in obvious disgust, then glared at him once more. "I still can't believe this. Have you gone fucking out of your mind!"

"Ah, now that's nice, Betts, that's really nice. That language goes so well with the designer dress, you know? And I have to tell you—it's fairly remarkable the way you can talk like that, what with your teeth slammed together. I'm impressed, really. Did you ever try throwing your voice? With one of those puppets? I think you might have a natural talent."

"You just go to hell, Doug. You may think you're funny, but you're not, and never were. Even when I had to babysit for you that summer we all took a beach house in the Hamptons, and you'd hide in closets and then jump out and scare me."

Doug smiled in remembered amusement, realizing there was a part of every man who still longed to be the boy who'd never had to grow up. "You screamed just like a girl, Betts."

"Oh, look at you—grinning! I never really forgave you for that," she said, waving away his response. "But enough of that, because you're not going to change the subject. Rob told me all about it, what you did. You fucking *hit* him. My God, if you'd hit him in the *face!*"

"I thought about that, Bettie. It was a very conscientiously placed punch, when you get right down to it, so feel free to thank me. Now, don't you want to know *why* I punched him?"

"Why would I want to know that from you, when Rob already told me everything? How you insulted his friends, calling them Midwestern hicks or some such thing, and when he defended them you *sucker* punched him when he wasn't looking. Big, macho man. What in hell could you possibly have been thinking? These two gentlemen are my *guests*. Granted, they're both a little strange—they really don't *match* with everyone else, do they? But that's no reason to be insulting. They can't help being from the Midwest."

"Now who's being insulting? And, Bettie, those two guys are about as Midwestern as the Statue of Liberty, unless the Jersey use of *youse guys* is taking off all over the country now," Doug told her, suddenly tired of this particular conversation. "As for the sucker punch? Possibly a bad thing, I admit it. And just so it doesn't happen again, you might want to tell your bought-and-paid-for groom to watch his mouth. Remember, I'm living on the mean streets of Philadelphia now, and can't really be held responsible."

"Oh, listen to you," Bettie said, rolling her eyes. "Big, bad Douglas Llewellyn threatening *me* now. You're a guest of the wedding, too, Doug, but that doesn't mean I can't ask you to leave. So just stay away from Rob. He never did anything to you."

"True. I just don't like the man you picked for Lili-beth on general principles. And, if you and *Snookie-oogams* ever really talked to each other, I think you'd find out that he doesn't like the whiny little prick, either—George's words, not mine. Although," he added, wishing he could keep his mouth shut but seemingly unable to do so, "the one I'd really be asking for an opinion is Lili-beth. You remember her, Betts—your daughter, your only child, the kid who's been holed up in her room all day crying?"

Bettie's face was beginning to clash with her coral or peach or whatever silk, and Doug was beginning to feel guilty. "She's not crying, she had some bad fish last night or something. So don't be melodramatic. And are you accusing me of being a bad mother?"

"No, Bettie, I'm not. Seriously, I'm not. But…hell, maybe you're trying too hard?"

She folded her arms across her waist. "Really. Trying too hard. And what's *that* supposed to mean?"

"I don't have a clue, to tell you the truth, Betts," Doug admitted, feeling most definitely out of his depth. "No, wait, I think I do. I remember asking a friend of mine about some of the plans for his upcoming wedding, and he told me he had no idea what his fiancée was planning—that all the groom is good for on his wedding day is as a handy arm for the bride to lean on. So maybe you could ask yourself, Bettie—is Rob the right man for Lili-beth, or just a convenient arm to hang the bride on?"

Bettie opened her mouth and then shut it again, shook her head as if to deny his words. "Lili-beth loves Rob, she's crazy about him. She *wanted* him the moment she saw him. We've been planning this wedding since she was a little girl, and—" She took a deep breath and raised her chin, defiance replacing the moment of worry he'd seen in her eyes. "So you just keep your mouth shut, Douglas, especially around George. You got that?"

"Yeah," Doug said quietly, lifting the wineglass to his supposedly soon-to-be-shut mouth, "I've got that, Bettie, loud and pretty damn clear. I don't know what I'm going to *do* with it, but I've got it. But you know, Bettie, I don't have to live with the consequences. *You* do."

Bettie's eyes narrowed dangerously…or at least Doug thought she was trying to make them narrow dangerously. But, since her skin seemed to be tied behind her ears, she just came off looking, well, looking like a woman who might *be* angry, but could never really *look* angry.

"Here's the deal, Doug," she told him quietly but fiercely, poking a long color-tinted nail into his chest to punctuate her demands. "You stay away from Rob, you stay away from his friends. You behave. Go play with Rosie or Ki-Ki or any woman who looks like a good time. Mostly, you stay away from George. Otherwise I'm going to have to ask you to leave…and *you* can explain that to your parents."

"Let's clarify, shall we, Bettie? I could be wrong, but I think you forgot to warn me away from Lili-beth."

Bettie pretty much raked him with her eyes, which was a little spooky. "Lili-beth, too. I don't want you within ten feet of any of them. I mean it, Doug. You all but ignore us for years, and then you show up here—and I know you didn't want to—and now you're sticking your nose in where it doesn't belong, telling us all what to do? How dare you? Who do you think you are? You screw this up for me and I'll kill you."

"Great talking to you, too," Doug called after her, waving at Bettie as she turned sharply on her heels and headed across the terrace to where Ear Waxx was setting up their instruments on a small, specially built stage. He wondered which band member was tonight's target.

"Excuse me. Hello there. Would you care for a cheese puff, or some breaded shrimp, Mr. Llewellyn?"

Doug turned to his left to see Delwood Armbruster standing there, holding a small round silver tray. "Thanks," he said, lifting one of the cheese puffs. "Bettie's commandeered you as one of the waitstaff, Del? You don't have a costume."

The boy blushed, shook his head. "Oh, no, no, I'm a guest. I'm the best man, actually, although I don't really know Rob all that well. He's an orphan, you understand, and an only child, so Lilibeth asked me to, um, to step in, since he doesn't really know anyone at all. But maybe you know that? I…I, um, I just wanted to talk to you and, well, and I…"

"Thought the cheese puffs were a good opening line?" Doug suggested, taking the tray and placing it on the table behind him. "What's up? Did Rosie tell you to come talk to me? No, wait, don't answer that yet. Let's go somewhere a little more private."

And cousin Bettie could just damn well go to hell—
Delwood wasn't on her list...

Delwood looked damn near overjoyed with the
suggestion, which made Doug wonder if the boy
got out much.

"We could walk down toward the tennis court,"
Delwood suggested. "I need to check the traps,
anyway. I caught five squirrels today. That's a
pretty good number, don't you think?"

"Hey, I know I'm impressed," Doug said,
smiling as kindly as he could. "You do know, of
course, that it would be next door to impossible for
you to rid this entire place of squirrels before the
wedding on Sunday. Plus, you're taking them
away from all their stored nuts and that sort of
thing, the food they've been gathering all summer
long." He shook his head, sighed just a tad theatrically. "Poor little guys, they're going to have to
face a long, cold winter in some strange place, and
all without their nuts. It's not easy, being without
your nuts." *Oh God, he was going to hell. Straight*
through, no stops along the way so he could beg
for leniency...

Delwood frowned, walking with his head down,
a stray lock of blond hair falling into his too-

innocent-to-live eyes. "You know, I never thought about that, Mr. Llewellyn. I'm going to have to stock up on nuts, and then take them over to the park and...and scatter them?"

Doug nodded his agreement. "Picking up some nuts is a good idea for you, Delwood. Definitely."

The boy sighed. "Good. Because they're just innocent squirrels, you know, just running around doing...doing squirrely things. I never liked this whole idea."

Doug wasn't completely cruel—so he didn't agree that the whole damn Squirrel Removal project was *squirrely*. Maybe he'd only be in purgatory for a couple million years?

"Then you know what I'd do, Del? I'd bag the whole thing as a bad job. Take back the traps, lose the pith helmet and rubber gloves and concentrate on more important business. You do have more important business at the moment, don't you?"

The young man blushed under his blond hair. "Uh...actually? Uh...well, I guess maybe I... seeing as how Lili-beth is...and I'm...I really think I should say something before they do that thing about if anyone here present knows of a reason...you know?"

"No, not yet I don't," Doug pointed out wryly, leaning against one of the corner posts of the cage around the tennis court. Was he enjoying himself? He might be, and that was definitely scary. He used to think of himself as a cosmopolitan man. Now he was…squirrely? And, yes, he was enjoying himself immensely. "Just take your time, Del. Take a breath, swallow, and then say what you've got to say."

The kid was an obedient sort, if nothing else. He took a breath. He swallowed. And appeared to choke on his own spit.

"This is about Lili-beth and Hemmings, isn't it?" Doug asked helpfully as he pounded Del on the back a few times. "You poor sap. You're in love with her, aren't you?"

Which may have been the wrong thing to say.

Delwood kept on coughing then held up one hand to wordlessly ask Doug to wait a moment as he reached his other hand into his pocket and pulled out a small inhaler.

"Asthma?" Doug inquired politely as the kid sucked on the business end of the thing.

Delwood shook his head. "Allergies," he said as he recapped the inhaler and slid it back into his pocket. "I don't know if it's the squirrel fur or the mold spores back in those woods, but something's really set me off the last few days. I sneezed twenty times this morning—my mother counted. Eight of them in a row. Sorry about that."

"No harm, no foul," Doug said, wondering when the last plane bound for the South of France left the Newark International Airport, and if Rosie would consider a topless beach. Probably not; she was modest. Except in bed, thank God.

"My mother said I used to have asthma when I was a baby. Baby asthma, she called it. But I grew out of it. Now I'm just allergic. Trees? I'm not good with a lot of them, and mold is even worse. A real pain. Lili-beth says I should move to a dry climate. Like Arizona, you know? I didn't want to go, but maybe now that she and Rob are...well, there's no real reason to stay here now, right?"

Doug figured he'd try again. "Because you won't be able to stand seeing Lili-beth day in, day out, once she's Mrs. Rob Hemmings?"

If Delwood looked any more appealing and pathetic he could be the new poster boy for Send This Child To Camp. "She's making a big, big mistake, Mr. Llewellyn. A *big* mistake."

"By not choosing you," Doug said, nodding his head.

"Oh, oh no, that's all right. I've always known Lili-beth sees me as her best friend, not as her…well, you know what I mean. She doesn't see me, you know…*that way?* I…I can live with that. I've been living with that for a long time."

Doug lowered his head a moment to hide his expression, pretending to scratch an itch behind his left ear. So much for Rosie casting the guy as Lancelot in her little fantasy because the kid didn't seem to be the mount up and ride to the rescue type. "All right, Del. What *can't* you live with?"

Delwood blinked several times. "That he'll hurt her, that he'll make her cry."

Oh, crap. Face it, Llewellyn, there's no backing out now, not if you let this boy talk to you, Rosie or no Rosie.

"You want to explain that, Del?" Doug asked, as he seemed constitutionally unable to clap a hand over his mouth and run like hell for the nearest exit. He could probably blame Rosie for that, sure, but only along with Cameron Pierce—his friend, junior partner and resident conscience for the past twelve or so years. And being a carefree, uninvolved, reasonable irresponsible bachelor on the prowl had been such fun, too. So far, forty was proving to be a real pain in the ass…

"He…Rob, that is…he borrowed money from me."

Okay. Rob Hemmings was slime on top of being a whiny little prick. But at least he wasn't an international assassin or something. "He did, did he? How much money?"

"I'd rather not say how much, betray a confidence or anything—forty thousand."

"Dollars?" Doug didn't shock easily, but this one seemed to come straight out of left field. Five hundred. One thousand. A little something to tide a pal over until the next paycheck. These he could understand. But forty thousand dollars? Was the kid insane? And rich, of course. Everyone around here seemed to be a lot more than just comfortably well-off. Not that he wasn't, but Doug didn't toss around forty thousand dollars like it was four hundred. Probably because he wasn't nuts—there was some small comfort in that. Verging on borderline squirrely, but not nuts.

"Well, yes. Dollars."

Doug didn't know if he should shake Delwood

senseless, or just send him home to his mother so she could count his sneezes. "And why would you do that, Armbruster? Did he have something on you? You know, was he holding something over your head? You don't get dressed up in that pith helmet on the occasional Saturday night to go clubbing in Greenwich Village, do you, and Hemmings somehow found out about it? I mean, I'm not condemning you or passing judgment or anything like that. I'm just checking here, trying to understand."

Delwood gave Doug that stunned-ox look again, but then began talking, fast, as if he needed everything said within the next ten seconds. "He won't pay it back, Mr. Llewellyn. He just won't. He just said he would so that I'd loan him the money. He said it was some cash flow problem, some mix up at his bank, and he was expecting a big check to arrive any day on the sale of his house in…in…well, wherever he lived. But now he says he's not paying me back, not one penny of the whole forty thousand dollars, and if I go to Mr. Rossman he'll tell him I'm lying, that I'm only *saying* he owes me money because I've got the hots for— Well, I don't want Lili-beth to know anything about this. And, and he threatened me, physically. I don't know what to do, Mr. Llewellyn, but Rosie said I should talk to you, since I didn't want to talk to her about my problem and she thought if I was bothered about something I should tell somebody and you'd be a good somebody to tell. You know—man-to-man?"

Doug waved Delwood a little closer, amazed at himself that he wanted only vaguely to strangle Rosie when he saw her. "But you've got his signed note, right? Come on, Del, tell me you took Hemmings to your bank with you and had the man sign a promissory note. Make me proud, Del, tell me about the promissory note."

"Uh...*wel-l-l...*"

CHAPTER TEN

ROSIE DANCED ONTO THE TERRACE in her black Dior strapless, floor-length A-line sheath to the beat of Ear Waxx doing a cover of Styx's "Renegade." Anvil was just getting into the second chorus, and Sticks was going a little too crazy for a wine-tasting gig, but that didn't stop Rosie from raising her arms over her head and doing her headbanger imitation as she two-stepped her way over to George, promptly shooting him with her six-gun index fingers.

"Come on, George, do it with me," she told him, motioning for him to follow her, and George Rossman had tasted just enough wine to do exactly what she said.

Anvil hit the lyrics hard in the rocking reprise, Sticks displayed a heavy foot on the bass drum, and Pied Piper Rosie had a pretty good line of followers snaking through the tables behind her by the time she ran up against Bettie, who looked ready to pull out a real six-shooter and drop Rosie right in her tracks.

"*Must* you?" Bettie said as Rosie punched her fists into the air with each pounding drumbeat, dancing in place now, while Fred Barnes smacked into the back of T-Three, the dancing guests stacking up behind Rosie and beginning to resemble a line of Dominos about to tip over.

"Sorry, gang. We've got ourselves a party pooper here," Rosie told the crowd behind her, then caught Anvil's eye and made a pained face as she slid a finger across her throat.

"Thank you," Bettie said as the sound level dropped almost immediately and Anvil began a Clay Aiken song that had something to do with measuring a man. Well, the *measure* of a man, which was different, and more important, except maybe to Bettie. "Now that you've made a complete fool of me, called me a party pooper. Listen to them all, muttering."

"Oh, come on, Bettie, you did that all by yourself. We were only having some fun. Anvil's really good." Rosie grinned. "Of course, you already know that, don't you?"

Bettie tried to narrow her eyelids. "A true friend wouldn't keep beating a person over the head with something like that."

Rosie lost her smile. "You're right, Bettie. I'm sorry. Oh, I stopped in to see Lili-beth before I came down here. She's not any better, is she? Have you talked to her?"

"No, I haven't had time," Bettie said heading toward the French doors that led to her private sunroom, assuming that Rosie would follow. Which she did, but only because she wanted to, not that Bettie knew that—and it was probably better that she didn't.

Rosie settled herself on a stool while Bettie went behind the bar to pour herself a neat Scotch. "You're not going to play wine taster with the rest of us?"

Bettie poured two fingers of the amber liquid, and tossed them back in one long gulp. "Wine's for amateurs," she said, winking at Rosie before leaning her forearms on the bar, clearly planning to be friendly, share a little girl talk. "That's one stunner of a necklace, by the way. What do they call that—a bib necklace? Beautiful. No woman can have enough diamonds, I always say. Now, tell me all about it. You were there, weren't you? Hiding out in the bathroom when we came in, right?"

"So much for small talk, huh? Who was hiding where? I don't know what you're talking about."

"Oh, come on, Rosie, don't try that with me. I know you were up there with him. Doug had that sleepy-eyed afterglow that only comes from great sex. So—how was he?"

Knowing Bettie never gave up, rather like a bulldog hanging on to a juicy T-bone, Rosie leaned an elbow on the bar and put her chin in her hand before running the tip of her tongue around her lips, her tone low, intimate, as she drawled, "The man is a freaking *god.*"

Bettie slammed her empty lead glass tumbler onto the bar top. "I *knew* it! I knew it! Tell me, tell me—what did he do? Does he like to talk while he's—you know. What does he say?"

Rosie clapped her hands together once and got down from the stool. "Sorry, the rest is privileged information. But I *was* dancing when you saw me, wasn't I?"

"*Oh*…that good? That's just wild. You should have seen him when he was ten. I was sure he was going to be a geek, always reading books, always building things. I don't know, something happened to that boy sometime in high school. Like...like he morphed. Into this *Playboy of the Western World* thing he's got going on now. Oh, I owe Millicent one, don't I? I owe her big. She's going to be *so* pissed when I tell her."

"Which you're not going to do," Rosie said coolly. "You're not going to say anything to anyone."

Bettie poured herself another Scotch. "Oh? And why not? You bagged him, Rosie. Took down a big one. I'm proud of you. Why shouldn't I say anything."

"Because then I'll tell George about Anvil, that's why," Rosie told her pleasantly. "I know he looks the other way a lot, but I don't think he'd much appreciate hearing about your not-so-discreet descent into the barely legal meat market. And in his own backyard, too? Literally? A man, even George, could get a complex."

"You wouldn't dare."

Rosie laughed out loud. Bettie was *so* easy. "Oh, sweetie, of course I'd dare, and you know that. I value my privacy, and you need to protect yours, so we'll both be good. Now, if there's nothing else? I promised Doug I'd meet him for drinks."

Bettie brought her glass with her as she hustled out from behind the bar to position herself between Rosie and the French doors. "But there is something else, Rosie. Something we need to discuss. Rob told me what Doug did. How he hit him with some sucking punch."

"Sucker punch," Rosie corrected, ready for Bettie's questions.

"Like I told Doug—I *don't care* what it's called, Rosie. He *punched* him. And you were there. I'm thinking of asking Doug to leave. Unless, that is, you can convince me to let him stay."

Always working the angles, that was Bettie. "No, I can't think of a reason," Rosie said, shrugging her bare, slightly freckled shoulders. "Shall I tell him to go pack?"

Bettie blinked. Rosie had been pretty sure she'd blink first.

"No! I mean—oh, all right. I'll forgive him, since having him stay means so much to you."

"Did I say it meant so much to me? Damn, I must have missed that. Oh, by the way? I found this earlier." She pulled the slim organizer out of the hidden pocket in her gown.

"My organizer! Oh, Rosie, you *doll!*" Bettie

grabbed the thing, immediately diverted like a child can cut a tantrum off in midscream when offered a cookie. She turned the organizer on, sighing audibly when it immediately came to life. "It's fine, everything's still on it. Where? Where did you find it, Rosie? No, don't tell me. I already know. Aunt Susanna copped it, didn't she? Damn klepto!"

"Excuse me?" Rosie said, truly not comprehending. "I found it on a table in Lili-beth's bedroom when I peeked in to see how she's doing. You must have taken it with you when you and your daughter had some warm, mother-to-daughter talk, and then forgotten it there."

"No, that can't be it." Bettie closed the organizer with a snap. "I haven't been in Lili-beth's room since—yes, that must be it. In Lili-beth's room. I even remember now. Lili-beth called me in to talk about how she wants both her father and I to walk her down the aisle on Sunday." Bettie pressed her hands to her chest. "I was *so* touched by that. George and I, both giving our little girl away to Rob. I simply must have forgotten the organizer."

"Right," Rosie said, pasting a smile on her face. "So that's that. Gosh, I think I'm getting all misty here."

Bettie's jaw set dangerously. "You don't believe me?"

"No, Bettie, I don't," Rosie told her affably. "And you know why? I don't believe you because I took your damn organizer the other day when I was angry with you. Not that I remember exactly what asinine thing you said that set me off. Probably something about your handpicked groom—whom you *bought*."

"For Lili-beth," Bettie countered, her cheeks coloring. "Remember that, Rosie, as you climb up on your high moral horse. If we bought him, we bought him *for Lili-beth*. Who *wanted* him. Who *still* wants him. I asked her, after you made those cracks about my motherly instincts or whatever you said, and she said she still wants him. So why don't you mind your own business and remember that Lili-beth is *my* child, not yours."

Rosie held up her hands in defeat. At least she hoped Bettie thought that. "Okay, okay, I was wrong then, wasn't I? If Lili-beth is truly happy, Bettie, then I'm truly happy. And you're truly happy. The whole world is truly happy. Now, let's put this all behind us, forget any unpleasantness and go have some fun. This *is* a party, remember?"

Bettie dropped her belligerent pose in obvious relief. "So we're settled here? No more smart remarks or meddling from you, no more of me teasing you to tell me about Doug? We both get what we wanted?"

"That only seems fair," Rosie told her, wondering if she could get Bettie to buy some swampland in Florida, or the Brooklyn Bridge. The woman sure was gullible.

"Thank you, Rosie. Because I shouldn't have said anything about Rob and money—that was the Scotch talking. And he had me so *mad,* needing money again. George is going to have another little talk with him."

"Tell him to leave his wallet and checkbook locked up somewhere when he does that," Rosie offered with a small smile. "And believe me, Bettie, this is none of my business. I will not interfere again, or even offer another opinion. Lili-beth gets married on Sunday, and that's that—without another single objection from me."

And that Anna Nicole Smith woman is a natural 44-E cup, Rosie added mentally as she left Bettie to her Scotch and her beloved organizer, heading out onto the terrace once more in search of Doug.

Only to have Antoinette find her.

"Did you hear the latest weather report, Rosie?" the woman said, fumbling with her reading glasses. "Eloise is changing course, regrouping. Not a lot of wind, not as far as hurricanes go, but she's just *sucking* up water she's going to just *dump* all over everything if she makes landfall on the East Coast—but not this part of the coast, please God, not here."

She took a long drink from something that looked an awful lot like the sort of soft-sided leather flask a Roman soldier would have carried into battle centuries earlier. "The tents, Rosie. Think about the *tents*."

"I would," Rosie said, pointing to the kidney-shaped thing Antoinette was in the process of re-capping, "except, right now, I want to know what *that's* all about."

"This?" Antoinette said, slipping the thing over her head, because it had a long leather strap, like a shoulder purse. "It's a genuine replica of a leather wine flask carried by Roman soldiers, of course. With Lili-beth's and Rob's names embossed on one side in gold—see? I'm just testing one tonight, that's all. For, um, for leaks?"

"I knew that," Rosie said, unsurprised that she had guessed correctly—but still not understanding what the wedding planner was doing with the thing. "Now tell me why you need to test a flask for leaks."

"For the toga party on Friday night, Rosie. Lilibeth's bridal luncheon is Friday afternoon, and Rob's bachelor party is Friday night. My understanding is that Rob wanted to have the bachelor party in Atlantic City, but Bettie nixed that, which is a shame, because I could have used a night off, frankly. Instead, we're having a Monte Carlo night here Wednesday night, with play money—didn't you get your schedule? I could have sworn you got a copy of the schedule. I may have an extra here on my clipboard. Do you want me to give it to you?"

"Not necessary, really. I know I have one in my room." Although getting it and reading all ten pages of it had been two different things, not that Rosie was going to tell Antoinette that her schedule was a tad lengthy as well as accomplishing the nearly impossible—making a week of endless partying come off as boring.

So she neatly changed the subject. "When are you going to give me that list of names for the calligraphy work you need? I'm free tomorrow until about ten, but then we're going golfing. I can meet you in George's study at eight? The printer is in there. Typing in the names and printing everything out won't take long at all, if you have the correct paper for me."

"Yes, I was able to drive into town this afternoon and—oh, my!"

Rosie tried not to jump in surprise as she felt strong arms sliding around her waist from the back, and then smiled as Doug whispered, just beside her ear, "If I looked in the dictionary, would a drawing of you in that dress appear next to the word *perfect?*"

"Ah, pick-up lines from the smooth-talking geriatric set. They're as painfully bad as I've been told." She leaned her head back against his shoulder, reveling in the sheer solidness of the man. "Besides, nobody's perfect."

"Not even me? Well, I'm crushed."

"Not yet, but if you're very, very good, I think that can be arranged," Rosie told him, turning into his arms, at which time Antoinette unscrewed the Roman flask and shot some Merlot at her mouth from about three inches away as she watched the interplay between Rosie and Doug. Some of the wine dribbled down her chin, unnoticed.

"Oops," the wedding planner said, giggling nervously as she belatedly wiped at her chin. "Uh, tomorrow morning's good for me, too, Rosie. I'll…I'll just go away now. Before I melt…"

"It is a warm night, isn't it? Hot." Rosie slid her hands up and over Doug's shoulders. "Oh, and Antoinette? Eloise won't show up here. Besides, I think I already told you that there's no sense worrying about something you can't change. Isn't that right, Doug? I mean, some things…just happen?"

"Am I supposed to answer that?" Doug asked her as the wedding planner scuttled away. He ran his hands up and down Rosie's sides, settling again against her waist. "You feel so good. I like that there's…enough of you."

"More than enough, some would say," Rosie told him as they moved slightly apart, holding hands as they stepped off the terrace and onto the thick carpet of grass.

"Then some would be fools. I sent one of the parking lot kids to get us sub sandwiches and a six-pack earlier. Or would you rather stick around and have dinner here?"

"A person can have poached salmon anytime, but sub sandwiches taste better fresh—before the bread goes all soggy," Rosie told him, lifting the hem of her gown as they picked up their pace on the way to his apartment above the garages.

"The store threw in two small bags of potato chips," he told her, reaching up to pull on one end of his black bow tie. "Barbeque style."

"Now *that's* perfect." She meant the untied bow tie, but he didn't have to know that. George Clooney looked great in a well-tailored tux, that was a given. But Doug Llewellyn looked even better. Stripping it off him would make him look ever better than that.

By the time they'd climbed the stairs, Doug behind her, playfully "helping" her up the steps, Rosie realized they were both breathing rather heavily, and not from the climb.

She pulled on one end of the bow tie, sliding it out from under his collar, and hung it over the doorknob just before Doug kicked the door closed behind him, then locked it.

Rosie stepped to within an inch of pressing her body against his and began working on the black onyx studs on his pleated white shirt even as she looked up into his smoldering gray eyes. "Are you sure you're not too old for this sort of exertion, Grandpa? Twice in one day?"

His hands found the concealed zipper at the center of her back. "Maybe we can take a good book to bed with us, and you can read to me."

Rosie's gown slid to her feet in a whisper of black *peau du soie* and Doug's eyes widened. Silly man, did he really think a gown like this called for undergarments?

"Or we could listen to my biological clock ticking while I tell you how wonderful it would be to see a baby with your gorgeous gray eyes."

"True," Doug said as she helped him out of his tuxedo jacket. "Or we could both just shut up and enjoy the moment."

Rosie's smile curved the corners of her mouth up in a way that made her feel decadent, delicious. "I love it when you talk sexy, Llewellyn."

He growled low in his throat. "And you should never wear anything but diamonds—and nothing else."

They'd be searching for small black onyx shirt studs for hours, but that was a problem that didn't seem to concern Doug as Rosie all but tore off his shirt as he lifted her free of her puddled gown and began backing her toward the bedroom.

Now that he was stripped to the waist, Rosie gloried in the rippling contours of Doug's tanned chest, the way his broad shoulders arrowed down to his tight washboard stomach and flab-free waistline. "You're holding up pretty good for an old man," she told him, sliding her hands over him before going to work on the button at the front of his tuxedo pants.

"Don't do that now or I'll land flat on my face when they fall down," he warned her, his palms splayed on her buttocks. "Not that I mind, but it might break the mood."

"Help, I've fallen," Rosie singsonged as she left him where he stood, to flop onto her back on the bed he'd already turned down—she liked that; the sign of a confident man. "I've fallen, and I can't get up."

"Luckily, only one of us has to," Doug teased, grinning as he unzipped his pants and pushed them down over his male-slim hips.

Rosie pressed her hands to her cheeks in mock shock. "Oh Grandma, what a big—Doug! You still have your shoes on!"

"So do you," he told her even as he began

nibbling on her earlobe. "Your legs look great when you're wearing high heels. I look at them, and all I can think about is how they'd feel, wrapped high around my back. The shoes are only a bonus…."

Rosie's insides went all tight and hot. "I suppose that can be arranged. Although…although spurs are out of the question, just in case you were going to mention them."

"Good. I'm lusting after you, woman, I admit it, but I hope I'm not depraved," Doug told her, reaching past her to the bedside table. "Tell me you feel what I feel…that I'm not moving too fast here, that you need some time to catch up."

Rosie wriggled beneath him, moving her pelvis up toward him as he fumbled with the protection. "I'm almost ahead of you," she said honestly. "We don't need no steenking foreplay…*oh!*"

He was inside her completely in one swift, intense thrust, and she clamped her arms around his neck, her legs around his waist, eagerly returning that intensity. That need. That undeniable hunger.

Ravenous hunger.

He jackknifed somehow into a sitting position, the two of them still locked together, their arms around each other as his mouth found hers, as he mimicked each thrust inside her with his tongue.

He was so deep inside her, taking her higher than she'd ever been, driving her onward, higher and higher.

And then he had a hand between her legs, spreading her with his fingers, lightly pinching at her throbbing center as stars burst behind her eyelids and her body opened to him even more of its own accord, then clamped around him greedily, again and again and again.

Rosie was wild with pleasure, nearly out of her mind with it, and all she wanted now was for him to find his own release…but he pulled away from her. "Doug…no."

"Again." That's all he said, and she opened her eyes to look at him in confusion and some maidenly shock (she could still do that at thirty-two? Imagine that!) as he gently pushed her onto her back and pressed his hands against the under-side of her thighs, raising her legs, spreading her legs wide. "All of you…again."

And then his mouth was warm and wet against her, his tongue doing things to her that had her throwing back her head as she purred then moaned in pleasure, giving in to the urge to raise her hips so that he could do more, take more, give more.

Who was she? She'd never been like this. Never felt like this. Never wanted this.

She'd die, simply die, if he stopped...

And then it happened. He found her secret, one she didn't know she possessed. One single spot, one very special, hidden part of her...and a shot of pure adrenaline coursed through her, a need so great, so overwhelming, that she reached down to grab at his head, all but grinding him against her. "Don't stop...please. I...I never...*don't stop.*"

There was a heat beyond red-hot. White-hot. And Doug was there, he'd discovered it, her white-hot center. The magic spot that switched off all her inhibitions and allowed her to need, to want, to take.

And take. And take.

And, at last, at last...yes, yes...give over...relinquish all control. Let it happen...

Then she was reaching for him, needing him more than she had needed her own release, dragging at his shoulders, pulling him upward, into her, all but attacking him as he sank inside her. Biting at his neck, her nails digging into his back, dragging across his skin. Her legs raised high and wide, then clamping him to her. Holding on as he drove into her, rode her, breathed her name over and over and over again....

CHAPTER ELEVEN

"ARE YOU SURE YOU don't want my pickle?"

"Positive," Doug said as Rosie held the large dill by its stem and wiggled it in front of his face. "Now be a good girl and finish your sub. We have to get back out there before somebody comes to get us."

"We still have to find two of your studs," she reminded him, tossing the pickle back into the paper bag that had held their meal before shoving the last bit of her sub into her mouth and getting to her feet.

He watched her as she gracefully moved about the room, dressed only in his tuxedo shirt—with only three studs holding it closed at the middle, a circumstance that pleased him more than a little bit—a killer pair of black satin high heels, and an equally killer diamond necklace. "By the way—that's real, isn't it?"

Rosie put a hand to her throat. "This? I adore costume jewelry. Big, chunky, fun stuff. But who'd wear fake diamonds? I mean, what would be the point?"

Doug shifted comfortably on the couch, his feet resting on the coffee table. She stopped near the door, and then bent over to pick up a stud. He knew so little about this woman. She had a great ass, he knew that, even as he admired it. But maybe it was time he learned something else about her. "So this Web site design stuff—it pays well?"

"Not Dior gown and real diamonds well, no. My great-great-grandfather took care of that, thank you. Like you—since Bettie filled me in on your background before you ever showed up—my money came to me the old-fashioned way. I inherited it. I work because...well, because I like to work, feel useful. Don't you? Ah, and here's the last one. All right, Mr. Llewellyn, you're good to go now."

"Not where I want to go, I'm sure," he said, reluctantly getting to his feet. "So, what was great-great-grandpa? Robber baron? Railroad tycoon? Shipping magnate?"

"Private banker," she said, opening the door to quickly retrieve his bow tie. "And he married his partner's daughter, a move you must agree bordered on the brilliant, at least as far as their descendants are concerned. I suppose you'll want your shirt back now. I'll leave it on the bed." She picked up her gown that had been spread out over a chair and headed for the bedroom. "I'm going to grab a quick shower."

Doug followed after her. "Private banker, huh? What's the name of this bank?"

"Sullivan-Kilgannon," she called back over her shoulder.

He shook his head. "Never heard of it."

She pushed the bedroom door almost closed, grinning at him as she said, "I told you it was private. Now go shower in the other bathroom and give *me* some privacy."

He could have pointed out that it might be a little late for modesty, but he was forty now, and had actually developed a brain. He was almost proud of that fact as he went off to shower, returning to the bedroom with a towel wrapped around his middle, to see Rosie fully dressed again—not that zipping up a gown took a lot of time—standing in front of the mirror, trying to fluff up the damp tendrils at the back of her head.

"I tried brushing off your jacket, but there's nothing I can do about the few wrinkles in your slacks. I'm fairly sure everyone is going to know what we've been doing—unless you brought an extra tux?"

"No, afraid not. You of course know I'm going to spend the rest of the evening looking at you, remembering what's underneath that gown. And what isn't. Which means it's time to get back to business, keep my mind from going places it shouldn't. You've had time to think about what I told you about our idiot friend Delwood. Any suggestions?"

Rosie fluffed her hair one last time, gave her head a shake and stepped away from the mirror, turning her back as Doug dropped his towel and reached for his underwear. "None, as far as Delwood and his money go—and it certainly went. What I think we need to concentrate on here is where all this money is going. According to Bettie, Rob has hit up George several times. He's hit up Delwood. He pulls down a supposedly considerable salary at George's company. Can anyone gamble *that* much? And that badly? And another thing—at what point do you say to yourself, hey, I'm not so good at this and find yourself another hobby?"

Doug danced around the floor a bit as he climbed into his tuxedo pants. Funny. He'd gotten undressed in front of women before, more times than he cared to remember at the moment. But never dressed again. Not in this way. Not together, just talking. Comfortable together, at ease in each other's company. He liked it. He liked it a lot. "People have been known to drop millions in AC. I can name a couple, just off the top of my head."

"I like to gamble," Rosie said, helping him slip into his shirt. "Roulette. My father tells me those are the worst odds in the house, but I still like to play. But not a million dollars' worth. That's insane, even if you had it to lose. So, you're thinking that Rob gambled away the money, then maybe borrowed some more from the Doublemint Twins who are hanging out here to protect their investment?"

"Or make sure he's not planning to leave town on his honeymoon and forget to come back," Doug pointed out, heading into the living room to put on his jacket. Rosie was close behind him, offering to tie his tie for him. "But—and it's a big but, Rosie—is that any of our business?"

"Nope," she said, handing him the tie as he turned up his collar. "Bettie said George got him to sign some sort of prenup for one thing, and if George and Bettie are dumb enough to loan Rob money—same goes for Delwood—that's their problem. No skin off our noses, right? Our problem—hold still will you, this isn't as easy as it looks in the movies—is Lili-beth. My student and friend. Your only cousin's daughter. She's not happy, and Rob Hemmings is never going to make her happy. Did you do what I told you to do, when you spoke with Del? Sicced him on Ki-Ki?"

"I did, General. But there's that old saying about how you can lead a horse to water…"

"He won't do it?"

"He sneezed six times, then pulled out his inhaler again. I don't know if that was a no, or an 'I'll try but I'm going to fail' answer. Are you *sure* Lili-beth loves this kid?"

"Positive. She worries about him all the time. She talks about him all the time. It's always Del and I did this, Del and I went there, Del and I— Ah, that's it, perfect! She just doesn't realize how empty her life would be without Del in it, Del to worry about."

"And Hemmings?"

"An aberration. Her bad boy. Every woman

needs a bad boy. Rob is Lili-beth's, and she's already regretting letting it all get this far, giving Bettie the go-ahead with her lifelong plans for the world's most unforgettable wedding, and all the while wondering what on earth she saw in the guy in the first place. I had one. A bad boy."

"Really?" Doug asked, going over to the small mirror beside the door to check on Rosie's expertise. "Not bad. Looks good, in fact. You may have a new career here, Rosie—dressing me. Undressing me wouldn't be so bad, either. So what did you see in your bad boy?"

"His motorcycle," Rosie told him as she gathered up the bag filled with wrappings and the two empty beer bottles, carrying everything to the small kitchen area. "It was," she turned to him, dramatically rolling up her eyes as she shook her hands in front of her, "the most totally *rad* bike. Oh, and that was my Valley Girl impersonation, in case you're wondering. Anyway, my parents hated it and him. I, of course, thought he was the sexiest thing on…well, on two wheels. And he was twenty-six to my eighteen, which was a *real* turn-on."

Doug grinned. "So why didn't you and cycle boy go riding off into the sunset together?"

"Because I wasn't the only rich man's daughter who thought the guy was James Dean come back to life, that's why. Do you know that James Dean posters still sell well? The ultimate bad boy—those smoldering eyes, that cigarette dangling from his lips. Posed astride that powerful, pulsing motorcycle of his. Oh, and that hair—a dark blond pompador beneath that cowboy hat he wore tipped back on his head as he squinted into the camera. Oh, my."

"If you need to stop a moment, compose yourself? Maybe fan yourself?" Doug teased, adoring her.

"Thanks, but I'm over it—mostly. Anyway, with my particular bad boy there was also a drug-store tycoon's daughter in Bedminster, a stock-broker's daughter in Dunellen—not to mention the wife and two kids living in a duplex in Wee-hauken. Hey—do you suppose that Rob…no. That just would be too easy."

"A bigamist would be too *easy?*"

"You know what I mean. Too easy to prove. Everything's on the Internet these days, you know. So we're back to Lili-beth being miserable, and made even more miserable by her parents, who are insisting she go through with the wedding because it's too late to call it off now. I mean, their names are embossed in gold on wineskins. How much more locked-in can a person get?"

Doug followed her out the door and down the staircase. "I think I could use another drink. Wineskins?"

"Never mind. You'll see them during the toga party."

"Toga party? Bettie's idea, right?"

"Considering that a gin rummy party would be George's idea, yes, I think we're safe in saying this is another one of Bettie's brainstorms. She's been planning this wedding since Lili-beth was born, remember. She's had lots of time to come up with some pretty spooky ideas."

"And unworkable ideas if she thinks I'm dressing up in a sheet the way we did in college."

"Tell her that, not me. She's supplying the sheets."

Rosie stopped a good thirty feet from the terrace, lit now with Chinese lanterns and rings of small lights wrapped around the posts of each umbrella. "Looks like we're just in time for dessert."

"I thought we had that before the subs," Doug teased, slipping an arm around her waist. "Hey, it looks like Anvil and the rest of the Q-Tips are about to play again. You know, they're pretty good."

"They should be. They all graduated from Juilliard. Those outfits, the band's name? Just youthful rebellion, considering all of them also earned their money the old-fashioned way. Poor kids—if they don't make it big soon they'll all be lawyers or insurance agents within another few years. Sticks starts medical school next week to keep his urologist father and podiatrist mother happy, and if that doesn't make you question the American medical system, I don't know what would."

"And you already knew all of this when we first sat down with them? How do you know all of this? Do you know *everybody?*"

Rosie only shrugged her magnificent bare shoulders…with their fantastic sprinkling of freckles that—who knew?—were a major turn-on. Hell, everything about her was a major turn-on.

"Oh, look, there's Lili-beth. I didn't think she'd come downstairs at all today. Ah, look at her, Doug. She looks so sad. The sad little bride, all alone at her own party." She grabbed his hand and led him toward the terrace. "Come on, we should do something. I know—I'll go tell Anvil to play something slow, and you go ask her to dance."

"I don't think the tables are set up for dancing, Rosie," he pointed out as they climbed the two steps onto the terrace.

"And that's going to stop you, old man? I guess you were still getting dressed when I was leading George in the conga line. Or are you afraid the dance floor police are going to arrest you?"

Doug opened his mouth to make a defensive comment on that old man insult. But Rosie was already on the move, and as she threaded her way in between the dinner guests she was doing an "Excuse me, pardon me, just passing through, just passing through" routine that he seemed to remember from a Bugs Bunny and Elmer Fudd cartoon in his youth. He lightly covered his mouth with his hand, and chuckled low in his throat.

God, where had this insane, wonderful woman been all his life?

Or had he finally arrived at a point in his life where he was ready for a woman like Rosie?

He'd think about that later. Probably all through a long, uncomfortable, sleepless night…

Three minutes later he was dancing with Lili-beth, whose protests he had overridden by the simple expedient of taking her in his arms and moving her into the dance.

"Do you have a smile for me tonight, Lili-pad?" he asked as he maneuvered her within a small circle of space that was all that was available in the midst of so many people and tables.

"I'm sorry, Doug," she said, her head bent as she watched her steps, clearly terrified she'd step on his toes. "I...I haven't felt well today."

"Yes, so I've heard. Is there anything I can do?"

"Do?"

Cripes, the kid was looking at him as if he'd just asked her if she wanted him to kill somebody for her. "Yes. Do for you. I'm your cousin, Lili-beth, even if I consider myself more your uncle. I know I'm never around, and that's my fault, my mistake. But I've been around enough to know that the Lili-beth I remember always had a smile for everyone, even back when your teeth were wired for sound. And I'm around now. You're not smiling now, honey, and you weren't smiling yesterday."

"I...I told you. I haven't been feeling well."

"And I'm telling you, I don't believe that." He was pushing, probably too hard, but it was Monday night, and the wedding was Sunday. It wasn't like he had a lot of time to get where he was going. Not to mention that, if the wedding was called off, he and Rosie could be on a beach in the South of France in less than ten hours. As in, when he faced the truth about himself, there was family affection, sure, and then there was real incentive…

"Oh, Doug," Lili-beth wailed, none too quietly, so that he quickly took her hand and pushed her into the room directly behind them before any of the guests in varying states of happy inebriation could take notice and follow after them.

Unfortunately, not before Rosie could notice, and she did follow after them, slicing Doug a *men—ask them to do one simple thing!* look of superior feminine disgust before taking a sobbing Lili-beth into her arms.

So Doug stepped behind the bar in the corner and poured himself the drink he'd wanted in the first place.

"Shhh, Lili-beth, shhh," Rosie soothed as she patted the girl's back. "It's all right. Everything's all right. Doug and I are going to make very sure that everything's all right. Now, tell us all about it."

Doug and I? He looked at the Scotch bottle,

wondering if maybe he should make a it a double, then decided that he was going to need all of his wits about him in the next few minutes. The Scotch bottle went back into the rack behind the bar and he reached beneath it to pull a soda can from the small built-in refrigerator.

"It's…it's…it's *Delwood!*"

Delwood? Doug mouthed as he looked at Rosie, who was still held tight in Lili-beth's damp embrace, although she was sort of goggling at him right now, which was nice.

"Delwood, honey?" Rosie asked, carefully disengaging herself and taking hold of Lili-beth's hands in order to lead her over to one of the couches and sit her down. "What's wrong? Is he ill?"

Lili-beth shook her head so hard that a few pins flew out of the ridiculous upsweep someone had foisted on her, poor kid. "He…he's not sick. That…that witch, Ki-Ki. He's…he's…oh, how *could* he?"

"I don't understand. How could Delwood do what, Lili-beth?" Rosie asked, looking hopefully at Doug, who decided that he might be justified in taking a small bow. *Go, Delwood. Holster that inhaler and make your move. What a man!*

Lili-beth sat up straight, sniffed a time or two and raised her chin in a watery show of defiance. "Well, if he wants her, then he can just have her. Everybody else has!"

Doug made a fist and gave a quick *aw-right* stab into the air, losing his smile when Rosie glared at him. Hey, what was this? Wasn't telling Delwood to pretend to make a play for Ki-Ki so that Lili-beth woke up and realized she was in love with the guy *her* idea? It sure as hell wasn't *his*. Women. Maybe he still didn't understand them.

"Douglas, don't you have somewhere else to be? Clearly Lili-beth and I are going to have a woman-to-woman chat. Besides, you've done enough damage."

He stabbed his fingers against his chest. "*Me? What do you mean, what I've* done?"

Without the benefit of having visited Bettie's cosmetic surgeon, Rosie's expressions were still fairly easy to read, and Doug was able to read *Go away, you idiot* quite easily as she looked at him now.

So he went. And this time he was by damn going to find himself a stiff drink.

He stepped back onto the terrace just in time to

see a skinny brunette toss the contents of her wine glass smack in the face of a guy he was pretty sure was Rosie's supposed seating chart partner, Quint.

Talk about your perfect cappers to an evening…

Five seconds later Bettie was in his face, snarling at him. "Did you see that?"

"Let me guess, Betts. That was Millicent? The ex?"

"Yes, and it's all your fault, Douglas, that they've been forced to sit together. They've been sniping at each other all evening, making everyone uncomfortable. What do you have to say to *that?*"

"Good night and good luck?" he offered as Antoinette rushed past him carrying a small towel. He snagged a half-full wine bottle from the table closest to him before retiring to his Bachelor Quarter, alone, where it might be safer for an uninvolved man to be right now.

CHAPTER TWELVE

ROSIE SPIED OUT DOUG already standing on the first tee, his legs spread slightly as he leaned on the grip of his driver, looking very professional and only slightly hungover in his golf glove and visor.

"Sorry if I'm late," she said as she joined the rest of their foursome. "I had to run over to my own course to get my clubs from the locker room. Good morning Rob and—Mr. Rizzo, Leslie."

"Just Rizzo," the man told her as he looked pointedly at his oversize silver watch, and then turned at the sound of a large golf bag crammed with clubs hitting the ground. "Damn, Leslie, you know what those titaniums set me back? You carry them, you don't drag them."

"Leslie's going to caddy for him? Oh, well, this could be fun," Rosie said, lightly bumping against Doug, who still hadn't said hello to her. What was his problem, other than the obvious? "Oh, come on. It's a completely gorgeous day, the course is in immaculate condition, and we're going to wipe these two amateurs all over it for the next four or five hours. *Smile.*"

"Maybe when my teeth stop throbbing," he told her quietly as Rob was teeing up his ball. "What the hell happened last night?"

"You were wonderful, that's what happened. You played the obtuse male as if you were born for the role. Once I pretended to chase you away, Lilibeth and I had a marvelous talk about how terrible you men are," Rosie whispered back to him as her caddy handed her a ball and her three wood. "Rob?" she called out just as Rob Hemmings was addressing the ball, so that he turned to her with a look that just might mean he'd rather be teeing up her head. "What are you hitting? We all need to declare our balls, remember? You know, in case we both happen to hit into the same area?"

"Oh, right. Callaway."

"Really? Me, too. What number?"

"What do I care what—okay, I remember." Rob leaned down and snatched up his ball. "A three. Mine's a three."

"And mine's a one, so we're good there."

"Isn't that just terrific. Now, if you don't mind, I'd like to hit my shot." Rob replaced his ball.

She turned back to Doug and said brightly, "So that's two of us. You want to declare your ball?"

"You have some kind of death wish, woman?" Doug asked her in a stage whisper, reaching into his pocket and pulling out his own ball. "Mine's a Titleist two. Rizzo?"

"Mine's got one of them monograms stamped on it, so it doesn't matter," Rizzo told them smugly.

"ATR?" Rosie asked. "Anthony T. Rizzo." She smiled at the man. "I was helping the wedding planner with some calligraphy earlier this morning. That's a lovely name, Anthony. But you want us all to call you Rizzo? We could call you Tony."

"It's Rizzo. People call me Rizzo." He motioned for Leslie to hold up the golf bag so he could pull out a club with a fuzzy gopher head on it. "My mother calls me Rizzo. You got a problem with that?"

Rosie shot him her best dumb-female grin. "Who, me? No. I've got no problem with that. Rizzo is a…a lovely name. And you're hitting a driver off the tee? On this narrow fairway? Wow, that's confidence. I can't wait until Rob tees off and you can go to it, show us amateurs how it's done."

Doug put his arm around her waist and pulled her to the back of the tee. "Are you always this obnoxious on the golf course?"

"What? I'm being nice. I'm being friendly." She winked up at him. "And I'm driving both of them crazy, partner, which should make you happy. It's like knocking two strokes off my handicap. Now be quiet, Rob's going to hit, and I have to interrupt him again."

This time, she waited until he's was in his backswing.

"Wait! Aren't there going to be any side bets?"

Rob pretty much twisted his body into a pretzel, trying to hold on to his backswing, but he managed it. Glaring at Rosie, he asked, "How much?"

Rosie shrugged. "I don't know. A little five-dollar Nassau all right with you boys?"

"Rizzo?" Rob asked, walking over to the other man, and the two of them began conferring…or asking each other if either of them knew what the hell five-dollar Nassau was.

"You watched *Caddyshack* a hundred times, didn't you?" Doug asked her as they waited. "And you look terrific. I kept hoping you'd come back to the Bachelor Quarter last night."

"I couldn't. We had an impromptu slumber party."

"That would have worked for me. Except for the slumbering part," he said, and Rosie felt her stomach do a small flip.

"Well, to tell you the truth," she told him, "I thought maybe we needed to slow down a little. We do have the whole week. Six more whole days."

"But only five more nights. Less, if Lili-beth pulls the plug on the wedding. Have you thought about that one?"

More than you know, Rosie thought, but she didn't say the words. "I did, I did. Then I wondered if I should ask you if you've had a stress test lately. You know…all this activity, and with you in your advancing years."

Doug hitched a thumb toward Rob and Rizzo. "Hey, lady, psych them out, not me. I'm your partner, remember?"

"I know. And we're going to beat them senseless, take all their money and then go back to the Bachelor Quarter and celebrate our victory. Now, how's that for psyching you up?"

"Works for me," he said, then put a finger to his

lips before pointing to Rob who was standing over his ball again.

"He didn't settle on an amount for our bet," she whispered. "I was sure he'd want to bet. He's a gambler, right? Gamblers bet."

"Excuse me?"

Rosie and Doug turned around to see Leslie hovering behind them, holding out a score card. "Yes?" Doug asked.

"Here's the bet. You're to sign the bottom, both of you. It'll be like your marker, Rizzo says."

"Don't sign that," Rosie warned, panicking just a little. "Who puts a bet in writing? Wait. How much is it?" She pulled the score card out of Leslie's hand and read the figure scratched on the back of it. "Five hundred dollars each nine, another five hundred for the match? Are they nuts? First the croquet, and now this? It's a *game*. Leslie, you look like a nice guy. Tell me the truth—is your friend Rizzo on the tour?"

But she really shouldn't have had to ask that question. All she needed was the first three holes to learn that, while Rizzo was pretty good, he wasn't great. And, with each hole lost, Rob's game disintegrated. Rob Hemmings was not a lump of coal that could be turned into a diamond under pressure. With Rob, it was more like the coal crumbled into coal dust, and then just lay there, not good for much of anything.

On the other hand, Doug was very good, and just kept getting better. He finessed a par by chipping the ball in on a par five after landing his drive in the water, never losing his concentration. She liked that.

She liked everything about Douglas Llewellyn, and each new thing she learned about him made her like him even more. And Sunday was only six days away...

"Rosie? Come on, Rosie, you've got honors."

She blinked at Doug, who she'd been staring at, actually. "Oh, sorry. I don't know where my mind was."

Except that she did. And her mind, her heart were looking toward Sunday night, and the moment she and Doug said goodbye and parted ways. Fun time over. He'd go back to Philadelphia and his life there, his nubile young things there, and she'd go back to telling herself that she had life by the tail and was enjoying every moment of it.

They won the match, but for the last seven holes, it was pretty much *hit the ball, drag Rosie* for Doug, because her mind was no longer on the game.

Because it was on *the game*...and on how maybe it might be safer if she didn't play it anymore.

She followed Doug back to the house, parking her car beside his in the field turned over to that purpose. She took hold of his outstretched hand as she walked around behind her Mercedes.

This wasn't going to be easy. Because he looked so cute—almost boyish—his thick dark hair rumpled from the visor, his skin flushed with the sun. He even smelled good: like grass and sun and good sweat. She could just eat him up.

"Doug, I've been thinking..."

"Hold that thought," he told her, reaching into his pocket to withdraw his ringing cell phone and flip it open. "Llewellyn here," he said, and Rosie tugged on his hand, ready to move away and let him have his privacy—give herself at least a momentary reprieve from being a responsible adult who had a great respect for protecting her heart.

But he squeezed her hand tightly, holding her where she stood.

"But I really need to..." she began, and then

shut her mouth, because she was standing close enough to hear both sides of the conversation.

"Hi, Doug. I tried the numbers you gave me, but someone told me you were on the golf course, so I tried your cell. It's hell here. I've got an inspector out at the Kline job telling me the rewire plan we used doesn't pass muster and he's giving me three days to fix it or he shuts us down. You and I both know damn well there's nothing wrong with that rewire—I think this hick town jackass is trying to shake us down. Like that's going to happen. You have to come back here, do your thing, pull some strings. The subcontractor tells me we've got the drywall showing up on Thursday morning, the crew all set to go. We can't take this kind of dip-shit delay."

"Yeah, right, Cam. You think I have you on speaker, or something? Nice try, and thanks, but I don't need you. You'll get your Oscar at the Christmas party."

Rosie frowned, wondering what on earth *that* meant.

"Doug. Douglas. *Boss.* I know what you said, but this isn't your requested Tuesday afternoon get out of jail free call. This is for real. You have to come back here, at least overnight. And what's the problem—you didn't want to be there in the first place. Oh, wait, don't tell me—you're still working your way through the bridesmaids, right? Doug, buddy, one of these days you've really got to think about growing up."

Now Doug did let go of her hand, and Rosie took off like a shot across the grass, hearing him call her name as she ran, but not stopping until she had slammed into the house and was upstairs in her assigned bedroom, the door locked behind her.

"Stupid," she told her reflection in the bathroom mirror a half hour later, once she was done with her weepy self-pity party. "Stupid, stupid, stupid. You knew what you were doing. He was right up-front with it, and so were you. Fun and games, that's all this is. Don't try to make more out of it than there is. Great sex is just that, great sex. Two consenting adults, just like everybody else around here. Isn't that what you told yourself just before you went crazy? And that's all there is here, and all there's going to be here."

She leaned in closer to the mirror. "So either stay or bail, Kilgannon, but stop being such a jerk."

Her reflection looked back at her, and she could

see the hurt in her eyes, and the embarrassment, maybe even the shame. Who had she thought she'd been kidding, anyway? Doug? Herself? Fun time?

Well, fun time was over.

She didn't do this. She'd never done this. See a man, go after him, make a damn fool of herself pretending she could do something like this and then just walk away, find herself someone else who looked good to her, and then do it all over again.

Rabbits did that. Cats did that.

Men did that.

Rosie Sullivan Kilgannon did not do that.

Except that she had. Somewhere between that first impulsive kiss and their conversation on the terrace, the part of her brain that had taught her a long time ago that touching hot stoves meant a nasty burn had decided to let her find this one out by herself.

And it hurt. She'd touched the stove and the stove was hot. And it really, really hurt.

She turned on the taps and splashed her face with warm water, then cold, before reaching blindly for a towel as the phone extension in her room began to ring.

"Hello," she said as cheerfully as possible on the

fifth ring, after debating whether or not to answer at all, because she was sure Doug would be on the other end of the line. "Kilgannon's House of Ill Repute and Taco Bar. How may we assist you?"

"Rosie? Rosie, it's Doug. Listen, about earlier—"

She cut him off. "Oh, I know. I'm sorry I just sort of left you standing there. My bladder suddenly realized I'd had two bottles of water on the back nine. Hey, do you mind if I kind of stick around here tonight, help Antoinette with more calligraphy, talk to Lili-beth some more and see if Delwood got off the dime, or what? I'm sure George will have a good gin rummy game going later anyway, and you might want to get in on it."

"Rosie, I have to go back to Philadelphia. I'm already on my way, as a matter of fact, and I'm calling you from the road. Just something I have to work out. But I'll be back. Tomorrow, or Thursday at the latest. I will be back. And you'll still be there?"

She forced a laugh to her lips, but it really couldn't move past them. "Well, of course. Where else would I be, if not here, trying to ruin Bettie's big day?"

"Okay then. I'm glad you understand."

"What's not to understand? Business calls and you have to go."

"Right. Business calls. Rosie—"

"See you then, Doug. I've got to run, I'm standing here naked, wet from the shower."

"Oh, Christ, don't do that to me, give me that visual picture. I already feel like hell leaving you. Rosie, I don't know what you thought you overheard Cam saying, but—"

"Now I'm getting goose bumps. I really have to go." *Before I start blubbering again.*

"Rosie…something's happening here. Between us. I don't know what it is, but something's happening here. Something good. Please be there when I get back."

She gripped the old-fashioned phone with both hands. Were all women as easy as she was? Because she actually believed him. She *wanted* to believe him. "I'll be here, Doug. Drive carefully."

"Do you think so, too, Rosie? That something good is—"

It wasn't until the sound of the dial tone finally reached her brain that Rosie realized he must have hit a dead spot on the highway and their connection had been dropped. Which was a good thing, because he was going to ask her something, and she was going to have to give him answer.

She wasn't ready to give him any answers. Not until she had some for herself.

"Rosie? Rosie, I've been knocking forever—I know you're in there. Don't make me go downstairs to get the key."

Bettie. The last person she wanted to see.

Rosie replaced the phone, then wiped at her eyes with the hem of her golf shirt. "I'm coming, Bettie, you don't have to resort to breaking and entering. I was on the phone."

Then, taking a deep, steadying breath, she opened the door.

"I know that," Bettie said, brushing past Rosie and into the room. "Who do you think switched his call to your room? What did he mean, that something *good* is happening? And why are you still dressed in your golf clothes? You said you were standing there naked, wet from your shower. You said you had goose bumps. My God, you *lied* to him? You lied to my cousin? Don't tell me you're going to let that man get away!"

"You were eavesdropping on our conversation?" Rosie asked, knowing it was a rhetorical question.

"Don't ever do that to Doug or me again, Bettie. You wouldn't like the way I'd react. Now, if you'll excuse me, I *am* going to take that shower now."

"No, wait, Rosie," Bettie pleaded, following her into the bathroom. "I'm sorry. I know I shouldn't have—but it's nearly time for dinner and I saw his car pulling out and I thought—well, I don't know what I thought. I haven't been very nice to him, have I? Or to you, either. We all just…we all just got off on the wrong foot on Sunday afternoon, that's all."

And then Bettie did her Lili-beth imitation. She plunked herself down on the toilet lid and dropped her head into her hands, sobbing. "Oh, Rosie…wha…wha…what am I going to do? George just told me wants a divorce! The…the moment Lili-beth is safely married on Sunday. I love him, Rosie. He's such a big, dumb lump…I love him *so much.*"

Rosie leaned a hip against the edge of the sink as she rolled her eyes toward the skylight in the ceiling. "Why me, God?" she asked quietly, pretty sure that was also a rhetorical question.

CHAPTER THIRTEEN

DOUG COULD HAVE BEEN BACK at the party by late Thursday afternoon. But he'd chickened out. He was pretty sure that was the correct technical term for what he'd done: chickened out.

He'd solved the problem at the Kline site by the close of business on Wednesday, but then told Cam he wanted to be back on the site Thursday morning when the drywall contractor showed up. Why? So that there were no more problems with the over-zealous inspector. So that he could calm the anxious home owner. So that he could speak with the subcontractor about another job coming up in Ardmore the following week.

So he could continue to chicken out....

By this time, he and Cam had shared several iced teas at their favorite watering hole, and his friend knew that his senior partner, boss, and friend was in it up to his knees. Maybe to his armpits.

Okay. Over his head. He was in over his head. Definitely.

"I'm not saying you're in love with this Rosie woman," Cam had told him. "You did the big four-oh thing a couple of months ago, Doug, and I've noticed the difference. You may be looking for something more than the—well, we both know what you've been hunting up until now. She sounds different. Older, more sure of herself and who she is—again, nothing like the, to be polite, pretty airheads you're used to. So maybe she's the right woman in the right spot at the right time, or maybe she's just what you *think* is the right sort of woman for you now that you're—hell, now that you're all grown-up. I'm just saying you have to be careful at what's probably a vulnerable stage of your life, and make damn sure you know the difference."

Yeah, that was it. Those were the words that had kept Doug in Philadelphia for another day. He'd even called up the woman he'd been dating semi-regularly, Kay Williams—she of the private beach and penchant for topless sunbathing—and invited her to dinner on Thursday night, refusing to see this as the gesture of a desperate man fighting the inevitable.

And nothing.

Kay was thirty now, and had been edging out of his asinine (or so it seemed now) date-age requirements, but that only made it easier for him to compare her to Rosie. And, because he had been dating her on and off for years, there must have been some attraction.

She was slim, gorgeous, fairly bright and definitely sexy.

And nothing.

She slipped off one high-heeled sandal halfway through the main course to seductively rub her bare toes up under his pants leg, and all he could think about was Rosie and her black satin heels digging into his back as she turned to liquid in his arms.

She leaned forward across the small table, her elbows pressed to her sides, exposing a fair expanse of her high real estate cleavage, and all he could think about was how he could see the outline of Kay's bones beneath her suntanned flesh, for God's sakes. Rosie's bones were hidden beneath soft, creamy skin; she had lush curves, not sharp-edged *planes*. Rosie had substance.

Hell, Kay didn't even have freckles. What was a woman's chest, if it didn't have freckles?

So he told Kay a funny joke Cam had told him, and Kay had laughed politely. *Politely.* Careful not to wrinkle her well-toned skin. Rosie would have thrown back her head and laughed out loud; she would have *enjoyed* the joke. Then told him one of her own.

By the time they'd had dessert and the check had arrived, he'd ducked Kay's suggestion he come back to her penthouse with her and was already planning to stop back at his own apartment to locate his other tuxedo, get a good night's sleep—his first in many days—and head for New Jersey before rush hour on Friday morning.

Dinner with Kay hadn't been a scientific experiment, but he had learned something. He looked at Kay, and wanted to see Rosie. He listened to Kay, and wanted to hear Rosie. Kay brushed up against him with practiced nonchalance, and he wanted to touch Rosie.

Everything he thought, everything he did, everything he felt…no matter what he factored into the equations, the answers all came up *Rosie.*

Love didn't come this fast and hard. He wasn't an idiot—he knew that much.

But there was something going on. There was something there between them.

The problem, as he saw it, was that Rosie knew that, too, and she was running in the other direction. He'd scared the hell out of her just as she'd scared the hell out of him.

Or, he told himself by the time he tossed his car keys to the kid playing a handheld computer game as he lounged against the bumper of somebody's prize Jaguar, she thought he was a certified, card-carrying, midlife-crisis jerk. There was always that.

Why had he been so damn honest with her about what even his best friend had none too politely termed his jackassed, fairly selfish way of looking at life? And why should Rosie think the week might end any differently than they'd agreed—so long, it's been fun, see you around.

"You're back!"

Doug had been heading toward the Bachelor Quarter, to get rid of the bag holding his tuxedo before searching out Rosie and taking her somewhere private to kiss her senseless, when the sound of Bettie's voice stopped him. "Hi there, Betts.

So, did you miss me? I told you I'd be—whoa, what happened, what's wrong? You look like sh— That is, are you okay?"

And why did he care? He had a mission: find Rosie, kiss Rosie, touch Rosie, be gloriously alone with Rosie.

By now Bettie had feverishly grabbed on to his forearm with both hands and was dragging him toward the terrace and the French doors that led to her private sunroom. "I called your office and somebody told me you were coming back this morning, and I've been standing out here for the past two hours, waiting for you. You have to help me, Doug. You have to talk to George, make him see reason."

"He wants to call off the wedding?" Doug wasn't really sure why that thought was the first to come into his mind, but it wasn't impossible to believe that George might have finally wised up about his son-in-law to-be, and what a pretty-boy loser schmuck the kid was.

"No!" Bettie collapsed into one of the couches, looking small and defeated, a wilted coral-colored flower. "He wants to call off the *marriage—our* marriage."

"Again?" The word was out before Doug could call it back, and he winced at Bettie's answering wail of despair.

He took a quick look around the room, checking all the exit routes, and then gave in, knowing he wasn't going anywhere. He might call it the Curse of Rosie, this feeling that he should be involved with other people's problems if those other people asked for his help...and maybe even if they didn't ask, but clearly needed help anyway.

Rosie. Of course. Why hadn't he thought of that immediately? This was clearly a job for Rosie, a woman-to-woman job. "Let me go find Rosie, Betts. You shouldn't be alone."

Bettie blew her nose in the handkerchief she'd pulled from her pocket. "Rosie can't help," she said piteously. "She tried, but George says he means it this time. The minute Lili-beth and Rob marry on Sunday, he's packing his bags and leaving. He says that's all he's been waiting for, and for a good ten years. Ten years, Doug. That's just...*cold.*"

"Did he find out about Anvil?" *And all the others?*

Bettie looked up at him, nodded her head. "He...he...he—" she hiccupped the word "—he doesn't *care!*"

"Wow," Doug said quietly to himself, remembering something he'd heard years earlier: the opposite of love is not hate, because that's also an emotion. The true opposite of love is *indifference*. "Maybe he's just saying that, Betts. He can't really mean it."

"You'll talk to him?" Bettie asked hopefully. "I can't walk down that aisle with him on Sunday, our arms around Lili-beth. It would be as if I was marching to my own funeral."

"Bettie, I want to help you," Doug said, at last sitting down beside her, putting a comforting hand on her knee and giving it a squeeze. "But you don't make it easy. I mean, you've been cheating on the man for years. Maybe he's just had enough?"

She wiped at her eyes, and then sat up straight. "Do...do you know why we separated for a while when Lili-beth was in high school? Because he was cheating on me, that's why. With one of his secretaries. Some skinny, opportunistic little bitch half my age. I forgave him, took him back, but it just wasn't the same, you know?"

No, he hadn't known the reason behind the separation—his parents seemed able to still keep some secrets from their son—but he also didn't want to interrupt Bettie. George had been catting around? *George?* In the words of the bard: Who would have thunk it? Doug had believed the man's entire life to revolve around golf, gin rummy and shirt collars, and there wasn't a lot of time left over for romantic adventures in that mix.

"I've...I've been *punishing* him," Bettie said brokenly, "that's what Rosie says, but now George just wants it all over. He's just been waiting for Lili-beth to get married."

"I know. You said that," Doug said, getting to his feet to go pour Bettie a drink. It was pretty early for Scotch, but Bettie looked ready to split into small, jagged pieces, and he'd think of the Scotch as purely medicinal. "It's a shame you and George didn't hash all of this out years ago—see a counselor, or maybe a psychologist."

"Rosie said that, too. And she's right, you're right. We've been...sublimating, or something like that."

"O-kay," Doug said, nearly pouring himself a drink, too, while he was at it, but deciding it might be a good idea if he got through this conversation without going anywhere near anything alcoholic. "So Rosie said a lot."

"She didn't *want* to say anything."

"She didn't?" *Rosie, who seemed to be involved*

*with everyone, everything, hadn't wanted to get
involved? Then why the hell was he getting involved?*

"No, she didn't. She said something about
having her own problems. It took me all day Wednesday to get her to go see George, talk to him.
And then she left."

The pull tab of the soda can Doug had pulled
out from the small refrigerator beneath the bar
popped with some force, soda fizz running out and
over his fingers—but Doug didn't notice. "She
left? What do you mean, Rosie *left?* She's gone?
Where did she go? And what does that mean—she
has her own problems? What do you know, Betts?"

Bettie waved off his questions. "Oh relax,
Romeo, she's coming back. One of the volunteers
at that dog pound she loves so much broke her
wrist in some fender bender, so Rosie filled in
yesterday and today. She's always doing *something.* But she promised she'd be back in time for
the bridal lunch, and that's in just a few hours."

Doug finally looked down at his soda-wet hand,
surprised to see that, damn, he was trembling. What
the hell was going on with him? Nothing meant this
much to him. Nobody meant this much to him.

Rosie meant that much to him. *Damn.*

"So will you go talk to George, Doug? It may have been a mistake to send Rosie. But you'd be man-to-man. *Please?* He's in his study, setting up tables for some Texas hold 'em for all the men." She frowned. "Rob isn't invited. Well, I had to tell him he'd been *dis-invited*. By George. Isn't that horrible? But he made such a fuss Wednesday night that George really isn't speaking to him right now, so he ordered him back to the office."

"What happened?"

"Oh, that's right, you missed Monte Carlo night, didn't you? Too bad for you. Rosie showed up in a man's white shirt over some real tuxedo slacks with black silk bands around her sleeves and a big leather visor, and dealt baccarat—whatever that is. The men were all over her. She made a lot of money for one of those charities of hers."

Doug smiled, relaxing somewhat. Rosie was still being Rosie, and that had to be a good thing.

"Anyway, Fred Barnes was dealing blackjack for his charity, and Rob accused him of cheating. It was all…very embarrassing. Lili-beth burst into tears and ran upstairs, and George told Rob to go somewhere and sober up. He'd been drinking fairly heavily." She pressed a hand to her forehead. "Oh, Doug, what's happening? Nobody's happy. I planned this week to be perfect, this wedding to be perfect—and nobody's happy. Except for Aunt Susanna but, hell, she's half-senile, what does she know?"

Doug decided to give sanity a shot. "Have you thought about calling off the wedding, Betts?"

"Call…calling off the—Douglas, are you out of your mind? The flowers, the tents, the caterers! The gowns, the music! All the guests, all those presents to be returned. I'd be a laughingstock—we'd *all* be talked about, laughed about…"

"Your husband is going to pack his bags and leave the minute the reception is over, Betts. You said so. There's going to be gossip, either way. Besides, if there's no wedding…?"

Bettie blinked several times before looking up at Doug with a watery smile and saying, in some awe, "Then Lili-beth wouldn't be married. And then George can't leave. Can he?"

Doug shrugged. "I'm not saying it would work, Betts. It's just a thought."

"And *brilliant!*" Bettie hopped up from the couch to hug him. "Why didn't Rosie think of this?

Why didn't I think of this? We call off the wedding! We can always get Lili-beth another groom!"

"Oh, now *that's* cold, Betts," Doug said as his cousin hung on his neck. "I'm not going to pretend that I like Hemmings, but that's cold. Let me go talk to George."

"Yes, yes," Bettie said, kissing him on the cheek before letting him go. "Go talk to George. I'll pretend I don't know anything. But you are going to fix this for me, aren't you, Dougie."

"Not if you call me Dougie, no," he told her, more eager than ever to find Rosie once she returned, now that he could tell her he'd found a way to call off the wedding.

He wondered why she hadn't thought of it—it was so easy, such an easy answer. Hell, they'd be in the South of France by Saturday night at the latest. If he'd thought of it, the same idea should have been a piece of cake for a woman with Rosie's devious talents.

Doug was still congratulating himself as he entered George's study by way of an interior hall, as the terrace was getting fairly crowded with chattering women in large hats.

"George?" he prompted when the man sitting

behind his desk didn't seem to notice him. There were several folded card tables propped against a wall, but that was about it, nothing else had been done. "Bettie told me you're setting up a few poker tables for the men so they can hide out in here, away from the women. Do you want some help?"

George looked up at him, blinking several times—a trait he and his wife seemed to share. "Oh, Doug, sorry, I didn't hear you come in. I'm going to miss this room. I had a lot of great times in this room. The night I took T-Three for his box seat tickets to the World Series with a great draw that filled an inside straight. Risky, I know, but worth it. It was the seventh game. The time Delwood's father scored a lid of pot from Delwood's roommate at Rutgers and we all got silly as hell, laughing at an old Jerry Lewis movie. It was only the one time, but hell, your kids are in college, they're trying it, so why not find out what the fuss is all about, right? I got married and responsible too young to try it in my own youth, you know?"

Doug sat down in the chair in front of the desk, enjoying this glimpse into George's private side. "Sounds like a lot of fun, George. You said Delwood's father?"

"Oh, yeah. Jim's nothing like the kid. Hell, Delwood would probably be allergic."

Doug smiled. "You've got a point there, George."

"Good kid, though. I like him. Solid, steady. For a long time Jim and I thought we were going to see a merger there, but then Lili-beth spotted her pretty boy, and that was that." George got to his feet. "Bettie told you about the divorce?"

"Yes, George," Doug said, standing up once more, because looking at George was beginning to depress him. "She told me."

George reached for the half-full tumbler on the desktop. "Figured as much. And she sent you in here to talk me out of it, right? Go ahead then, get it over with, say what you have to say. But like I already told Rosie when she tackled me yesterday—good kid, you could do a lot worse than Rosie Kilgannon, Doug—the minute Lili-beth is married, I'm gone, outta here."

"I know you and Bettie haven't always had it easy between you, but are you sure you really want to do this? You and my cousin have been married for a long time."

"Twenty-eight years next month," George said as he stepped out from behind the desk and the two men began setting up the card tables. "And doing nothing but hurting each other for the last ten of them." He put down one of the tables and leaned his palms on it. "I don't want that happening to Lili-beth. It's been hard enough on the kid, being here, watching her mother and father fall apart. Me hiding out in here. Bettie—well, we know what Bettie's been doing, don't we? I pushed her to it, I know that. But it still hurts."

"I'm sorry about that, George, I really am. So, you think Rob's the right man for Lili-beth?" What the hell, he was here, he might as well give up trying not to be involved.

"That little prick," George said, showing his first real emotion other than sadness. "Making an ass out of me in front of my friends—*accusing* one of my friends of cheating? I blame Bettie. Lili-beth wouldn't be in such a hurry to marry the first guy who asked her if she wasn't so much in a hurry to get out of here. Hell, if she waited for Delwood to get off the dime, she'd still be waiting when she was fifty. But Bettie and I—well, we fight. A lot. Lili-beth's smart to get away."

"I wonder if Doctor Phil makes house calls," Doug muttered under his breath. "So you and

Bettie still care enough to fight?" he asked as George started opening a few new decks of cards.

"Care enough?" George repeated, tossing cellophane toward a trash basket beside his desk. "I don't know what you mean."

Neither do I, Doug told himself. "I'm not sure I do, either, George, but I had the flu last year."

George paused in the middle of opening another deck. "Huh?"

Doug held up his hands. "I was sick in bed and watched some daytime television. Doctor Phil. You ever hear of him?"

George shook his head. "What does a doctor have to do with any of this?"

"He's a sort of family counselor. I'm no expert, George, but I think you and Bettie and Lili-beth could have used a family counselor."

"That touchy-feely stuff? No way in hell. I told that to Rosie when she suggested it," George said, returning to his seat behind his desk. "What good would that do?"

"I don't know. Maybe it's too late. But it seems to me that you and Bettie still care enough to yell at each other, and I know I just left Bettie, who is really broken up about your plans to leave. And, as long as I'm sticking my foot in here, you both look like shit. If divorce is such a good idea why do you both look like shit?"

George smiled weakly. "We were good together once. Really good. I don't know what happened."

"Too bad you already told Bettie that you'll be leaving right after the wedding."

George nodded, his bottom lip caught between his teeth. "She confessed to me about some affair she had this week. Tried to apologize to me, or something. So I opened my mouth, and it just came out. Lili-beth gets married, and I'm gone. You know? And now I'm stuck with it."

Doug smiled. Rosie was going to love him so much. How would she thank him? He could suggest several ways. "Well, you know, George, that's the thing. You and Bettie might have made some mistakes, but you wouldn't want Lili-beth to make a mistake of her own because of that, would you? I mean, the three of you might have more time to sit down, work all of this out…if there wasn't going to be a wedding on Sunday."

"I don't like that little prick, Doug. I tried, for Lili-beth's sake. Gave him a job, loaned him money, promised them a house right here on the grounds—

the whole nine yards. But he still turns my stomach," George said, rubbing his chin. "I could toss him— I'd enjoy that. But no…Bettie would have a stroke or something. She's been planning this wedding forever. We have to have the wedding."

"True," Doug said, settling back in his own chair, hoping like hell that Rosie was right about Lili-beth and the Squirrelmaster. "But what about the groom, George? Do you have to have *that* groom?"

CHAPTER FOURTEEN

HE'D COME BACK. Rosie knew he'd come back because she'd seen his car when she'd parked hers. She'd nearly rammed a Range Rover as she stared at his car.

After a ridiculous five minutes spent checking her makeup and reciting Lincoln's Gettysburg Address in the hope of regulating her heartbeat, she finally climbed out of her own car.

He'd come back.

Holding her black-and-white-striped, wide-brimmed straw-hat against the breeze that had been blowing in off the water for a few hours now, she half walked, half ran toward the terrace, hoping to find him before George rounded up all the men for the Anything But A Bridal Luncheon Poker Party.

She stood on tiptoe on the very edge of the terrace, trying to see over the sea of straw hats; it looked like race day at Churchill Downs. She was still holding on to her own hat when she saw him on the grass about fifty feet away, standing with his back to her.

And then something very strange happened.

He'd been talking to Delwood, gesturing about something, and he stopped in midgesture, turned and immediately saw her across the sea of partygoers between them. As if he had sensed her, felt her presence. He smiled, and without so much as excusing himself to Delwood, headed in her direction.

As turn-ons go, Rosie was fairly certain she'd never experienced anything that had ever given her such a visceral punch in the stomach.

"Hi," he said, taking hold of the hands she offered him, squeezing her fingers. "Do you know how the breeze is outlining that damn dress against your legs?"

"No, but maybe if you could hum a few bars...?"

His smile turned into a grin, and he leaned in under the brim of her hat, to lightly kiss her mouth. "God, I missed you. I never know what you're going to say next."

"Me, too," Rosie said, feeling nervous, feeling foolish. "I mean, I know what I'm going to say next, most of the time. I meant I missed you, too. This zoo just wasn't the same without you. Did you make everything right again in your business world? How do architects solve problems, anyway? Threaten people with their slide rules?"

"Not me. I just narrow my eyes like this, growl a little, like this—" and he did, low, into her ear "—and everyone scurries to do my bidding. It's fun to be the boss."

Rosie stepped back slightly, grinning at him. "I'd just laugh at you…boss. So I guess it's a good thing I don't work for you."

"Oh, Rosie," he all but drawled, reaching up to help her hold on to her own hat as the breeze intensified, "you do work for me. Everything about you works for me."

"Oh, the devil with it," Rosie said, yanking off her hat and sliding her arms around his neck as she stood on tiptoe, which put her mouth a whisper away from his. "You've been gone for more than two days. This time, I want a *real* kiss."

She staggered slightly backward, as Doug abruptly bumped against her, and needed to hold on while he turned his head, cursed low in his throat.

"A little pushy, aren't you? What was that?"

"Marmie sideswiped me. Come on, this isn't going to be good," Doug told her, taking her hand to lead her through the crowd of people that had parted with the efficiency of the Red Sea as the huge dog cut a swatch through them. "I think he's after a squirrel."

"Oh, God, no," Rosie said, slamming her hat back on her head and holding it there with her free hand as Doug pulled her along across the grass in the ridiculous high heels she'd thought he'd like, but that definitely weren't built for running on soft ground. "He's heading for the tents. We have to stop him before he gets to the tables and—uh-oh."

The sound of feminine yelps, mixed with a few screams and several curses—all from the ladies—was quickly followed by Marmie reappearing, heading toward Rosie and Doug again, his face and back covered in white cake and coral frosting.

"What in hell?"

"The cake," Rosie told him as they quickly stood back, letting Marmie go without trying to stop him. "He must have knocked over the bride's cake. Lili-beth's was to be white with coral icing. Rob's groom's cake is chocolate with chocolate icing."

"Do I really need to know all of that?" Doug

asked before dropping down into position much like a second baseman waiting for a ground ball, because Marmie was heading back their way again, a terrified squirrel only slightly in the lead.

"Probably not, but you did ask," Rosie told him, taking off her hat yet again, with the idea of employing it like a bullfighter's cape in hopes Marmie's attention would be diverted away from the squirrel. And the people. And the tents.

King Kong loose on the streets of Manhattan had created less havoc than Marmie as he barked and ran, weaving in and out between an increasingly panicked audience—most of them still trying to hold on to their straw hats and blue martinis.

The dog neatly evaded Doug's outstretched hands and shifted into third, picking up speed.

Rosie and Doug made it as far as the first of the two huge white tents that had been set up on the lawn before catching sight of Marmie once more. It wasn't hard to spot him. He'd run beneath one of the large tables, dragging the tablecloth and several chafing dishes down as the tablecloth caught on his long, bushy tail, so that he now dragged it behind him.

"He's destroying everything, poor baby," Rosie

said sympathetically. "The squirrel's gone, but Marmie's so upset, he just can't seem to stop himself, can he?"

"There goes the ice sculpture," Doug pointed out unnecessarily, as the sound of the huge carved heart hitting the portable wooden tent floor and smashing almost exactly in half was more than enough notice. "Bettie's going to gut him and stuff him."

"Can you blame her?" Rosie asked, trying not to laugh as Gina Thompson hopped up onto one of the folding chairs topped with a white slipcover, and overshot her target, so that she went sprawling face-first on top of yet another table, this one loaded with presents. "Oh, that's not going to be good. I hope Lord and Taylor has a lenient return policy. Look, there's Delwood. Oh, what a genius!"

They watched as Delwood made his way to where Marmie was now running in circles, chasing after the tablecloth dragging on his tail. He was holding up a whole, roasted chicken. "Here, boy. Look what Del's got for you. Just for you. Chicken, Marmie. Come get yum-yums."

Marmie stopped chasing his tail and looked at Delwood. Tipped his massive head to one side and looked at the chicken, raised what actually looked like quizzical doggy eyebrows. *Chicken? For moi?* his big brown doggy eyes seemed to ask.

"He's got him," Doug said as Marmie sat down on the grass, his tablecloth-free tail thumping hard on the ground as Delwood held up the chicken with one hand and pulled a leash from behind his back with the other hand, to attach it to Marmie's collar. "I'd probably still be chasing the mutt. That was brilliant."

"That's Delwood," Lili-beth said, standing beside Doug. "He's such a nerd."

Rosie looked at the girl, who was smiling rather dreamily as she watched Delwood lead Marmie away toward the tennis courts. "And that's a good thing? Del being a nerd?"

Lili-beth smiled at her. "Oh, yes. Delwood always has the answers, you know? Always knows just what to do." And then her smile faded and she sighed rather theatrically. "At least he used to. I...I'd better go check on the caterers. They're probably pretty upset."

"We should help," Rosie said, looking around to see that everyone seemed to be just milling about aimlessly, now that the figurative dust was settling, like cattle set out to graze.

"I can see that Ear Waxx is set up in the second tent," Doug told her. "You go tell them to play something—and not 'Hound Dog'—and I'll get the waiters moving, passing out more drinks. There's nothing so bad at one of these parties that enough free-flowing booze can't fix."

"Wait a second, Doug. Something important might have just happened here." Rosie put a hand on his arm. "Did you hear what Lili-beth said just now? That Delwood *used* to have all the answers? She's angry with him, isn't she? She loves him, and she's angry with him because he's not making any moves. Maybe she even started dating Rob in the first place just to get Delwood to finally declare himself. And then?" She shrugged. "Things just sort of got out of hand, Bettie and George and their checkbook stepped in—and here we all are. What do you think?"

"I think you could be right," he told her. "Or you could be wrong. Look, much as I want to get you alone and indulge us both in every fantasy I've had for the past three nights, I think we both need to help Bettie and George this afternoon—do the friend thing, the cousin thing."

"I know," Rosie said, wincing as she saw Antoinette making a beeline straight at her, a nearly wild-eyed look on her face. She turned Doug in the other direction. "Here's the drill. The toga party starts at seven, out here, at the tents. Your costume is already hanging in your closet, and it's not that bad, really. Don't forget your sword."

"I wouldn't think of it," he said, leering at her comically.

"Ha-ha, I walked straight into that one, didn't I, you dirty old man? Now listen up. We'll show our faces, have something to eat, and then go somewhere private and talk. Because we really do need to talk, Doug. You don't know what's been going on here. It's been bizarre."

"I'm beginning to understand that term— *bizarre.* So let me take a stab at it. George is leaving Bettie right after the wedding we're sure shouldn't happen, but he wouldn't leave if there wasn't a wedding—plus, he doesn't really want to go. Oh, and that you and I are still on about stopping the wedding, except that there still could be a wedding if we just found a way to switch grooms, something that should have occurred to both of us a whole hell of a lot sooner, and now all we have to do is figure out exactly how to do that between now and three o'clock Sunday afternoon."

He kissed the tip of her nose. "Or am I going to be depressed because we're not actually operating on the same wacky wave length, and you have something else in mind?"

Rosie was flabbergasted. "No, I think that about covers it, actually. I thought it would take me forever to talk you into doing something like that. You'd do that? You'd help me do that? Because the whole idea is fairly crazy. And because the only thing I've come up with so far to get rid of Rob is kidnapping him and stashing him somewhere until the ceremony is over, and I think that might be a federal offense. So we probably should put our heads together and think of something else."

Doug shook his head. "Yeah, we'll have to work on that last part. I'll meet you right here at seven o'clock." He looked at her then, his expression difficult to read, before he kissed her hard on the mouth. "God, I've missed you," he said intensely, and then took off at a trot toward the drinks table inside the first tent.

Leaving Rosie to stand there with her hat once more plastered on her head with one hand, pretty sure her smile bordered on the idiotic. He'd missed her. Wasn't that wonderful?

"Rosie?"

"Hmm?" Rosie answered, turning around slowly, still rather lost in a delicious daydream only to lose her smile as she looked at Antoinette—who wasn't looking so good. "What's the matter, Antoinette? This mess? Hey, things happen. We all knew Delwood couldn't have caught all the squirrels. We'll get it all sorted out, I promise."

"This?" Antoinette said, gesturing at the slowly winding-down mayhem that had once been a well-planned, excruciatingly well-thought-out bridal luncheon. "I don't care about this. I mean, the way things have been going around here all week long, I'm *way* past getting bent out of shape over this one. Not that the blue martinis aren't helping a lot. Oh, and neither does Bettie. Care, I mean. I found her in her sunroom and she told me she didn't give a flying—well, she doesn't seem to care."

"I think maybe she picked up a touch of whatever Lili-beth had earlier this week, and may be feeling a little under the weather," Rosie suggested helpfully. "So, Antoinette, if you don't care about the chafing dishes, the cake, the ice sculpture, the presents, the unhappy guests and the general mess—what do you care about?"

"Are you kidding? Haven't you noticed this wind? It's Eloise, Rosie. They don't call her Eloise anymore. She's been downgraded to a tropical storm, not a hurricane anymore at all. But whatever she is, she's heading this way, and she's got buckets of rain left in her. Buckets, Rosie, that's what the girl said on Accuweather at noon. A deluge is coming—she said that, too. By Saturday afternoon, we're going to be in a deluge. It's going to be hot, muggy, windy and *deluging*. Oh, I hate garden weddings. You can plan forever, but rain is rain and nothing can stop it."

Wasn't it the strangest thing? Doug, who'd told her he didn't like to get involved with other people's problems, seemed to be in his glory now as he took on everyone's problems…while she, who was used to juggling everyone else's personal dilemmas, and liked doing it, suddenly was wishing for nothing more than a deserted island populated by Doug, herself and a huge feather bed. Clothing optional.

"All right, Antoinette, so it's going to rain all weekend," Rosie said, putting her arm around the older woman's shoulders as they walked up toward the terrace. "There's nothing so bad it can't be fixed. Let's think. You said Saturday afternoon?

Okay, so that only leaves tomorrow night's rehearsal dinner and the ceremony on Sunday, right? So, we direct everyone in through the front door instead of laying the walkway leading around the side of the house. From the house we move them outside to the covered terrace, and from the terrace to the tents."

"But it will still be raining. A *deluge.*"

"Yes, but look at those tents. Those are some damn fine tents, Antoinette. They've got high, pointed tops—with flags on them, for God's sake. They've got sides that are tied back now, but those can be moved so that they keep the rain and wind out. They've even got fake windows."

"And chandeliers," Antoinette added, seeming to cheer up a bit. "And those temporary hardwood floors. They really are great tents. Once everyone is inside, they'll be fine. Dry. I think there's even a way to cover the passage between the tents. You're right, Rosie, we can do this."

"Yes, we can," Rosie said bracingly. "All we need to bridge the gap between the house and the tents are some canvas tarps to walk on, and about three dozen golf umbrellas. Didn't Bettie say part of the favors was umbrellas for the ladies?"

Antoinette shook her head. "Parasols. Paper parasols with Lili-beth's and Rob's names on them."

"Oh. Well, scratch those, huh? In fact, Antoinette, I think I'd like to see everything you've got for the big day that has Lili-beth's and Rob's names on it, okay?"

"Why?"

"Antoinette," Rosie said sternly, "you need help. I've offered to help you. This is going to be the wedding Bettie asked you to put on—a wedding no one will ever forget—and I'm going to help you pull it off. So don't look a gift horse in the mouth, okay?"

CHAPTER FIFTEEN

"'Friends, Romans, countrymen, lend me your ears. I come to bury Caesar, not to praise him'—and all that crap."

Doug turned around to see Bettie walking toward him a tad tipsily, waving a glass of Scotch in the air.

He snagged the tumbler from her and poured its contents on the grass. "And that's enough for you tonight, Cleo," he said, taking in the slightly askew black wig, the ruby-red gown and the fairly impressive gold collar at Bettie's throat.

She leaned against his breastplate. "George was supposed to be Mark Antony, but he won't do it. He's such a pity popper—party pooper." Then she stepped back, looked at Doug admiringly. "You look good. Most men don't, not when they're showing their knees. But you're cute. You've got cute knees. George has pudgy knees, with little dimples in them. They're so adorable. Itty-bitty little dimples—right *there*."

Doug caught Bettie before she could pitch forward onto his sandaled feet. "Okay, Bettie, time for beddie-bye for you, I think. Although I doubt your guests will think it's a real party if their hostess isn't here."

"Yeah well, they'll get over it," she said, allowing herself to be led up onto the terrace and into the house before the rest of the Roman senate and their ladies could see her. "Where are we going?"

"To bed, remember?"

"We are? No, that's not right. That can't be right. You're Doug. That's just a joke. But we could dance. Hear the music?" She leaned in close to whisper to him. "That's the Ear Waxxes-ses-ses. They're playing my swan song. Come on, Doug, it's a party. Let's dance!"

He was trying to fend off Bettie's lazily waving arms—and her Scotch-sweet breath—when Lili-beth came running down the stairs, holding up her long white toga with the Roman key design at the hem. "Mama! How did you get out?"

Doug was finally able to grab hold of Bettie's small wrists. "You had her locked up?"

"What else could I do?" Lili-beth asked as she guided her mother up the staircase. "I've never seen her like this before. Nobody else can see her, she'd be mortified when she, when she—"

"Sobered up?" Doug suggested. "Are you sure you don't need any help getting her upstairs?"

"No, thank you, Doug. Rosie's still in her room. She'll help me. Come on, Mama, let's go lie down for a while, okay?"

Bettie smiled at her daughter, cupping Lili-beth's cheek with one heavily be-ringed hand. "You're my baby, aren't you, Lili-bethy. My own little girl. You're happy, aren't you, Lili-bethy? Please say you're happy. Somebody should be happy, don't you think?"

"I'm happy, Mama," Lili-beth told her, looking down the stairs at Doug, her expression bleak as she guided Bettie up to the landing. "It's a wonderful party. Just your best ever."

"Screw the party," Bettie spat, her mood changing yet again. "It's you I care about, sweetheart. Remember…remember when you were little? We'd sing songs, and I'd read to you? I even remember your favorite. You remember, Lili-bethy? Georgie porgie, pudding and pie."

"Because of Daddy. Yes, I remember. He kissed the girls and made them cry."

Bettie stopped just at the end of the balcony overlooking the foyer, to peer down at Doug for a moment before she and Lili-beth disappeared down the hallway. "Georgie porgie ran away…"

"Well, that was fun," Doug told his reflection in the large mirror to the left of the foyer. Then he winced at that reflection. Look at him. He looked like an extra in that movie *Gladiator* for crying out loud. But Rosie was bound to love dressing up for the party, so he'd gone along with it, right down to the sheathed sword at his waist.

He wondered if he could do the Russell Crowe thing and use the sword to convince Hemmings the climate was healthier in California. Pulling the sword out of its sheath, he brandished it in the air, trying the look on for size.

"Oh, my, don't you look all early Roman Empire-ish?"

"Rosie," Doug said, quickly lowering the sword, more than a little embarrassed. And then he looked at her, standing on the third stair from the floor, and forgot his embarrassment. "Who the hell are you supposed to be? Not that I'm complaining, you understand."

"You like?" she asked, coming down the last few steps, her long, straight legs visible to a good two inches above her knees. The one-shouldered toga was tied at her waist with a gold cord, and she'd piled her hair loosely on top of her head, threading it through with golden thread. "I'm a slave girl, ruthlessly seized from her home in Ireland and brought to Rome to be sold to the highest bidder in the marketplace."

"In that case, excuse me a minute, will you? I think I left my *Visa* card in my other tunic," Doug told her, taking her hand and raising it to his lips. "Maybe this evening isn't going to be such a debacle after all."

"Meaning Bettie Blotto," Rosie said, sighing. "I was going to help Lili-beth pour her into bed, but it wasn't necessary. She hit the mattress and passed right out. Lili-beth asked me to find Rob and tell him she'll be down in plenty of time—for what, I have no idea. In the meantime, I'm to cue Antoinette to run the film for everybody in twenty minutes."

"All this, and a film, too? How did we get so lucky?"

"I know. Don't you wonder what the little people are doing tonight—and envy them? Still, these costumes could come in handy...later, when we're alone?"

Doug leered down at her comically. "Don't toy with me, woman. I'm armed."

"Yes," Rosie all but purred, rubbing up against him before dancing away again. "I'm counting on that."

"That does it. Let's go somewhere."

"Really? Where?"

"I don't know. To the Bachelor Quarter? To somewhere that isn't here? To the South of France?"

"I *love* the South of France. But to tell you the truth, right now I'd settle for anywhere that isn't here. But we can't. Believe it or not, we're the adults here. We'd never forgive ourselves if we let Bettie and George and Lili-beth—and Delwood—down, now could we?"

"I could probably find some way to assuage my conscience," Doug told her, then shook his head. "No, you're right. I don't know how it happened, but we are the adults here. So just let me lodge my protest with the Commissioner of Grown-Up, and we'll get back to the game."

"You got it, slugger."

By now they were back out on the terrace, and heading for the larger tent that was now strung with flowing purple banners, a pair of hulking, broad-chested, blank-faced centurions guarding the main entrance. He had to hand it to Bettie. When she did something, she didn't go halfway. Unfortunately, tonight that trait had carried over to her Scotch consumption.

"There's Hemmings standing with Delwood. Not a good idea, Delwood standing alongside our boy Hemmings, especially considering we can see their knees. The comparisons are much too easy to make."

"I know Rob is handsome, in a smarmy sort of way," Rosie said, "but Delwood's cuter. In that nerdy, young Bill Gates sort of way. Rob looks a little red in the face, don't you think?"

"Pissed," Doug corrected, taking her hand and leading them over to where the two men were standing just outside the tent. "The boy looks pissed. I don't think this party can take another problem."

"Yet you and I are at this very moment planning to give it a big one," Rosie reminded him.

"Don't confuse me with facts," he told her,

grinning at her, then said hello to Hemmings and Delwood.

"Lili-beth will be down soon," Rosie told them. "Delwood? Could you do me a favor, please, and go find Antoinette, tell her to start the movie in fifteen minutes?"

"Sure thing, Miss Kilgannon. Rob? That means you should be out front in ten minutes. I've got it all computerized—the music, everything. No later, or you'll ruin the timing."

Rob rolled his eyes. "I still think this is the stupidest thing I ever heard of. And give me your watch, if you want me to be on time. I don't have *mine* anymore, remember?"

"Caesars is in Atlantic City as far as you're concerned, Hemmings, right?" Doug said as Delwood ran off to find the wedding planner.

Hemmings actually smiled at him. "Right. In AC, or out in Vegas. Not this happy horse—"

"We've got a lady present," Doug interrupted, and Hemmings looked at Rosie, and then looked at her legs, and then smiled. Doug felt a definitely immature yet almost overwhelming urge to clock him, maybe rearrange his capped teeth a little bit.

"Uh, right…sorry," Hemmings apologized, his smile fading. "It's just…it's just that it's been a bad couple of days, you know? All Lili-beth and I want is to get married. Not all this happy horse—sorry. And now, just for the capper, somebody made off with my watch. That thing cost me a mint, and now somebody's copped it."

Doug looked quickly to Rosie, who had looked just as quickly to him. "Copped your watch, Hemmings?" he asked. "Are you sure? Maybe you just misplaced it somewhere."

"No, I did not misplace it as dimwit Delwood kept trying to tell me. I know where it was—on my nightstand, upstairs—and now it's not there. One of Bettie and George's hotshot friends took it."

"Well, that's too bad, isn't it? Maybe it will turn up," Doug said, taking Rosie's hand. "We'd better leave you alone now, so you can watch your time and we can go watch the movie. Right, Rosie?"

"Absolutely. And only two more days, Rob, and this will all be over and you can try to forget everything but the wedding itself. That is what this is all about, isn't it? You and Lili-beth, starting your lives together?"

Hemmings looked down at Delwood's watch,

which was now on his arm. "Yeah, right. Can't wait. Excuse me…"

"Aunt Susanna," Doug and Rosie said in unison, once Hemmings had left them, walking over to where Rizzo and Leslie stood looking uncomfortable in their white togas. Leslie looked as if the costumer had been forced to compromise to cover the man's bulk, and the guy was wearing a king-size sheet over his bulges.

"I know where she keeps her stash," Rosie told Doug as they headed back into the house, and up the back staircase to the guest rooms. "Lili-beth and I spent a good hour yesterday returning jewelry to the proper rooms."

"So where does my larcenous aunt keep her swag?" Doug asked as they entered Aunt Susanna's bedroom after knocking loudly a few times and getting no answer…only to see that the old woman was asleep under the covers, her toga still laid out at the bottom of that bed. "Oh, hell. We'll come back later," Doug whispered, taking Rosie's arm.

"Don't be silly. Look—her hearing aids are on the nightstand. She wouldn't wake up if we moved Ear Waxx up here for a couple of choruses of 'When The

Saints Come Marching In.' Just come on, follow me. It took us awhile, but Lili-beth and I figured it out," Rosie said, entering the en suite bathroom.

Doug was right behind her, holding on to the hilt of his sword so it wouldn't bang against the doorjamb. "Somehow this doesn't quite compare with the sacking of Rome, does it?"

"Oh, hush, we're on a mission. And if she does wake up and ask who's in her bathroom, we can both raise our hands and say *I, Spartacus*. I've always wanted an excuse to say that line. Now look here—Aunt Susanna has two of those plastic containers for her false teeth when she only needs one. That was the clue Lili-beth and I finally figured out. She keeps what she takes in the pink one. Or is it the yellow one? Oh, gosh, Doug, now I don't remember which is which. You look."

"Me look? Not in this lifetime, I won't," he told her, backing up two steps. "Her mouth is wide open back there, and I didn't see her molars. If I don't see them there, I sure as hell don't want to see them here."

Rosie reached up to kiss his cheek. "My brave centurion. All right, I'll look. Close your eyes if you think you'll faint."

Fifteen seconds later they were back in the hallway, Rosie giggling and Doug feeling more than a little foolish. But they had Hemmings's watch— and a silver tie tack in the shape of a golf club.

"This has to be George's, don't you think? I'll just hide it here for now, behind this photograph. Ah. One crisis averted among many," Rosie said, handing the watch to Doug, who looked at it for a moment, just out of idle curiosity, and then turned it over.

"Rosie?" he asked as they headed for the back staircase once more. "Didn't someone say that Hemmings is an orphan?"

She turned to look at him. "Antoinette did, I think. To explain why nobody will be sitting on Rob's side of the aisle on Sunday. Except Rizzo and Leslie, I guess. Why?"

"Because, my intrepid Doctor Watson, it would seem that there's an inscription engraved on the back of this watch," Doug told her, handing over the watch. "Read it. Out loud."

"Doctor Watson? Let me guess, that makes you Sherlock Holmes? Consider a protest lodged over the casting, if you don't mind. We wouldn't have the watch at all, if I hadn't known where to look for it. Okay, okay, don't make a face—give me that."

He leaned a shoulder against the wall, feeling faintly smug, and waited while she read the few words. "Out loud, Doctor Watson, remember? For the benefit of the viewing audience at home."

"We've got him, don't we?" Rosie asked, grinning at him. "Oh, all right, I'll read it out loud. *To Bobby. Happy birthday, Mom and Dad.* And the date—ta-da!—six months ago. He's a *liar.*"

"And if he'd lie about that…?" Doug prompted as they descended to the kitchen once more.

"Then he'd lie about anything. Maybe even everything."

"There might even be a wife and two kids in a duplex in Weehauken—but that's probably too much to hope for," Doug said. "I think it's time I had a small talk with our pals Rizzo and Leslie."

"Are you sure? What if they're what we think they are?" Rosie asked him as they headed outside, to see that the movie must already be playing inside the tent, as light was flickering through the white canvas, and a loud soundtrack could be heard.

"Don't worry, Doctor Watson—I'm armed. And I don't believe this," Doug said, still holding Rosie's hand as they entered the tent to see a chariot race in progress on the front wall of the tent. "Isn't that—?"

"Charleton Heston in the chariot race in *Ben Hur,*" Rosie said, shaking her head. "I wouldn't have thought Bettie would go for anything so obvious. I mean, it's been *done,* most recently at Sheila Barton's wedding last year. Oh, wait—now *that* hasn't been done. Leave it to Bettie to win any game of Can You Top This?"

Doug turned to look where Rosie was pointing as the centurions pulled back the tent walls on the far side of the tent, to show a full-size, honest-to-God Roman chariot pulled by a pair of white horses coming slowly into view—preceded by the bridesmaids in their flowing white togas, all of them tossing rose petals in the air from the golden baskets they carried.

In the chariot stood Hemmings and Lili-beth, waving to the crowd that had rushed out to meet them.

"Hail, Caesar! Hail Caesar!" someone yelled, and the partygoers took up the chant that soon segued into "Kiss her! Kiss her!" Sticks took up the cadence on the drums, and the chanting just got louder.

Doug felt Rosie's hand slip into his as Hemmings

grinned at the crowd, then pulled Lili-beth back and over his arm before planting a big one on her mouth, his right hand boldly roaming over the front of her gown as everyone cheered him on.

"And the orgy portion of our program has now started. Damn it!"

"Oh, Doug, look at her. She looks absolutely mortified," Rosie said, leaning against his shoulder.

"You're right, Rosie. She looks almost as miserable as the Squirrelmaster over to your right."

"Delwood," Rosie said, blinking back tears as she looked up at Doug. "We have to stop this, we really, really do. Lili-beth's too miserable and too timid to say anything, plus she's probably feeling too guilty about all this money her parents have spent—and Delwood won't get off the dime. Bettie and George are too wrapped up in their own problems to be of any real help, either. So you know what that means."

"Kidnapping Hemmings is out as an option, Rosie. You're right, it's definitely a federal offense."

"I know, I know. Which leaves us only one person who can stop this. One person who has to stand up, take charge and *stop* this."

"Delwood? You mean Delwood?"

"Who else is there? We know Rob is a...a con man, or something like that, at the very least. We know that he's entirely wrong for Lili-beth, and that he loves George's money, and not her. And we know that Delwood and Lili-beth were made for each other, that they're in love. But logic doesn't mean anything at a time like this, Doug, and publicly bringing out Rob's dishonesty would only embarrass Bettie and George, and most especially Lili-beth, who would come off looking like the poor, gullible little fool, even if she doesn't love him. We can't let that happen. So there's only one answer. Delwood has to declare himself. Openly, publicly. He has to stand up and show Lili-beth that he's the man for her!"

Doug looked toward Delwood just in time to see him sucking on his inhaler. "Are you sure you don't have a better idea? One that actually might *work?*"

"We'll sleep on it," Rosie told him, tugging him toward the Bachelor Quarter.

"Good idea. Well, everything but the sleeping part..."

"Rosie! Oh, Rosie, thank God I've found you!"

"Curses, foiled again," Doug said as they turned to see Antoinette jogging toward them. He wasn't happy, but he wasn't all that badly broken up about the interruption, all the interruptions, because he and Rosie were going to last way beyond this weekend. Years and years beyond this weekend. For the rest of their lives, if he had anything to say about the matter, and he hoped he did.

"I know, I know, but I promised her I'd help, if she promised me she wouldn't ask any questions," Rosie said, visibly sagging. "Do I have to keep my half of the bargain if she doesn't keep her half of hers?"

"I'd say no, but then, I'm prejudiced. And selfish."

"No, you're not. You only think you are. What you are is all grown-up now, Peter Pan. Otherwise, you wouldn't be helping Lili-beth."

"You can pin a medal on me later. Go on, sweetheart, see what she wants. I want to get out of this stupid costume anyway before I'm tempted to invade some country."

"Yes, but I wanted to *help* you out of it," Rosie told him, putting a hand to his faux breastplate. "I mean, I had *plans*."

"Oh, well, in that case," Doug said, grinning widely, "let's make a break for it."

"Rosie—I can't find George or Bettie, and someone has to talk to the man who brought the chariot. He says he won't leave until he's paid, and he won't believe me when I tell him it will be taken care of tomorrow. One of the horses just made a mess all over the lawn, and we need to get them out of here. Can you help? You said you'd help."

"I can do that," Doug told Rosie.

"No, that's all right. You go, and I'll see you in a little while. I promise. Just as soon as I can get away. Hey, you're heading in the wrong direction—the Bachelor Quarter is that way."

"I know. But if you're going to be working, I might as well work, too. I'm going to go find Delwood so we can have a little man-to-man talk."

"Don't scare him," Rosie called after him, and then went to see a man about some horse poop.

CHAPTER SIXTEEN

THEY MET AT THE POOL at the bottom of the large yard after midnight, Rosie's promised *little while* having stretched out over two hours one way or another, and only ending when Ki-Ki had decided to be the belle of the ball and begun an impromptu striptease on the portable band stand. That's when George, who had finally surfaced in his Mark Antony costume, had pulled the plug on Ear Waxx's amps and called it a night.

Rosie sat on the far side of the pool, facing the back of the house. Her bare toes dangled in the water at the deep end of the pool that was built to resemble an ancient grotto, complete with rock-wall waterfall and a hot tub that, sadly, had developed some sort of algae and was temporarily off-limits. That's what happens when you distract the pool boy….

She felt rather than saw Doug as he sat down beside her, lowering his feet into the pool.

"I got your note," he said, then sighed. "This feels good. When did it get so hot?"

"About two seconds ago when you showed up?" Rosie teased, kicking her feet, splashing water into the air, where it seemed to be caught by the pool lights before falling back down into the crystal blue water. "Seriously? It's the remnants of hurricane Eloise, and those remnants are definitely heading our way. We, and I quote any of the hundreds of weather forecasts Antoinette related to me, will be in the middle of a *deluge* by tomorrow afternoon." She pushed her hair up off her nape with both hands. "But it is hot, isn't it, even with this breeze. There's even a mist coming off the water. Pool fog. September can be such a goofy month. So, where have you been?"

"A minute ago? A minute ago I was shoveling a drunk but determined Delwood into the spare bedroom in the Bachelor Quarter because he's in no shape to drive himself home. He's going to do it, Rosie. He's going to stop the wedding. Somehow."

"Somehow? You didn't suggest a way?"

"I did run kidnapping past him—Lili-beth, not

Hemmings—even offered to drive the getaway car, but Delwood nixed the idea. He says he wants to do this on his own."

"Okay. Just tell me this much—do you think his plan involves a pith helmet?"

"Because we've decided that Hemmings is a little squirrely? We can only hope not," Doug said, smiling at her in the reflected ripples of light rising from the pool. "Now ask me about our friends Rizzo and Leslie. I dare you."

Rosie took the replica Roman wineskin Doug had placed on his lap and unscrewed the top. "I take it you spoke with the gentlemen? My, haven't you been the busy boy. Did they tell you that they're loan sharks? Mafia? Come on—give me all the juicy details."

"Poor Rosie," Doug said, shaking his head. "You're going to be so disappointed. One—Leslie. The guy is nothing more than one more high school football player who didn't make the pros and went to seed."

"I beg your pardon?"

"You know, Rosie. It's like a seven-foot-tall guy who once played basketball. Once the glory is gone, he's nothing but a guy who needs to bend over to get through normal doorways, has to sleep with half his legs hanging off the bottom of a bed. Leslie's just big, and running to fat. But bad? Nope."

"But…but what about the gun?"

"Oh, okay. That's real. But that's because our friend Rizzo is a diamond salesman, and Leslie's his bodyguard."

"No!" Rosie took a drink from the wineskin. *"Rizzo?* Rizzo's a *diamond* merchant? You're kidding."

"He'd like to meet with you sometime," Doug went on, still grinning. "He greatly admires the piece you wore the other night and thinks he may have some stones you'd appreciate."

"I saw him looking at my necklace. But I thought he was planning to steal it. Oh, I'm so embarrassed. I judged by appearances, didn't I? But wait a minute—what does a diamond merchant have to do with Rob Hemmings? And don't tell me they're buddies because *that* I'm not going to believe."

"And you shouldn't. It seems, sweetheart, that the three-carat rock on Lili-beth's hand, among various and other sundry gifts Rob showered her with to make himself look good to George, are all on loan from Rizzo. And, if Hemmings doesn't cough up the money for them before he and Lili-beth leave on their honeymoon, Lili-beth will be traveling sans glitter."

Doug took the wineskin from her and shot some of the liquid into his mouth, then smiled at her. "You know, people don't feel as if they're really drinking, not when they're playing around, shooting this stuff into their mouths. But they still really get drunk, and talk too much. Anyway, that's what Rizzo told me. He's here, playing wedding guest, to watch his diamonds."

Rosie thought about everything for a few moments. "So why didn't Rob pay him? He's certainly borrowed enough money to pay him."

"True. But that's where Hemmings's small problem with gambling comes in. If he gave the money to Rizzo, then that's just diamonds for cash, an even exchange. Ah, but if he were to take that money to Atlantic City he could double it, even triple it, and then pay Rizzo *and* take a nice profit."

"Except that's not what happened," Rosie said, grabbing the wineskin and screwing the top back on. "Rob *lost* the money. All the money George gave him."

"And all the money Delwood loaned him. But

Rizzo's okay with that, because Hemmings told him that he gets a huge check after the wedding—a present from George and Bettie."

"But he won't be, will he? Bettie all but told me there's an ironclad prenup, and George cut him off a month ago. Rob isn't getting any money on Sunday. Is he?"

"I don't think so, no. Not unless Hemmings tells George, and he pays for the diamonds his daughter is wearing. If not, the diamonds go back and, to tell you the truth, I have a feeling Leslie would also leave Hemmings with a few parting gifts—maybe a couple of broken knee caps, courtesy of Rizzo—in lieu of the twenty percent interest he's been charging him."

"Then he and Rizzo *aren't* on the up-and-up."

"I won't pass judgment, sweetheart. But how many diamond merchants do you know who operate out of the back of their Lexus? He took me out to the parking area and showed me his stock. He has a two-carat pink diamond out there that would look wonderful on you, but I resisted. Probably my Boy Scout training."

Rosie unscrewed the top again and took another drink. "Lili-beth is wearing *hot* stones? Ohmigod, Doug. We have to tell her. Don't we have to tell her?"

"Only if Delwood chickens out," he said. "We've got to give him a chance to fix this his way. He seemed serious, Rosie. At least up until the moment he turned green and ran into the bushes for a few minutes. And I already made a deal with Rizzo to return all the jewelry after the wedding. He isn't happy, but the guy knows when to cut his losses. Not to mention the fact that George and Bettie don't want any scandal, I'm sure. Now, back to important things."

"Such as," Rosie asked him as he edged in closer. "No, wait! I wanted to meet you out here for a couple of reasons. One, I was hot and wanted to cool off a little. And two, I thought we could cool off together. In the pool."

Doug looked down at the pool, then up at the house. "Okay, I admit it. I'm old. Too old to go skinny-dipping where someone might see us. I'm so ashamed."

"Don't be," Rosie said, holding the remote control she'd picked up earlier in the pool house. "Just watch."

She hit a button and the pool lights, both those above and below the water, slowly went out. Every last one of them, pitching the entire area into complete darkness. "See? No moon, no stars, no light. Just...us. What do you say now, old man?"

"Last one in is a rotten egg?" he asked, getting to his feet and quickly stripping out of his shorts and briefs, then pulling his shirt off over his head before diving in while Rosie was still unsnapping her bra.

She dove in after him, coming up gasping, even though the pool was heated, and tried to see through the faint mist of that warmed water colliding with the warmer, heavily humid air. She used her arms to swivel around, looking for him. "Doug?" she called out in a loud whisper. "Doug, where are—"

He pulled her under by grabbing at her ankle, and the game was on. He was a strong swimmer but, then, so was she, and they swam and teased and splashed for a good fifteen minutes before Rosie retreated to the side of the pool, resting her bent arms on the tile pool surround, breathing heavily. "Uncle, uncle. I give up."

"Good. Then I've got you where I want you," he told her, coming up directly behind her, pressing his naked body against hers, his hands on the tile on either side of her. "At least I will, as soon as I can catch my breath."

Rosie turned, sliding her arms around his shoulders. It was so dark she could barely see his face, although she delighted in the features she could make out, and the way his black hair was all sleekly plastered to his head "Now this is interesting. Have you ever…you know."

"Done it in a pool? No. You?"

Rosie shook her head, suddenly shy. She was naked in a pool with a man she'd made love with…made very intimate love with…and she was shy? How was that for ridiculous?

Doug's smile curled her toes. "I guess there's a first time for everything. It's all a matter of logistics. For starters, may I suggest we move to the more shallow end of the pool?"

"Probably a sensible thought," Rosie told him, breathless once again as they edged along the side of the pool until Rosie could stand with her head out of the water. "I…um…I'm on the pill."

Doug's hands, which were in the process of cupping her full breasts beneath the surface of the water, stilled for a moment. "Damn, Rosie, I didn't even think about that. I always think about that—but not tonight. Not with you. Are you sure you're all right with this? Because I'll stop. We can go up to the Bachelor Quarter and—"

"Delwood's up there," she reminded him, and then, because she really, really didn't want to talk anymore, she reached a hand below the surface of the water and wrapped her fingers around him. "Besides, I don't think either one of us is going to make it back to the Bachelor Quarter…."

The next thing she knew, Doug had lifted her partially out of the water and his mouth was fastened on her left nipple while his free hand slid wetly over her right breast, finding her, teasing her, mist rising all around them, the now cooler air helping to tighten her nipple into a hard bud of desire.

She was buoyant, floating, anchored only by her legs as they clamped around Doug's waist. She grabbed on to either side of his head as he kissed her breasts, tugged lightly at her nipples, even took her underwater with him before lifting her with the help of the water, so that she could then slide down his belly as he unerringly guided himself home.

They were making love. Hard, fast, furious love.

Standing up!

The sensations were beyond her experience. Their bodies reacted underwater, that feeling of weightlessness that left them free to concentrate on the sensations, the warmth…that all-enveloping warmth.

And the driving need.

He covered her startled outcry of pleasure with his mouth as they climaxed together, both of them letting go, slipping below the surface and into the welcoming cocoon of the water.

When they surfaced again, two once more, not one, it was to sweep the water out of their eyes and look at each other. Just look at each other.

"I need a pool," Doug told her at last in some awe. "First, I need a house. Then I need a pool. We have to have a pool, Rosie."

We. Did he realize what he'd just said? Probably not. But that was all right. They both knew where they were going, even if he hadn't said so, she hadn't said so.

They'd just take their time. They weren't young and foolish, there was no huge rush. They'd get there....

WHEN ROSIE AWOKE the next morning, wrapped in Doug's arms, she smiled again at the memory of the previous evening, and snuggled closer. It was so right that she was here, so right that he held her this way.

What a remarkable week. She'd come here to possibly stop a marriage, and here she was, thinking about the possibility of her own wedding. Someday. Not just now. But someday.

Someday soon. Because, poor guy, he wasn't getting any younger, was he?

Rosie laughed low in her throat, and Doug squeezed her shoulder. "You're awake? What's so funny?"

"Nothing," she said, levering up to kiss his mouth. "I just feel delicious, that's all."

"So do I, or at least the male equivalent of delicious. Listen, do you hear that? It's raining."

Rosie struggled upright to look at the clock on the bedside table. "And it's only eight o'clock. So much for the deluge at noon. I guess we should get up? I should leave before Delwood wakes."

"He's already gone. I heard him leave about a half hour ago. Since then, I've just been lying here, listening to the rain while I mentally sketch out our pool. What do you think—kidney shaped? Typical rectangle?"

She happily settled back against his shoulder to begin playing with the light sprinkling of hair on his chest. "Can it have a sliding board? You really should consider a sliding board, you know. A pool's not a real pool without a curvy sliding board."

"I'll take that under advisement." He turned onto his side, slipping his arm around her. "Now, speaking of curvy things…"

The next time Rosie woke up it was to the sound of voices coming from the living room. A fast check of the clock told her it was nearly noon, and she quickly slipped out of bed and grabbed one of Doug's shirts from the closet before tiptoeing to the closed door and opening it a crack.

Bettie. What did she want?

"So he says we'll talk," Bettie was saying, and Rosie leaned closer to the crack in the door. "He isn't promising anything, but he will talk. Well, we'll talk to a counselor. It's going to be very embarrassing, Doug. I don't know if I can do this."

"If you want George, you'll do it, Bettie," Doug said, and Rosie nodded her agreement. "More coffee?"

"Yes, I suppose so. But I don't know if there's enough coffee in the world to get through this headache. I'm never going to drink again, I swear it. I'll…I'll take up scrapbooking, or something," Bettie said, and Rosie felt a pang of sympathy for the woman. And just think—she still didn't know her big hotshot wedding wasn't going to come off. How many pots of coffee would it take to fix that headache?

Rosie quietly shut the door and tiptoed into the bathroom to brush her teeth using her finger as a brush, wash her face and then use Doug's comb to tidy her mass of once again unruly curls. They'd showered together last night to get rid of the smell of chlorinated water. Rosie's new lack of inhibitions had made blow-drying her hair the last thing she wanted to do, as Doug's lovemaking under the large rain shower had left her too limp and depleted to do anything except fall into bed and go to sleep, and the hell with her wet head.

Satisfied that Doug's shirt was long enough to cover her decently, she then walked out into the living room, drawn by both the aroma of freshly brewed coffee and a desire to see if Bettie was really all right.

"Please say that isn't decaf," she said, heading for the pot sitting on the kitchen counter. "Morning, everyone. Or afternoon, everyone. Whichever works."

"Rosie?" Bettie turned on her chair to stare at her. "I didn't know you were here."

Rosie shrugged, full coffee cup in hand. "And

yet I am. How are you doing this morning, Bettie? And how's Lili-beth?"

"Fine," Bettie said, blinking. "Everybody's, um, fine."

"Good. We've got appointments for manicures and pedicures at two. Will you tell her I'll be ready in time?"

"Sure, I suppose so. So, you spent the night here? So you two are still…still…?"

"Looks that way," Rosie told her brightly as Doug leaned against the kitchen cabinets, grinning as he saluted her with his coffee mug. Hey, if he could say *our pool,* she could lay a little claim of her own with his cousin. "Now, if you'll excuse me, I'm going to go grab a shower."

She stopped in the hallway, out of sight, to hear whatever Bettie might say next. And it didn't take long for the woman to find her voice.

"I wish I were more like Rosie, Doug. Men like her. Hell, they drool all over her. But women like her, too. Even me. Women don't really like me. I never understood why. But everybody loves Rosie. Men, women, kids. Puppies? I bet they lick her hand. Sunshine seems to follow her wherever she goes, for some reason, for crying out loud."

Rosie pressed a fist to her mouth as she heard Doug say rather facetiously, "You're right, Bettie. That's Rosie, all right. Did you ever notice? Flowers bloom as she walks past."

"Stop it, you know what I mean. And she's *fat*. I starve myself, and everyone looks at *her*. I don't get it."

Rosie looked down at herself. Fat? She wasn't fat. Just because you can't count somebody's rib bones...

"Bettie, you're thinking like a woman," Doug said, and Rosie came to attention once more. "I, on the other hand, think like a man. And as a man, I'm here to tell you, Rosie Kilgannon is *not* fat. She's perfect."

I love you, Rosie mouthed toward the living room as she turned to reenter the bedroom, grab up her clothing and head for the shower. She suddenly didn't want to miss a moment of the rest of her life....

CHAPTER SEVENTEEN

ANTOINETTE MAY HAVE seriously considered making an offering to the Rain Gods for some sun—she probably would have offered up Bettie on a platter, with an apple in her mouth—but Lilibeth's wedding day dawned without it…. Well, it was a sort of hit or miss thing, trying to say when dawn arrived, since everything around them was gray, gray and more gray.

And wet. Very, very wet. Soaked. Sodden. Drenched. Basically…not good.

By noontime, the huge white tents were looking a little sad, banners dragging, many-pointed roofs just a tad heavy looking. The sides had been down since Saturday morning, protecting everything inside the tents, but the see-through plastic-paned "windows" constantly fogged up as the humidity climbed, and the temperature climbed along with it.

Rosie had taken over dressing the bride for her big day since Ki-Ki couldn't be found anywhere ever since she'd disappeared with Anvil after the boring rehearsal dinner the previous evening, and it turned out that nobody cared enough to go look for her.

"Are you *sure,* Lili-beth?" Rosie asked, at least a half-dozen times.

And Lili-beth had answered, variously, that she didn't have a choice, that her parents wanted this, that everyone was waiting for her and, lastly, that if Delwood didn't care then she didn't care, either!

So Rosie, left without options, and praying Delwood knew what he was doing after their private chat after the rehearsal dinner—and before leaving him at one of the tables with Leslie, of all people—clasped Rizzo's diamonds to Lili-beth's throat, lifted the train of the designer gown that couldn't be allowed to touch the wet tarp between the terrace and the main tent, and they all headed down the stairs.

"Oh, she looks so beautiful," Bettie said, standing at the bottom of the stairs. "George, doesn't she look beautiful?"

And George, bless him, and forgive him many of his lapses, cried.

And the photographer took another two hundred photographs.

Rosie handed Lili-beth over to a slightly unsteady Ki-Ki and the rest of the bridesmaids, took hold of Doug's arm and headed out to the tent, sitting on the groom's side, because nobody else did, except for Rizzo and Leslie, the latter looking quite spiffy in a powder-blue tux.

The tent had been decorated beautifully not to mention within an inch of being ostentatious. There were flowers everywhere. Pillar candles. Tulle and trailing ribbons. Pristine white slipcovers on each chair. A small, makeshift altar covered with even more candles.

It could have been a centerfold spread for some bridal magazine. Except for the sound of rain pelting the tent, splashing in puddles outside the tent. Oh, and the wind. The wind really wasn't helping matters much....

"No luck, huh?" Doug whispered as Anvil stepped to a microphone over to one side to sing "Sunrise, Sunset," a song calculated to bring everyone in the tent to tears, whether they had an affection for the song, or if they were just wishing for some sun.

"Not a bit. She's like a lamb, being led to the slaughter. I wanted to strangle her with those damn diamonds. Where's Delwood?"

"I don't know. But I saw him a little earlier. He is here. And no pith helmet, in case that makes you feel better."

"It doesn't. She's really going to go through with it. And all because Delwood is such a wuss. Oh, and Bettie and George know this is going to be a fiasco, but they're going through with it, too, because Lili-beth *says* she wants to go through with it. If they'd only *talk* to each other."

"Shh, don't worry, my money's on Delwood. And you look beautiful, by the way."

"Thank you." Rosie held out her hand, palm up. "Is that— It is." She leaned close to Doug and whispered, "The tent's leaking. Doug—*the tent's leaking.*"

He looked up to see that they were sitting just to the left of one of the many poles holding up the vaulted roof. "Relax. It's just getting in a little bit, around the poles."

Rosie looked up as they all stood because Ear Waxx was now playing "The Wedding March." "Just a little bit, huh? And what do you have to say about the *sagging?* Just a little bit of sagging? I don't think so."

Doug checked again. "I hope there isn't much of a sermon."

Rosie slipped her hand into his as Rob Hemmings came out from behind a bank of flowers followed by his best man, Delwood, and several other interchangeable young men Rosie didn't recognize.

All heads turned as Lili-beth finally made her appearance to oohs and aahs, her mother on one side of her, a still weeping George on the other, and it was showtime.

"Nothing's happening," Rosie complained through gritted teeth as some preliminary prayers were said. "You know I'm going to have to do something, don't you? I can't just stand here and watch this."

"It's all right. Delwood's got it."

Rosie's eyes got big. "You're kidding. He's actually going to do the *if anyone here present objects* thing?" She stretched her neck to look around the perimeter of the tent. "Man, I hope her videographer is getting all this. Rizzo could sell copies on the black market and make a mint."

"Rosie, you're being incorrigible," Doug said, but he smiled as he said it. "And quiet—here we go."

"If there is anyone here present who has any objection to this marriage, let him speak now, or forever hold—"

And that's when Delwood pulled out the gun.

"Ohmigod!" Rosie exclaimed as women screamed, men cursed, and most everyone ducked for cover.

Leslie turned around, his hands still folded in front of him, to say, "It's all right. We had a little talk earlier, me and Rizzo and Del, seeing as how we notice things. Well, Rizzo notices things, I just go along, and Rizzo says that Del's the better man. It's my gun, by the way, and it's not loaded. Del just wanted to make sure he got everyone's attention. He told me that people often don't notice that he's around, and I told him I had a way to fix that." He grinned, showing the gap between his front teeth. "It's working, isn't it?"

Both Doug and Rosie nodded their sincere agreement.

"I object!" Delwood shouted. "I most strenuously object! This man is an impostor, a *thief!*"

"What in hell are you talking about?" Hemmings

asked, taking Lili-beth's hand. Hiding behind her, actually, if anyone wanted to get technical about the thing.

Delwood pointed the gun at him, and anyone still standing ducked. "You stole George Rossman's *tiepin.* The solid silver tiepin in the shape of a golf club. The tiepin he won in the club championship last year. His *most prized possession. That's* what I'm talking about! We found it this morning in your room. Admit it—you're nothing but a *common thief!* You're a thief, and I love this woman! I love Lili-beth Rossman, and I want her to be my wife! Dragoons—take him away!"

And damn if those two huge, brawny, blank-faced centurions who had "guarded" the tent on toga night didn't march in from the rain, carrying their long, impressive spears, ready to march Hemmings off to the stockade.

"Rosie?" Doug asked, looking at her, and she had the grace to blush.

"Well, it is George's most prized possession. And I thought Delwood might need a little help." She raised her eyebrows at him. "What? Did you think I tell you everything? Oh, and both Brian and Scott volunteer at the animal shelter. They're big, but they're harmless. They're both on the track team at the community college—javelin tossers, or whatever they're called. Those are their javelins, naturally. I didn't know the timing. I just gave Delwood the tools, and hoped he'd use them."

"Will you ever tell me everything?"

She grinned at him. "Probably not. I like to think of myself as an independent thinker. Do you mind?"

"No, I don't think so. I'm beginning to like surprises."

Then Doug started toward the front of the tent as Hemmings tried to fight off the centurions. There was a small struggle…and then disaster.

The tip of one of the javelins made contact with the sagging tent roof, and the sound of ripping material was quickly followed by a waterfall, the force of the water trapped on top of the tent increasing the tear inch by inch then, more quickly, foot by foot.

"Everybody—*out!*" Doug shouted, unnecessarily as it turned out, because the entire wedding party was already heading out any way they could, slamming into pole posts as they went, further weakening the structure.

Just as Anvil and the rest of the band cleared

the tent with their instruments, and as everyone stood in the *deluge,* watching, the tent gave a mighty groan, listed to one side, then the other... and then came down.

Somebody cheered.

Everyone was wet to the skin, but nobody seemed to be moving, attempting to shelter under the roof over the terrace. They all just stood there.

Except for Millicent and Quint, Rosie noticed.

"Are you all right?" Millicent was yelling.

"I thought I wouldn't reach you in time."

"I'm fine, Quint. You rescued me. You're my *hero.*"

"When I thought I could lose you...Millicent! What fools we've been! Oh, Millicent!"

Doug folded his arms and watched as the two embraced in the rain. "Call me a cockeyed romantic, but that's nice. That's really nice. Laughable, fairly nauseating, but really nice."

As one, the crowd seemed to belatedly realize that they were all wet, and getting wetter, and that the second tent, the one housing the food, the cake and, most importantly, the booze, was still intact, and they began running toward it. Mostly toward the booze.

"Care to join them?"

"No," Rosie said, shaking her head, then wiping her face as rain ran into her eyes. "Look, there go the Rossmans. And Delwood. They're heading for the house."

Doug watched as the four walked arm in arm, Lili-beth and Delwood in between George and Bettie. "They're going to be all right," he said, feeling satisfied. "Neurotic, but all right."

"And here comes Rizzo, chasing after them," Rosie said, pointing in the man's direction. "I guess he wants his diamonds back, huh? Well, Bettie wanted to put on a show nobody would ever forget. You know what, Doug? I think she's pulled it off."

Holding hands, the rain still a *deluge,* they slowly began walking toward the Bachelor Quarter.

"I'm officially on vacation for the rest of the month," Doug told her as they walked.

"That's nice. Going anywhere special?"

"I was just going to wing it, but lately I've been thinking a lot about the South of France. Do you think you could come along?"

"I'll have to think about that. But aren't I too old for you?"

"Actually, I think you're just the right age for me."

"Oh? But then maybe you're too old for me?"

Doug grinned at her, rain dripping off his nose. "After what happened this morning? And last night? Etc., etc.?"

"Well, there is that, isn't there? The South of France, huh?"

Doug linked his hands behind his back, and just let it rain on him. "Yup. South of France. I'm crazy about you. You do know that?"

"I've been hoping you were. We're going to take this slow, right? I don't want to scare you off."

"Anything you want—and I'm not scared easily."

They stopped at the bottom of the stairs leading to the Bachelor Quarter, to look back at the fallen tent.

"But not too slow," Rosie said. "We aren't getting any younger."

They turned, and began up the stairs. "True. We can give it a month, see how we're doing."

"Because we're doing pretty well," Rosie said, waiting for him to open the door.

"I'd say better than very well."

"Me, too." Rosie stepped into the living room of the Bachelor Quarter, then shook herself like a wet spaniel. "So, bottom line here, Llewellyn, you're going to let me and my ticking biological clock chase you?"

He stepped closer. "I am. And I plan to walk very, *very* slowly."

She began helping him out of his tuxedo jacket. "Yes, of course. It's that old age thing. You probably can't run any faster."

Doug grabbed her, pulled her close against him. "Is this going to be a running gag, Kilgannon, until we're both in our nineties?"

Grinning, Rosie snuggled her wet self against his shirtfront. "Could be, Llewellyn. Could be…"

Happy the Bride the Sun Shines On...

"WHERE ARE THE RINGS? I can't find the rings. Rosie, I can't find the rings!"

"Calmly, Antoinette, calmly," Rosie told the wedding planner as she leaned in toward the mirror, retouching her lipstick. "Cameron Pierce has them, remember? That's what the best man does. That, and making sure the groom doesn't bolt at the last moment."

Antoinette collapsed into a green-on-green slipper chair and began fanning herself with her carefully planned schedule of events. "I don't know how you can be so calm. The last time someone in this family got married—well, almost got married—it was the disaster of the year. I've never been an advocate of elopement. It would cut horribly into my income, for one thing. But in this case, Rosie, I think I would have held the ladder for Doug."

Rosie tipped her head to one side as she stepped back from the mirror to inspect her appearance one last time. She had chosen to wear her grandmother's bridal gown, the A-line style straight out of the late forties, and composed of a satin sheath underslip that skimmed her curves topped by Chantilly lace that had aged to a lovely ivory. Her something new was her headpiece, a circlet of palest yellow tea roses with the veil attached only at the back, and trailing down to meet the hem of the small train.

Antoinette was just handing her the nosegay of matching tea roses, the handle wrapped in long, thin satin ribbons, when the bedroom door opened a few inches and Bettie Rossman peeked in her head. "Am I being bad, coming up here with Lili-beth? Can I take a quick peek at the— oh, Rosie, you look *fabulous*. So retro." She pushed the door open all the way. "Lili-beth, look at Rosie!"

"Coming, Mama," Lili-beth said a little breathlessly from the hallway, then entered the room belly first, one hand to the small of her back. "Climbing stairs is like climbing mountains these days. Oh, Rosie, Mama's right. You look wonderful."

"And you look ready to pop," Rosie told her, accepting air kisses from both women. "You shouldn't have flown all the way here from Phoenix, just for my wedding."

Lili-beth smiled sweetly. "Delwood said the same thing, but I convinced him. After all, some of the best hospitals in the world are only about an hour in nearly every direction. Besides, he's been taking classes in childbirth. I almost think he hopes he'll be the one to deliver Delwood Junior."

Bettie bent to fuss with Rosie's veil. "I have to show you last week's *U.S. News and World Report* at the reception, Rosie. Delwood's new company has been named one of the top five start-ups to be watched this year. The boy is brilliant with all those computer gadgets. But then, of course, he did marry my daughter."

Lili-beth rolled her eyes even as she reached in her small purse and pulled out a bag of cleaned baby carrots and began munching. "Did you know Daddy's selling his business and he and Mom are moving to Phoenix to spoil their grandchild? Well, and he says there are great golf courses in Arizona, and he can play all year there. I can't believe he's actually retiring."

"We want to spend more time together," Bettie said, actually blushing. "He's bought me my own golf clubs."

Antoinette clapped her hands together three times in quick succession. "All right, ladies, it's time. Bettie, you'd better go downstairs and sneak into your seat, as Rosie's mother is already seated. Lili-beth, here are your flowers. You lead the way. Rosie, I'll fluff your veil as you start down the steps."

"Wait." Rosie looked at the women. "Maybe I should think about this some more."

"Rosie!" The exclamation had come from all three women.

"Just kidding," Rosie said, grinning. "I've never been so sure about anything in my life."

"Well, that's good," Lili-beth said in a small voice, "but I think you'd better hurry this up. I'm pretty sure my water just broke. *Mama...*"

And so, while Bettie helped her daughter to a chair and Antoinette slipped down the hallway to the back staircase to find Delwood and alert him, Rosie stepped out onto the landing of her parents' house all by herself, and began walking down the center of the curved staircase and toward the gathering of guests in the large living room visible beyond the opened double doors.

Doug was already standing to the right of the small aisle, and he looked up to see her hesitate at the bottom of the staircase before her father stepped forward to offer her his arm.

"My God, look at her," he breathed quietly, feeling humbled, his knees actually shaking as he watched her approach, her smile as bright as if she'd brought the sun into the room with her. There were birds singing in the rose garden outside the opened French doors, the world was perfect, and everything was coming up Rosie. His Rosie. Now and forever, his Rosie. "Cam, how did I get so lucky?"

Cam shrugged as he whispered back, "I'd say it was clean living, except I don't think that fits. Go get her, pal. *Now* your life really begins."

Doug nodded, blinking back unaccustomed tears as he stepped forward to take Rosie's hands in his, because his friend was right. Now his life really began. His life, and Rosie's life. Together…

* * * * *

Watch for Kasey Michaels's next release
A MOST UNSUITABLE GROOM—*the latest
in her historical saga,* **THE BECKETS OF
ROMNEY MARSH**—*on sale March 2007
from HQN Books.*

If you enjoyed what you just read,
then we've got an offer you can't resist!

Take 2 novels FREE!
Plus get a FREE surprise gift!

Clip this page and mail it to The Reader Service

IN U.S.A.	IN CANADA
3010 Walden Ave.	P.O. Box 609
P.O. Box 1867	Fort Erie, Ontario
Buffalo, N.Y. 14240-1867	L2A 5X3

YES! Please send me 2 free novels from the Romance/Suspense Collection and my free surprise gift. After receiving them, if I don't wish to receive any more, I can return the shipping statement marked "cancel". If I don't cancel, I will receive 4 brand-new novels every month, before they're available in stores! In the U.S.A., bill me at the bargain price of $5.24 plus 25¢ shipping and handling per book and applicable sales tax, if any*. In Canada, bill me at the bargain price of $5.74 plus 25¢ shipping and handling per book and applicable taxes**. That's the complete price and a savings of over 10% off the cover prices—what a great deal! I understand that accepting the 2 free books and gift places me under no obligation ever to buy any books. I can always return a shipment and cancel at any time. Even if I never buy another book, the 2 free books and gift are mine to keep forever.

185 MDN EFVD
385 MDN EFVP

Name	(PLEASE PRINT)	
Address	Apt.#	
City	State/Prov.	Zip/Postal Code

Not valid to current subscribers of the Romance Collection, the Suspense Collection or the Romance/Suspense Collection.

Want to try two free books from another series?
Call 1-800-873-8635 or visit www.morefreebooks.com.

* Terms and prices subject to change without notice. Sales tax applicable in N.Y.
** Canadian residents will be charged applicable provincial taxes and GST.

All orders subject to approval. Offer limited to one per household. Credit or debit balances in a customer's account(s) may be offset by any other outstanding balance owed by or to the customer. Please allow 4 to 6 weeks for delivery.
® and ™ are trademarks owned and used by the trademark owner and/or its licensee.

BOB06R   © 2004 Harlequin Enterprises Limited

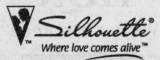

Kasey Michaels

77059   STUCK IN SHANGRI-LA   ___$6.99 U.S.   ___$8.50 CAN.

(limited quantities available)

TOTAL AMOUNT	$_____
POSTAGE & HANDLING	$_____
($1.00 FOR 1 BOOK, 50¢ for each additional)	
APPLICABLE TAXES*	$_____
TOTAL PAYABLE	$_____

(check or money order—please do not send cash)

To order, complete this form and send it, along with a check or money order for the total above, payable to HQN Books, to: **In the U.S.:** 3010 Walden Avenue, P.O. Box 9077, Buffalo, NY 14269-9077; **In Canada:** P.O. Box 636, Fort Erie, Ontario, L2A 5X3.

Name: _____
Address: _____ City: _____
State/Prov.: _____ Zip/Postal Code: _____
Account Number (if applicable): _____

075 CSAS

*New York residents remit applicable sales taxes.
*Canadian residents remit applicable GST and provincial taxes.

HQN™

We *are* romance™

PHKM0906BL